"Wicked" Women on Top

"Wicked" Women on Top

Tina Donahue
Jen Nicholas
Jordan Summers

BRAVA

KENSINGTON PUBLISHING CORP.
http://www.kensingtonbooks.com

BRAVA BOOKS are published by

Kensington Publishing Corp.
850 Third Avenue
New York, NY 10022

All Kensington titles, imprints, and distributed lines are available at special quantity discounts for bulk purchases for sales promotion, premiums, fund-raising, educational or institutional use.

Special book excerpts or customized printings can also be created to fit specific needs. For details, write or phone the office of the Kensington Special Sales Manager: Kensington Publishing Corp., 850 Third Avenue, New York, NY 10022. Attn. Special Sales Department. Phone: 1-800-221-2647.

ISBN 0-7582-0935-5

First Kensington Trade Paperback Printing: February 2005
10 9 8 7 6 5 4 3 2 1

Printed in the United States of America

CONTENTS

LET THE
GAMES
BEGIN

Tina Donahue

One

Nick Marlow looked at the note that had just been slipped beneath his door.

Nick, it began rather nicely, then got straight to the point.

My office, this morning, at 9.

Be there.

It was signed *T.T.*

It was also scrawled in what looked to be lipstick or lip liner that was a deep rose color.

Nick opened the door to his penthouse suite and looked into the hall. Behind the potted palms and lush tropical flowers, he caught movement as the elevator doors closed on the note's messenger.

Her fragrance lingered. It reminded Nick of the scent of skin baked hot from the Las Vegas sun and washed clean with perfumed soap. Delicate, yet provocative.

He smiled at that enticing thought until he looked back to the note. Lifting it to his nose, he sniffed. Oddly enough it had that same delicious scent, despite the fact that it had been written on the back of a used Keno ticket.

The player hadn't won.

Nick tried to picture *T.T.*—Tiffany Taylor—playing anything more rousing than tournament chess, and could not. She was his partner's only child and so damned smart she had been holed up at Oxford before entering the real world as the CEO of a Hollywood cosmetics firm that just went belly-up.

Maybe it was the way she wasted lipstick.

Not that it mattered, since Daddy had just given her controlling interest in this casino, with Nick owning the next largest block of stock in Piacere. Italian for pleasure.

He looked at the *Be there* on the note. Very commanding for a young, inexperienced businesswoman who not only considered herself his boss, but fully expected him to accept her as such. Bad boy that he was, he had not. If anything, he had worked very hard to avoid her—hell, he still hadn't laid eyes on her. And was she ever pissed. She had pressed so hard while writing this love note, she actually ripped the paper . . . unless those were claw marks.

Hmmm. Pleasure probably wasn't something T.T. was anticipating for him this morning, but as far as Nick was concerned, it was definitely time that they met on his terms. And that was not going to be in her office, nor was it going to wait until nine.

Twenty minutes later, Nick adjusted the collar of his Polo shirt, smoothed down his khakis, then exited the elevator near Tiffany's suite. Just ahead were reproductions of *Venus de Milo* and Michelangelo's *David*. From this angle, David's vacant gaze fell on Venus's naked breasts.

Nick gave the kids two thumbs-up.

This was not lost on Mae, a room-service employee. Mae was only forty, but had always treated Nick as if he were the son she never had.

"You should be arrested," she said.

Nick grinned. "I'm working on it." He followed as she wheeled her cart past. "Here, let me help."

Mae gave him a sidelong glance as he eased the cart toward himself, then lifted the metal covers from the plates.

Besides the usual female fare of fresh fruit, there was a steaming white egg omelet and a toasted bagel with cream cheese.

"Would you care for a paper with that?" Mae asked.

Nick smiled sweetly at her sarcasm, then glanced at the papers Tiffany had obviously ordered. There was the *New York Times,* the *Wall Street Journal,* and one he couldn't read since it was in French.

"Ms. Taylor's *very* smart," Mae said.

As if he were stupid enough to challenge that. Of course, he *was* tempted to show Mae Ms. Taylor's lipstick-written note, while bragging about his mathematics degree from MIT.

Before he could, Mae tried to take her cart back.

He held firm. "I'll deliver the goods."

For the first time ever, Mae smiled.

It wasn't pretty. She obviously knew something about T.T. that would make him unwilling to deliver anything. Despite that, Nick bribed Mae with a generous tip, then pushed the cart to Tiffany's door and pressed the buzzer.

A voice over the intercom murmured, "Please come in."

Nick didn't move. Dear God, but that voice was so deliciously throaty it conjured up an image of a sultry brunette in a tight leather dress, stiletto boots and quite possibly a delicate rose tattoo.

Before his stiffened shaft got too excited, Nick warned himself that the voice couldn't belong to Tiffany. It had to be an automated answering system, or one of her executive assistants who had probably been told to hate him.

Reluctantly, he went inside. To his surprise, the room was empty, but drenched in sun and filled with real art, broadleaf banana plants, whispery ferns, a bronze leather sofa and matching chairs.

It also smelled faintly of sun-baked skin that had been washed clean with perfumed soap.

Nick lifted his face to get a really good whiff when that same voice called from down the hall, "Please set up breakfast in the dining room, Mae."

Nick glanced in that direction before looking back down the hall. A shaft of light spilled from the open doorway of a bedroom or bath.

There was the brief tinkling of glass containers as they were being lifted, then returned to a counter. Beneath that was the faint whirr of the air-conditioning and music.

One of Aretha Franklin's old hits.

As Aretha belted out how some guy made her feel like a natural woman, Nick finally paused.

What had seemed like a good idea just moments before, didn't now. Even if Tiffany Taylor had a nice voice (and by God, she must since no one else was here), Nick thought it might be best to keep avoiding her, especially at this ungodly hour, in particular if she were still getting dressed. Quick as can be, he rolled the cart to the dining room table, set up her breakfast (so Mae wouldn't get blamed), and was turning to leave when he heard footfalls coming down the hall.

As he froze, she said, "Good morn—"

Her delicious voice paused. So did Nick's heart.

Before turning around, he warned himself not to expect a sultry brunette, a tight leather dress, or a tattoo.

He was right on two out of three counts.

The tattoo was on her right thigh, just below her silk boxer shorts. It was a cluster of tiny stars that appeared to be falling down her taut, bronzed flesh.

Sweet Jesus. When his gaze finally inched up, he saw that those white boxers rested on the flare of her hips exposing a gold waist chain that was so delicate it sparkled like glitter dust. Each time she breathed it gently rolled over her flat belly.

Nick was quickly transfixed, but forced his gaze to her silk camisole. Edged in antique lace, the fabric whispered over her firm breasts and pebbled nipples. He noticed the right strap had fallen off her shoulder. He couldn't see the left strap, because it was hidden by her shimmering curtain of hair.

She was a real blonde—even her hairline had a silvery tint—the same as those silky-straight brows. Her nose was delicately shaped, her mouth plush, her eyes blue-gray and held by his.

In the pause that followed, the ice in her orange juice cracked, then tinkled. The air-conditioning hushed.

Nick's heart hammered. He stepped closer.

Her gaze never wavered, nor did it leave his. There was a surprising look of recognition in her eyes, as if they had known each other forever, and then a flicker of desire, a surrendering that flushed her throat and cheeks.

In all of his days, Nick had never been more intrigued, and not only by what he saw in her eyes. She looked unbelievably sexy, yet elegant, and seemed completely unaware of it. In a town where most women flaunted their physical gifts, this woman didn't have to. Those silky PJs conjured up images of her lovely hair tousled from bed play. He pictured those amazing eyes sated from love and heavy with sleep.

This was little Tiffany? *Damn.* Suddenly Nick never wanted to leave. He wasn't going to. ". . . hi."

Her lids fluttered, and then her gaze slowly cleared. It was as if his voice had brought her back to the moment, because she glanced at her breakfast, then looked as if she couldn't believe he was here.

Nick figured he'd better say something, just in case she was also thinking of screaming. "I thought I'd help Mae deliver your order."

Her gaze drifted to his mouth, before returning to his eyes. ". . . I see."

Dear God, but her voice was sultry. *This* was little Tif—

She broke into his thoughts. "Do you usually help Mae like that?"

Nick was briefly silent as she pulled her robe from a chair and slipped it on. ". . . I'm not usually in this part of the casino."

Her gaze took in the room before returning to him. "My suite, you mean?"

He cleared his throat. "For the last few weeks we've just kept missing each other, so I thought—"

"You did?" Her eyes briefly widened. "We have?"

Momentarily, time stopped. Nick wondered if he had somehow gotten the wrong suite. Dear God, had Mae known that all along, and that this gorgeous woman wasn't little Tiffany? Was that why Mae had finally been smiling? "Let me start over," he said.

Her gaze swept up and down him. "If you think it will help."

Nick opened his mouth, then closed it without saying a word.

Was she making fun of him? He searched her face, and was quickly lost in the way she continued to regard him. At last, he extended his hand. "I'm Nick Marlow."

She didn't jump for joy. Of course, she didn't threaten to call security, either. After a lengthy pause, she finally approached and slipped her hand into his.

Nick locked his knees to keep standing. Her skin was surprisingly hot, moist, and so achingly soft he could barely breathe.

She moistened her lips.

Okay, now he was beyond dizzy.

". . . Nick Marlow," she said.

He nodded slowly, then felt his heart really race as her thumb starting stroking his. To Nick's surprise, that stroking didn't seem calculated, but oddly tender, which certainly didn't match her initial confusion or that *Be there* on the note. Because of that, he still wasn't entirely certain who she was, so he hedged his bets. "How would you like me to address you?"

That stroking stopped. She seemed to be considering her response before she pulled back her hand. "I'll leave that up to you."

Well, that certainly helped. Even so, Nick kept his tone casual, while he continued to sweat. "Good. So, you read French?"

She followed his gaze to the newspapers he had hastily tossed on the table. Peeking out from the French-language one (which Mae claimed little Tiffany could read) was something Nick hadn't noticed before—*The Enquirer.*

He looked at her.

Her cheeks and throat had already flushed pink.

He couldn't help but tease. "I generally have mine delivered in a plain brown bag."

A smile tugged at her luscious lips. "I'll have to remember that the next time you show up for breakfast."

Next time? "Does that mean I'm staying?"

She fingered her robe's silk tie. "Don't tell me you're hungry, Nick?"

He couldn't tell her anything. His scalp tingled at the way her voice suddenly caressed his name as if she just couldn't help it, which only confused him further. This *couldn't* be little Tiffany, could it? "Actually, I am, Ms . . ."

As that word hung in the air, Tiffany's smile paused. She waited for him to continue, only he did not.

A moment before, when he had asked how to address her, she thought it was because she was the new CEO and he was simply being polite.

Only he wasn't. He didn't know her. Even after all the meetings he had avoided having with her, even after showing up in *her* suite, with *her* breakfast, he still didn't know her.

Dear God, that was depressing. Dear God, his eyes were really something . . . pale as honey and fringed with long, dark lashes, just as she remembered. Of course, Nick Marlow wasn't a man she could easily forget. His gaze had fueled her fantasies from the moment her father had introduced them eleven years before.

Even then, Nick had seemed so adult, so *worldly,* although he had only been twenty-two. At the time, she was just fifteen and thought the glasses he had worn were outta-sight sexy, while his tall, lanky frame had seemed truly buff.

Now that he was thirty-three, he had definitely filled out with only hard, muscled flesh on his six-three frame. He wore his light brown hair a bit shorter, though it still tumbled over his forehead. And the glasses were gone. Only a shadow of beard darkened his rugged features.

He wasn't a conventionally handsome man, but he was damned masculine, a living endorsement for testosterone and how it could turn a woman inside out.

He had always done that to Tiffany and wasn't even aware of it. In the years since they first met, she had often visited the casino, but Nick never noticed her. His attention had always been fixed on beautiful women. Exciting women.

Women he would never forget.

"Tiffany Taylor," she finally said, stating what to him wasn't entirely obvious.

The briefest look of surprise flickered across his face, before he slowly nodded. "Forgive me."

Tiffany wasn't so certain she should. "For what?" After all, there were so many moments to forgive, including all those weeks when they *just* kept missing each other.

Given the expression on his face, he seemed to realize that. "I didn't know."

"That I would actually be in my own suite?"

He sighed. "Tiffany, you've changed."

He was speaking of her at fifteen, of course. Since then, she had done everything she could to make herself attractive and interesting. "Well, maybe." She softened her voice even further. "How about you?"

"I'm not certain what you mean."

Uh-huh. "I sent you numerous e-mails so we could meet to discuss business, all of which you ignored."

"I didn't mean to," he quickly said, "and I am here now. You ready?"

Since she was fifteen. Even so, that didn't mean she was going to throw herself at him now. "I hadn't planned to be ready until nine."

"Tonight?"

He seemed almost eager. Unless she was misreading that, too. "This morning," she said. "You did get my note, right?"

"The one written in lipstick?"

"Lip liner—I was hoping to get your attention."

"Believe me, you did. That's why I'm here."

Tiffany couldn't help but tease. "And here I thought Mae asked you to deliver my breakfast . . . or is it that you're still hungry, Nick?"

"Actually, I am . . . how about you?"

He had no idea. Tiffany slowly nodded, then figured she'd better go to the table before he knew what she meant. To her surprise, Nick actually followed and was soon close enough for her to touch. As she considered the wisdom of that, he said, "I was in kind of a hurry when I put out your food."

Tiffany looked. The silverware had fallen onto one of the chairs, the orange juice had sloshed out of the glass, and the covered plates were stacked like the tower of Pisa.

She finally looked over her shoulder at him.

His gaze fell to her lips before returning to her eyes. "I'll do better next time, all right?"

Her heart caught on that *next time.* "You did fine," she

said, then turned back to the table. "And I suppose we could talk while we eat."

"Whatever you want."

Tiffany stopped herself before she told him exactly what she wanted. After removing the metal covers from the plates, she asked, "What would you like, Nick?"

"Whatever you're willing to share."

Now *there* was a dangerous statement, given that she was prepared to offer her heart. Spearing a bit of the omelet, she prayed for a steady hand and the look of seduction before turning to him. "I think you'll like this."

Nick's gaze met hers, then lowered as she slipped her fingers beneath his chin and eased the food into his mouth.

He swallowed it whole.

She stopped stroking his neck and brought her fingers back. "Good?"

His lids fluttered; he nodded.

She slowly licked the fork clean, hoping to taste him on it.

As Nick watched, his nostrils briefly flared. "If I had known our other meetings would be like this, I wouldn't have missed them."

Tiffany pulled her tongue back into her mouth and lowered the fork to the table. "And that's why you did?"

He was back to looking uncomfortable. "I was busy."

Uh-huh. "As the new CEO, I'd really like to know what you were busy at." *Or with whom.*

He paused as if weighing his words. "Look, Tiffany, I know your dad wanted to retire, so—"

"I thought he wanted time to spend with his fifth wife."

Nick cleared his throat. "That, too. But just because he gave you controlling interest and made you CEO doesn't mean—"

"That I didn't earn it?" she interrupted.

He quickly shook his head. "I didn't say—that is—"

As he continued to stumble over an explanation of why he considered her incompetent, Tiffany finally sighed, "Afraid of a woman boss, Nick?"

His mouth finally closed over the rest of his words. He quietly regarded her, then leaned close. "Nope."

She was glad of that. She trembled at his scent. "Good, then we'll get along just fine."

He smiled, and softened his voice just as she had. "That's what I'm hoping for."

"You don't have to hope, Nick. I'm just pleased you're going to follow my directives."

His smile paused; he leaned back. "I didn't say that—I don't think you want to be calling the shots with the gaming."

"And when I think I do?"

He stepped back. "We're going to have a very big problem."

Tiffany couldn't imagine a bigger problem than him dismissing her judgment, *and* continuing to move back. At last she followed, then looked down as the edge of her big toe touched his moc. Dear God, even that sent shivers down her spine despite his lack of confidence in her and his previous behavior. Suppressing a sigh, she finally raised her face to his.

His gaze lifted from her robe to her eyes.

To her surprise, his eyes were hooded as if he was honestly aroused.

Suddenly, she couldn't think. ". . . what were we talking about?"

It was a moment before he seemed to understand the question. ". . . the fact that you really shouldn't—"

"But why shouldn't I, Nick?"

He paused, then sighed. "Before you can run something you have to learn about it first. If you don't," he said, interrupting her, "you'll be using Keno crayons to write early-morning notes to your next set of employees."

Okay, that stung. She arched one brow. "I'll have you know Wonder Cosmetics had its best quarter ever when I was running the place, and I'll do the same for Piacere."

"You seem fairly certain of that."

She moved past him to the other side of the table. "Eminently so."

"Uh-huh. Then you're willing to put your title and everything else on the table?"

She paused, then looked at him. ". . . what do you mean?"

"Exactly what I say." He moved to her side. "I'll wager that you can't learn this business well enough to satisfy me."

"Oh, Nick. Who says I have to satisfy you?"

His gaze moved from her mouth to her eyes. "Well, if I win, Tiffany, *I* do. And believe me, I don't satisfy easily."

Her face flushed. Before he guessed just what she was thinking, she grabbed a spoon, scooped up a glob of cream cheese and flicked it at her bagel.

It landed on his hand instead.

Nick cleared his throat, and scraped it off.

She dropped the bagel and ran her finger over the spoon, then just had to ask, "You want controlling interest?"

"Not in this casino."

Her finger shook as she lifted it to her mouth. "You want to be CEO?"

"Nope."

"You want to run the show?"

"Tiffany, I already do, at least when it comes to the gaming."

"So, if you win you want to continue doing that?"

"*When* I win. And that would be yes."

She slipped her finger into her mouth, sucked off the cream

cheese, then watched as he finished wiping off his hand. "And when you speak of everything else . . ."

This time he didn't help.

Tiffany finally pulled her finger out of her mouth, and just had to ask. "Are you referring to sex?"

He finally met her gaze.

Her head quickly spun. He *had* been flirting. She *had* aroused him. She leaned against the table.

He looked at her trembling fingers. "Are you all right?"

". . . never been better."

"You sound a little breathless."

Only because she was so dizzy. Never had she expected her first meeting with Nick to go like this. Good sense warned that once this bet began, there would be no turning back. The most primal part of her said it was high time she experienced something other than academics or work.

She cleared her throat. "Let me get this straight—"

"The straighter the better."

Tiffany looked at him. He looked right back.

God, did she want him. "If I don't win your wager—"

"*When* you don't win."

Uh-huh. She pushed away from the table and went to him. "Then you're saying you want my cooperation in something like this?"

His gaze darted down as she moved into him until their bodies touched. And then his gaze jumped up as if he were genuinely surprised.

That didn't even begin to address what Tiffany felt, and yet she couldn't help herself. Eleven years of wanting drove her forward as she slipped her arms around his neck. Her heart caught at the feel of his thick, silky hair and how good it felt to guide his head down to hers. His warmed breath stirred her as nothing else ever had. The obvious restraint in his powerful body comforted and thrilled. She wanted him badly; she always had.

Brushing her lips against his, Tiffany sighed at how soft a man's mouth could be when surrounded by the roughness of his coming beard. Her skin felt slightly scoured, used, and she liked it. So did he. As she teased the seam of his mouth with her tongue, his arms tightened around her. As she eased her tongue inside, she tasted a hint of his morning coffee, and a maleness that was his alone.

It weakened her body and nearly did in her resolve. She wanted to bury her face in his chest, his taut belly and glorious groin. She wanted to experience all of him, but now was not the time. She had promised herself a slow, steady seduction, and so she kissed him just a bit longer before forcing herself to pull away.

Nick's lids fluttered open. He continued to breathe hard, then drew her right back into himself.

His eyes were hooded, his voice husky. "You're wrong, you know."

Her heart beat hard. Her voice hushed, "About what?"

He cradled her face in his free hand. "I want your cooperation in something like this."

Before she could comment, his mouth was over hers, his tongue plunging inside.

He pulled her close and she willingly surrendered.

At that moment, his hardened rod thickened even more, while his kiss grew deep and unrestrained, demanding all that she had to give.

Tiffany gave it without pause, softening to his passion, opening her mouth still further, offering a home to his tongue.

Nick took full advantage filling her as no other man ever had. When she arched her back, inviting him to touch, he did. One hand caressed her buttocks, while his other sought her breast.

As he enjoyed her, she whimpered.

As she enjoyed him, his kiss turned unexpectedly tender, and Tiffany responded in kind, resting her fingertips on his cheek.

At last—almost reluctantly—he ended the kiss, but didn't let go. Their foreheads touched as they both breathed hard.

Outside in the hall, there was the sound of voices.

Not now, Tiffany thought, knowing if anyone jabbed her buzzer she might just fire them. On. The. Spot. And without severance.

No one buzzed. She sighed.

Nick murmured, "You okay?"

Was she ever. "Uh-huh."

"Tiffany, you shouldn't be."

She was about to shake her head, when she understood his comment. "What?"

"You shouldn't be," he repeated, pulling back. "This is what happens when you foolishly play with fire, Tiffany. Not to mention being in over your head."

Her cheeks burned. He thought she was *foolish?* He thought she was *playing?*

She opened her eyes. "And you're the fire I'm in over my head with?" She moved back. "Well, in that case, Nick, I'm the gasoline."

He sighed.

"*And* your boss."

He closed his eyes for a second. "You're not my boss," he said, then continued to speak above her, "not until you win our wager. Unless, of course, you're scared."

At this moment, she was pissed. When that passed, she would be scared. "You must be joking."

"Then we agree on this."

"I haven't agreed to anything."

He looked at her, then stepped back. "I'll give you till ten this morning. When you're ready to talk terms, you can come to my penthouse like you did this morning when you pounded on my door, waking me up, then ran a—"

"I did not run away."

"Have it your way. But the deadline's ten this morning. My penthouse. Be there."

Before Tiffany could respond, he turned and left her suite.

TWO

As Tiffany's door slammed behind him, Nick turned and nearly ran into a tall, blond guy who was blessed with a face as good-looking as Michelangelo's *David*'s and wearing a name tag that read *George*.

"Whoa," George said. Despite his snug T-shirt and jeans, he moved gracefully to one side to avoid a collision. With that accomplished, he offered a million-watt smile that could have brought Venus to life.

"Whoa," Nick said, grabbing George's gorgeous arm before he could deliver that wattage to Tiffany. "What do you think you're doing?"

His hand fell away from her buzzer. "Working."

"*You're* room service?"

"No. I'm here to give Ms. Taylor her morning massage."

Nick's gaze zipped up and down this guy. Hell, he was better-looking than *David*. "What happened to Christina?"

"Nothing." That smile had returned. "Ms. Taylor prefers me."

Now *there* was a surprise.

"If you'll excuse me," George said.

Nick released his arm.

George lifted his finger to the buzzer, then sighed as Nick grabbed him again.

"Is there a problem?" George asked.

Damn right there was, because Nick knew this was none of his business. If Tiffany wanted this guy to give her a massage, pedicure, shampoo, and rinse, that was her right—after all, she was everyone's boss. "No."

The kid looked down to Nick's fingers still clamped around his arm.

"Give Ms. Taylor whatever she wants," Nick said.

George's gaze jumped up.

"Make her happy—treat her with respect, understand? Or you'll be answering to me."

"Yes, sir. Are you her brother?"

Nick arched one brow. "Of course not. I'm the fire and she's the gasoline."

"What?"

"Never mind. Just do whatever she says."

"Yes, sir." He jabbed the buzzer.

Tiffany's intercom'd voice was just a shade off sultry as she said, "Yes?"

The kid announced himself.

As the two of them talked, Nick strode to the elevator.

It had just reached this floor when Tiffany's voice shot out of her suite. "Mr. Marlow said *what?*"

Maybe she no longer wanted to be the gasoline.

Nick slowly shook his head. Only an inexperienced woman would have said that. Only an inexperienced woman would have kissed him so sweetly as she first had.

Only a maniac would have insisted on this wager, and with his partner's daughter, no less.

Suppressing a groan, Nick went into the elevator and slumped against its mirrored wall. He imagined Tiffany's father finding out about this. Knowing Eddie, Nick figured the man would be concerned about one thing, and it wouldn't be Tiffany's wager on her sexual future. If anything, Eddie would want to see the statistics that proved this wager was going to be good for business. And dammit, that was the problem.

Eddie should be here offering his support to Tiffany's new corporate role and keeping Mr. Massage away, rather than honeymooning in Fiji with wife number five.

Sadly enough, it was a choice that had not been lost on Tiffany. Nick had seen the lingering hurt in her eyes, and the resignation, too. Her father had always been too busy making money and the ladies to even notice that his daughter had grown into an amazing young woman who could read *The Enquirer* in French.

Nick smiled as he thought about that, and her sass.

Afraid of a woman boss?

The answer was still *nope*. Nor was Nick afraid of a woman with a good mind. If anything, that made her worth the trouble, and added fuel to the passion. Or, as Tiffany had said, the gasoline.

She was really something.

Nick exited the elevator on his floor and wondered if she'd actually show up by ten, or a few minutes after that just to drive him nuts, to show him who was really boss.

Unless . . .

He stopped just inside his door. What if she didn't show up at all? What if she called his bluff, dug in her soft, pink heels, and forced herself on him, but *only* as his boss?

He could picture it now. She'd show up for all of their meetings wearing silk camisoles, boxer shorts, and an array of new tattoos on varying body parts. Once she had his attention (like she'd lose it after today), she'd lean across the conference table until their noses just about touched; she'd stare at him with those vulnerable blue-gray eyes; she'd point at him with fingers that were sticky from cream cheese, then

murmur directives punctuated with *I'm not only the gasoline, I'm your boss.*

She'd drive him fucking nuts.

Either way, nothing was going to be the same from this
moment forward. Nick knew if he weren't very careful,
he'd be walking bowlegged from a perpetual hard-on like
the one he was sporting now.

Frowning down at his stiffened cock, he hissed, "Patience."

It twitched in defiance.

Suppressing a sigh, Nick bypassed the living room, kitchen,
his bedroom, and stopped at the indoor swimming pool. It
was fed from a waterfall that looked surprisingly real, given
that this was the desert and the water cascaded from a hidden pipe in the floor before tumbling over a series of art-
fully sculpted rocks.

Those splashing sounds mingled with the whisper of air-
conditioning, while the shimmering water reflected off the
glass ceiling and walls. From here, Nick could see jets flying
overhead and all of Vegas below. As always, it seemed tamed
by the early morning light . . . unless Tiffany had subdued it
because she had dominion over that, too.

Suppressing a smile, Nick stripped to skin, then dove
into the cool water and did lap after lap. Back and forth he
went, round and round, until he was dizzy, exhausted, and
still pretty damned hard, because he kept thinking about
delicate gold waist chains and starry tattoos.

Which were currently being stroked and massaged by Gorgeous George, otherwise known as *Ms. Taylor Prefers Me.*

Frowning, Nick hauled himself out of the pool and headed
for the shower.

Once the cold water was on full blast and pelting him
like jet-propelled icicles, he rested his forehead against the
slick tile and tried to focus on the new games he was devis-
ing.

By the time he was finally able to concentrate, he was

wrinkled from the cold water, shivering pretty damned bad, but about twenty degrees too cold to be aroused.

Switching the water to hot, Nick scrubbed every inch of himself, exited in a plume of steam, and stopped dead at what he saw.

What the—?

Behind the clouds of moisture there was a pair of shapely, very long legs parted enough to make an inverted V. They were perfectly balanced on strappy stiletto sandals in a hot coral shade.

His gaze bumped up. Hugging those slender thighs was a short coral skirt that was just this side of dangerous and topped by a matching silk jacket with a neckline that plummeted south.

Nick tried to remember what the housekeeping staff was wearing these days, but could not.

Fingering water out of his eyes, he breathed hard, then snuck another look.

At that moment the steam parted like the Red Sea, showing Tiffany Taylor in all of her glory.

Holy fucking moly.

Her hair hung straight and loose to her shoulders; her tawny skin looked buffed.

And yet, it was her gold, rectangular-framed glasses that captured most of his attention. They made her look decidedly intelligent, unbelievably sexy, and ready for *anything*.

As if to prove it, she gave him a throaty "Hi."

Nick gave her one right back.

"I'm a little early," she said.

He lifted his arm and looked at his watch.

Damn, he was still nude. Somehow he had forgotten about that. His gaze jumped up.

Hers was already well past his face, chest, and navel. As she stared at his stiffened cock, he said, "Only by a few hours."

She moistened her lips, then forced her gaze up. "What?"

"I was just agreeing with you." He paused and squinted. Was that a new mole near the corner of her mouth? "About being early," he finally added.

She slowly nodded. "Your door was open, and since you were expecting me, I just came in." She gave him a tiny shrug, then struggled to keep her gaze up.

Nick wasn't about to look down since every cell in his body knew what she was doing to him. So, he stated the obvious. "I should get dressed."

"If you want to."

If you want to? He lowered his face so she couldn't see his smile. *Damn.* Watching her trying to act sexy while being so obviously vulnerable tugged at his heart. He felt a surprising tenderness for Tiffany he had never felt for another woman. Oddly enough, that didn't make him sappy, but mischievous. He looked at her. "Do you really think *you* would be able to discuss anything while *I'm* like this?"

Her gaze dropped to his groin, lingered briefly, then moved back up. "You mean aroused?"

Okay, that did it. He moved toward her. "You think *this* is aroused?"

She seemed momentarily surprised. "Don't you?"

Of course he did. If his rod got any harder, or her voice got any lower, she'd have him in tears. "Didn't I warn you about playing with fire?"

That got her color up. "Who says I'm playing?"

Nick breathed hard. If he didn't do something physical and soon, they both might regret it. And that was definitely not a chance he was going to take with this woman. When they made love, and they would, it was going to be on his terms and fucking special. It was going to be something that they both *earned.*

Tiffany turned as he strode past. "Nick?"

He stopped at the plaintive note in her voice, then looked over his shoulder to her. "What?"

"You're leaving?"

How could he? He was *naked*.

"No, I'm going to take the swim I had planned to take before you got here."

Her eyes widened slightly as she glanced at the shower. "You bathe before swimming?"

"Doesn't everyone?" He strode to the pool.

A moment later, her high heels clicked against the tile as she followed, bringing that sun-washed, earthy fragrance with her.

Just as he reached the edge of the pool to drown himself, she said, "Nick, haven't you forgotten something?"

He looked over his shoulder to her.

She had a death grip on his Speedo, while her gaze was glued to his buck-naked ass.

"We can talk while you do your laps," she said, then threw the suit.

It landed in the pool.

"Sorry," she said.

She sounded as if she really meant it. Even so, no way was he going to get down on his knees to fish it out. "It's okay," he said, "I'll just do without."

He dove into the pool and swam hard. Back and forth. Round and round, until he was dizzy, but not even close to getting rid of his hard-on. *Dear God.*

At last he treaded water, breathed hard, and looked up.

Tiffany was sitting at the shallow end of the pool, regarding him through those glasses. Her left leg was dangling in the water, her right outstretched with his Speedo hanging from the tips of her naked, coral-polished toes.

From this angle, he could see clear up her thigh. Either she was seriously naked beneath that skirt, or wearing a skimpy thong.

His heart just about stopped. And here he thought *she* was the vulnerable one. Breathing hard, he knew it was definitely time to get down to business before she drove him completely nuts.

He swam to the shallow end of the pool, then walked through water to her side. "Thanks." He lifted the Speedo from her toes, threw it on top of her stiletto heels, and cupped her ankle in his palm. "Ready to set the rules of engagement?"

Her lids fluttered widely, a coral blush crept up her throat as Nick ran his forefinger from the tips of her toes clear to that starry tattoo on her thigh.

"About learning this business?" she asked.

"And how to seduce a man."

She paused in mid-sigh and leveled her gaze at him.

"Uh-uh," he said, holding onto her leg when she tried to take it back. "You've been trying to seduce me since—"

"Oh, *please*. I have—"

"Very little experience in this area." Reaching up, he gently peeled that fake beauty mark from the side of her mouth.

She looked at it resting on the tip of his thumb. "Was it about to fall off?"

"It was unnecessary. You don't need it."

Her gaze lifted to his. She seemed genuinely surprised. "Research at Wonder Cosmetics indicated that men like it."

"Well, I don't, and I'm a man."

Her eyes glazed as she glanced at his chest. "So what do *you* like, Nick?"

He rested his hand on her smooth, hot thigh. "Bare flesh."

Her lids fluttered.

"And starry tattoos."

She blushed. "You really like that?"

God, did he ever. "Yep."

"Then it appears I do know how to seduce a man."

"Not entirely. But don't worry, I intend to teach you everything I know."

Her laugh was as throaty as her voice. "About seducing men? You surprise me, Nick. So, how often do you seduce—"

"You know what I mean. I'm going to teach you how I like to be seduced by . . . well, you know."

Tiffany wasn't entirely certain that she did. Had he been about to speak the name of another woman, *his* woman, one he might have lost and still loved? Her heart caught as she quietly regarded him, then leaned closer to study his face.

Beads of water clung to his lush lashes, there was a touch more color in his tanned cheeks, and a muscle in his jaw suddenly twitched.

He cleared his throat. "What are you doing?"

"Looking."

"For what?"

Something other than his current embarrassment—specifically, his feelings for her. Did he think she was still playing at this?

Did he think she looked ridiculous?

Once more, Tiffany's heart caught, but she had to know. "You didn't finish, Nick. Seduced by whom?"

"You," he said, without pause.

Her entire body flushed with heat and victory. "*If* you win," she said, leaning back.

He arched one brow at her sass, but finally smiled. "Ready to talk terms?"

"Since you claim to be the expert, you first."

"Fine."

Tiffany's gaze lowered as he rested his hands on her knees, then parted her legs so that he could move inside. Once there, he planted his hands on either side of her and leaned close.

Her heart raced. Swallowing hard, she lifted her gaze to his mouth, then to his eyes.

They seemed momentarily transfixed.

Her belly fluttered, her voice hushed, "What?"

"I was just thinking of the terms."

Her throat got red. "What exactly do you have in mind?"

"What else? You have a week to learn gam—"

"*A week?*"

He arched one brow. "Do you think either of us will be able to withstand more than a week of this foreplay?"

She followed his gaze to her legs, which had been hugging him. She unwrapped them. "I'm certain you won't."

There was a smile in his eyes, but he kept his voice businesslike and calm. "Okay, here's the deal. You learn the games we offer here, and then we play. If you win—"

"When I win."

"O-kay. Each time you win I'll bow to your CEO decisions for one week with as little argument as possible."

"How about none?"

"Make good decisions, and you got it."

She tapped her forefinger against her lips as she thought about that. "So, you're saying that if I win fifty-two games, I'll be running the show—and you—for a year?"

"If your decisions are good, that's right."

"Great."

"Not so fast. When I win—"

She pressed her forefinger against his lips, stopping him. "*If* you win."

His nostrils briefly flared before he wrapped his hand around hers, eased her finger from his mouth, then licked its length.

Tiffany's toes curled.

"Each time I win a game," he continued, "I'll be running the show *and* you, nothing forbidden, nothing held back, for one hour."

He released her hand.

It fell to her lap as her mind zipped over what he had just said. ". . . that's a little lopsided, don't you think?"

"One hour of your time is fair since I have far more experience in gaming than—"

"I was referring to the *nothing forbidden, nothing held back* part." *God, what did he have in mind?*

"Worried you won't win?" he asked, then ran his forefinger over the edges of her jacket, the deep V that dipped between her breasts. "Or are you worried that you will?"

Her eyes fluttered closed; she continued to tremble. "I'm not worried at all."

"That's my girl."

Tiffany liked the sound of that. She opened her eyes and looked at him from beneath her lashes. "So, that's it?"

"Uh-uh. We haven't even started."

She liked the sound of that, too.

"In order to make this completely fair," he said, "we'll only be playing those games that require some level of skill."

"There is such a thing?"

"It's called blackjack and poker. As CEO of this place, you should know that."

"I do. You have to count cards to be good at blackjack."

"It certainly helps."

"And with poker . . ."

"Uh-huh?"

"Would we be talking seven-card stud or draw?"

He seemed genuinely impressed. "So, you *do* know about this stuff?"

Not really. Before coming here she had researched a few terms on the net so she could dazzle him with her clothes *and* her knowledge of gaming. "As you so aptly said, I do run this establishment, Nick. So, which game do you prefer?"

He leaned so close their noses just about touched. "You tell me."

The words were out of her mouth before she could stop them. "Ever hear of strip poker?"

He stared, then moved back. "Huh? What?"

"Strip," she said, with more confidence than she felt. "We'll not only play for creative control of the gaming, but for our clothes."

He looked down at his obvious nudity.

So did she. Good Lord, the water made his erection look three times its usually enormous size.

Nick cleared his throat. "That's a little lopsided, don't you think?"

No, his stiffened rod was simply perfect. Inhaling deeply, Tiffany sighed out her words. "Look at it this way, you'll get to see me *if* you win."

His gaze lifted. "Believe me, you don't have a chance."

"Are you going to play fair or not?"

He glanced down to her Frederick's of Hollywood business suit.

She fidgeted. "You know what I mean."

"I always play fair," he said, then met her gaze. "And we'll do this your way. Strip poker for our clothes, mixed in with blackjack for everything else. Once you're totally bare—"

"Excuse me?"

"O-kay. Once one of us is totally bare, we'll tally up the weeks of my time that you've won, and the hours of your time that I've won, and—"

"Wait a sec—we're mixing apples with oranges here. We should tally up the hours of *everyone's* time. With 24 hours times seven days a week, I would have 172 hours each time I won."

"168," he corrected. "And no, I'm offering a handicap, not giving you the keys to the castle."

She ran her forefinger over his chest, making his pecs dance. "What's the matter, Marlow, you scared?"

He grinned. "Only that you won't last the night." He drew lazy circles around her starry tattoo. "Looks like you've got some serious studying ahead."

She laughed. "How hard can gambling be?"

"Gaming," he corrected. "And you better find out if you want to run this show."

Her laughter paused.

"Would you like a kiss for good luck?" he asked, his voice unexpectedly soft. "Or don't you think you need it?"

"You tell me."

Smiling, he lifted the glasses from her nose, perched them on the top of his head, and cupped her face in his hands.

Tiffany's lids fluttered closed as Nick covered her mouth with his own. His lips were still chilled from the water, but his tongue was achingly hot as he slipped it inside.

She whimpered as his kiss grew increasingly tender. She moaned when he stopped too quickly, as if he wanted her to crave more.

She did. As he pulled back, Tiffany kept leaning forward until she was in danger of falling into the pool.

"Good luck," he said, then slipped the glasses back on her face.

She went briefly cross-eyed as she looked at the water spots on the lenses. "Can I ask you something?"

"About gambling?"

"Gaming," she corrected, "and no." She lifted her gaze to his. "My dad won't ever know about this bet, will he? I mean," she quickly continued before Nick could speak, "I don't want him to know. He put me in charge here. I don't want to let him down. I don't want him to get angry. He's very protective of me, you know?"

"Yeah, I know."

Tiffany was stunned. She knew Nick and her dad were close, but she hadn't imagined they ever talked about her. Although she loved her father dearly, Tiffany had long given up hope that she was on his list of priorities. In fact, she had only mentioned him so that Nick wouldn't guess the brutal truth. "Dad actually discussed me with you?"

"Well, not discussed . . . but he does talk about you all the time."

Tiffany considered such a thing. "Is that talk good?"

"The very best."

"And did you listen?"

"I should have."

She smiled. "Then I forgive you."

That meant more to Nick than everything else he had achieved, and he didn't feel bad about lying just now. He wouldn't have hurt Tiffany for the world. And when he next contacted Eddie, he was going to tell the damned fool to pay attention to his beautiful daughter. "Thanks. Now, get going. I'll see you at today's meeting."

Her smile paused. "Meeting? What meet—"

"The one you call each week with the senior execs."

"You're actually going to come to that?"

He smiled. "You sent me fifteen email invitations all ending with *be there*. So, I intend to be. But don't worry, I won't say anything about *this* meeting. As far as the rest of the staff's concerned, you and I have never even set eyes on each other."

Her gaze dropped to his chest and lower. "But you never came be—"

"I want to now."

Tiffany looked torn between raw panic and dread.

It was definitely going to be some meeting. "Need help getting up?" he asked.

She shook her head. "I'm a bad-ass chick."

Nick smiled. "You're an intelligent woman, and don't you forget it."

"Like I said, a bad-ass chick."

He laughed and moved back.

Tiffany pulled her legs out of the pool, swung them around, grabbed her high heels, and gracefully pushed to her feet. Looking down at him, she asked, "Next week, here, for our wager?"

"You bet."

She stepped away, turned, then paused. "Can I ask you something else?"

Nick's gaze lingered on that damp coral silk stretched across her firm butt. "I won't tell my parents about this, either, all right?"

She turned around. "They live in Vegas?"

"Lord, no. They never go west of New Hampshire."

"Then they've never even seen what you do here?"

Nick smiled at the indignation in her voice. "They're molecular biologists, Tiffany."

"God, they must be as smart as you."

He paused to that endorsement. "Actually, they're even smarter."

Her indignation was back. "Even if that were possible, that doesn't mean they can't have some fun."

"You don't know my parents."

"Aren't you guys close?"

Nick wasn't certain how to answer that. Over the years, he had had more heart-to-heart talks with Tiffany's dad than his own, a man who was so brilliant being human simply didn't come easy. And when it came to his mom, well, she could barely hide her embarrassment over her son's choice of a career. They loved him, he knew; they just didn't approve of him.

"We do all right," he said.

"Forgive me for saying this, but it's their loss."

Nick put his left elbow on the edge of the pool and rested his head against the heel of his hand. "You know, that's the nicest thing anyone's ever said to me."

"It shouldn't be. You deserve the very best."

"When I win you, I'll be getting just that."

Those delicate nostrils flared, but her voice was all sass. "*If* you win."

Nick smiled, then ran his fingers across her naked toes until she jumped back, giggling. "Oh, I will. Believe you me. See you in the meeting."

Three

Tiffany left Nick's penthouse tingling with excitement, and pretty much scared to death.

She couldn't imagine what might happen at today's meeting, except that it would hardly erase the memory of him stepping out of the shower naked, stunned, and very hung.

Dear God. With that image invading her thoughts, how was she supposed to concentrate on business?

Just as importantly, how was she going to survive this bet that was surely no more than a game to Nick? After all, he had been surrounded by beautiful women for a good part of his life when she had only wanted him.

As far as Tiffany could see, her only chance of winning his love was to give him something all those other women could not. And that meant dazzling him with her gaming skill that was currently nonexistent.

Suppressing a sigh, Tiffany entered the elevator and pressed her forehead against the mirrored wall. How in the hell was she going to keep up with, much less beat, an MIT-educated mathematics whiz?

How in the world could she settle for anything but winning his mind and heart?

From the moment they had met, Tiffany had loved the thought of Nick Marlow. He had seemed dangerous, seductive, exciting.

A few minutes ago, she learned better.

He was a genuinely nice guy. His innate class had allowed him to treat her like a lady despite the things she said, how she acted, and what she wore. His honor was no less impressive. In order to spare her feelings, he had so easily lied about her dad's disinterest in anything she did.

For that alone, Tiffany had pretended to be fooled. For that alone, she loved Nick.

But she also craved his male beauty. Nick Marlow easily surpassed all those male models in beefcake magazines, not to mention the less-than-beefcake guys she had seen in real life. After all, she wasn't a virgin. There had been lots of men. Okay, *some* men. Okay, two men. But neither of them had been Nick.

Dear God, his body was lean but muscular with hair in all the right places. His round-the-clock shadow was unbelievably arousing, just like his heavily furred chest, though neither came close to the wonder of that dark, silky thatch above his stiffened penis.

"You think this is aroused?" he had asked.

A lusty moan escaped the back of her throat. Tiffany tried to picture his rod being any longer or stiffer, and what would actually be lost if he won.

He'd collect on their bet, smile for three seconds, and that would be the end of it. Unless she could convince him how seriously she did take his work, and how much she craved his love.

Tiffany chewed her lower lip and was out of the elevator before the doors had fully opened on the executive-level floor. Running down the hall, she nearly knocked down her personal assistant.

The young woman pressed against the wall, her dark

eyes on her boss's streetwalker suit, an article of clothing Tiffany had purchased in anticipation of seducing Nick.

He hadn't bought it, but he had been really sweet. *Don't worry, I intend to teach you everything I know.*

Tiffany's head swam, before she realized her assistant was speaking. "I'm sorry, what?"

"I said, good morning, Ms. Taylor."

"Good morning, Carla. I need to see you in my suite now. Let's go."

As Carla dutifully followed Tiffany back to the elevator, two male executives watched.

Tiffany breezed past them without a word. No sense in explaining she wasn't a lesbian, which was the current gossip making the rounds. It seemed her lack of interest in any of the men here was more noticeable than she had thought, and probably wouldn't be helped by what she wore now.

During the elevator ride, Carla's gaze kept darting to Tiffany's reflection in the mirrored wall, at least until Tiffany smiled back.

After that, they both kept their gazes averted. Once they reached her bedroom, Tiffany tossed her glasses on the bed and removed her stiletto heels.

Carla remained in the doorway as her gaze bounced over the room's jungle décor. Earthy, sensual colors mixed with cool, feathery ferns. Nestled in all that foliage was a king-sized bed with gold-slashed copper linens, and a canopy that was gossamer thin, just like those plumes of steam that had followed Nick from his shower.

At one time, Tiffany had hoped to impress Nick with this den of passion. Now she knew better. She was going to have to get him with her gaming skills.

Before depression completely overtook her, she spoke to Carla. "Please take notes while I get ready for my meeting." Grabbing a notepad and pen from the nightstand, Tiffany tossed them.

Carla glanced over her shoulder to where they had landed in the hall. After retrieving them, she returned, but not one step closer than the doorway.

Apparently Carla had heard those lesbian rumors, too.

Ignoring that, Tiffany said, "I need all the info you can find on blackjack and strip poker."

Carla stopped writing.

"Stud poker," Tiffany said, correcting herself. "Draw, too. And whatever other kinds there are."

As Carla continued writing, Tiffany pulled a conservative pearl-gray business suit, a white silk blouse, and sensible heels from her closet. "After you compile that data, I need a spreadsheet detailing wins using various strategies—in particular card-counting—along with all the available statistics during the last ten years or so of what else makes a person get the most favorable hands. Break the winners down by gender, occupation, age, locale, education, and if pertinent, IQ. You might want to put that in a detailed table, or a PowerPoint presentation. Please have it on my desk before noon."

Carla glanced at the clock on the nightstand. *"Today?"*

Maybe she was pushing it. "Have it to me by two today. I know how thorough you like to be."

Carla muttered something beneath her breath, then pointed over her shoulder. "Mr. Marlow knows everything there is about gaming. I'll ask—"

"No. You say *nothing* about this to Mr. Marlow, understand?"

She frowned. "But I don't see how I'm going to finish by—"

"I'll call HR and have them send you some help. How's that?"

"I could use two assist—"

"I'll get you three. What are your plans for tonight?"

"After work?"

"I really need you to stay and play cards."

". . . with you?"

Tiffany nodded.

Carla touched her Peter Pan collar. "My boyfriend was kind of expecting—"

"Can I be honest with you?"

Carla's expression said *please don't.*

Tiffany sighed—there was simply no other choice. "Since this is a casino, I need to learn about gaming, at least to some degree, but I want to do it without the other execs knowing."

Carla's short, dark hair skimmed her cheeks as she quickly nodded. "Good for you."

"Excuse me?"

"Well, I might be out of line here, but if you allow them, the other execs will try to put one over on you. They can't if you know the business—so, good for you. Still, I don't play cards, so I don't know how I can possibly be of any—"

"You have all afternoon to study. And each time you beat me at poker or blackjack, you get a hundred-dollar, tax-free bonus."

". . . and if I lose?"

"You still get it, minus taxes."

"What time do we start?"

"Seven. And we're here working late, not playing cards, understand? So, please don't tell anyone."

As Carla hurried down the hall, Tiffany called HR and ordered a team of assistants. After that, she pulled on her CEO duds, went to her office, and worked as hard as she usually did.

At eleven-thirty sharp, she swallowed down panic, grabbed her meeting materials, and headed for the conference room.

Inside, a group of conservatively dressed men and women stopped laughing and chatting the moment Tiffany put her stuff on the table. They looked at the mountain of data she intended to go over today, then greeted her with a cautious or hostile, ". . . Tiffany."

At any other time, that might have wounded. At any other time, Tiffany would have felt eager to begin, to learn as much as she could about Piacere's many operations.

But today, her attention was on Nick.

He stood next to Tom Hawkins, an older exec. As Tom resumed pointing to and talking about the report he was holding, Nick's gaze suddenly lifted to Tiffany.

Her tongue paused halfway across her lips.

Nick's gaze lowered to it. There was a flicker of mischief and unashamed passion in his honey-colored eyes.

Before she started to seriously drool, Tiffany pulled her tongue back in and glanced over both shoulders. To her surprise, no one was currently watching.

When she looked back to Nick, he had already donned his corporate face and was saying something to Tom. He then left the man's side and came around the table to her.

"I don't believe we've met," he said, taking her hand in his own.

His grip was strong, his skin heated, his clean scent damned near intoxicating.

Tiffany's face flushed. She looked down to their hands while Nick introduced himself as if she had yet to see him nude or aroused—in other words, as if they were still strangers.

Tiffany nodded, playing along as she studied the dark blue suit, white shirt and gold silk tie he wore. Dear God, he looked nice.

He was also still talking.

She cleared her throat. "I'm sorry, what?"

"I said, I've been wanting to meet you for a very long time."

She nodded absently as she continued to stare at his gold silk tie. Somehow, she just couldn't get past the thought of him pulling that tie from his collar, then slowly wrapping it around her wrists so he would have full control while he stripped her naked.

"For weeks and weeks, in fact," he said.

Her gaze finally lifted to his and the world went blurry. "You look good dressed."

His smile froze. His brows lifted.

Tiffany was briefly confused before the blood drained from her face. She lowered her voice so only he could hear. "Don't tell me I said that out loud."

Nick worked his mouth so he wouldn't smile. She looked so adorable he couldn't help but tease. "Said what?"

She continued to speak in a lowered tone. "About liking your tie—your clothes."

Uh-huh. "Which is it?"

She looked down.

When her gaze remained fixed, Nick finally glanced down, too, then spoke in a lowered tone. "Would you like me to wear this suit next week for our bet?"

"Just the tie," she whispered, "and your Speedo."

He laughed.

Her gaze jumped up.

As the other execs glanced over, Nick released her hand and spoke in his normal voice. "I've never heard that particular story before. Your father is really something."

Tiffany twisted the top button of her blouse. "He is, isn't he?"

When the other execs resumed their own conversations, Nick leaned a bit closer and spoke in a lowered tone, "My tie and Speedo?"

She nodded, then paused as she twisted that button off. Slipping it into her jacket pocket, she kept her voice lowered. "Is that a problem?"

"Only the tie. Why do you want that?"

Her face flushed. She whispered, "If you win, I'll tell you, all right?"

Now he whispered. "Oh, honey, I think you misunderstand. *When* I win we won't be using our mouths to talk."

Those delicate nostrils flared.

"So," Nick said, as another exec neared, "are we on the same page with that?"

Tiffany slowly nodded as her gaze said they were on the same page, paragraph, sentence, and word.

"Good," he said. "How about we eat?"

Tiffany's gaze trickled down him, then edged back up. ". . . huh?"

He inclined his head toward the buffet.

She looked back to his tie.

Before anyone noticed her peculiar fixation, Nick spoke in his normal voice. "Shall we?" He gestured toward the refreshments.

She sighed deeply before heading in that direction.

Nick's first reaction was to follow so they could continue to arouse each other, but he forced himself to hold back. As she reached the buffet, his gaze swept over her. Unlike before, her hair was now in a French roll, her gray skirt was mid-calf with a matching jacket, and her white silk blouse reached practically to her ears. In other words, she looked unbelievably sexy *and* elegant.

And was obviously still thinking about their conversation (or his tie), as the serving spoon hung limply from her hand while she simply stared at the food.

Nick finally joined her.

Tiffany looked from the bagels to him.

Her expression was so guileless, so wanting, his heart quickly melted.

She noticed. "Are you all right?"

His balls hurt, his cock was trying to break free of his briefs, and he was having trouble concentrating. "Never been better."

She slowly nodded, then glanced at the buffet as another exec neared. "This looks really good."

"Enough to eat."

She hesitated for a moment, then met his gaze. "You hungry?"

"Starved. You?"

Her gaze dropped to his mouth before returning to his eyes. "You wouldn't believe my appetite."

His balls twitched. "If you'll allow me . . ." He covered her hand with his own, then eased the serving spoon from her and dug into the cream cheese. "Is this enough? Would you like more?"

She glanced down. He had scooped up half the bowl. "That's perfect. Thanks."

He slapped it onto her bagel. "You're welcome. What else would you like?"

Her eyes got unfocused as she thought about that.

Before anyone noticed, Nick suggested fruit, slapping that on her plate and some meat on his own before suggesting they return to the conference table.

Once there, he pulled out a chair for her.

She looked briefly disappointed that she wouldn't be sitting on his lap. "Thank you."

"You're welcome." He rested his hand on the small of her back. Her lids fluttered. She sank like a rock, then looked to either side. Both chairs were being taken.

"Excuse me, Frank?" Nick said.

The man looked up, then down as Nick pulled the chair from him. "There's a seat over there," Nick said, gesturing with his head.

As Frank backed away, Nick sat. He struggled for a moment, then looked at her.

Tiffany quickly averted her gaze and bit into her bagel.

Nick looked from that back to her.

She slowly chewed, then starting writing on her notepad. Easing it to him, she said, "Is that calculation correct?"

He looked down to what she had written:

Nick, you're staring at me.

"I think it might be a bit off," he said. Pulling out his own pen, he wrote: *There's cream cheese on your chin.*

Tiffany blushed to the roots of her hair. Clearing her throat, she fingered the cream cheese from her chin and forced herself to look at the rest of the crew.

Most of the women were watching Nick. The men, on the other hand, seemed far more interested in the food than her.

Nick continued writing on the pad, then pushed it toward her. "Try this," he said.

She glanced down to what he had written.

I was staring—but not because of the cream cheese. You look lovely. Forgive me?

Even her bones went soft. If they had been alone, Nick would have been breathless from her forgiveness. Given that they were surrounded by her hostile staff, Tiffany wrote: *Well, I don't know. Are you going to behave?*

He wrote: *Are you?*

Am I what? she wrote.

Nick click-click-clicked his pen, then wrote: *Going to behave. What did you think I—*

His pen skidded across the pad, then fell out of his hand as she wrapped her leg behind his.

Tiffany watched as the pen rolled off the table. "You better get that." She pulled back her leg. "We're ready to begin."

As Nick pushed his chair away from the table and leaned down, Tiffany looked back to the staff. "Adam," she said, "why don't youuuuuuuu—"

Even the men who were still eating looked up.

Tiffany didn't dare look down since she could feel Nick's pen skimming the back of her knee. Before she got too giddy, she covered it with a cough.

Nick straightened, grabbed a glass of water, and handed it to her. "You all right?" he asked.

She drank fast, then said, "Fine." After clearing the gravel from her throat, she looked at Adam Blake. "Let's have your report."

Nick took back his glass. As Adam went into his spiel, Nick's long fingers stroked, stroked, stroked that glass.

Tiffany was transfixed.

She imagined the magic those fingers could work on a woman's breast, or between her legs. *Mercy.* Shivers of delight coursed down—

"—page three of the report," Adam said, his voice suddenly breaking into her naughty thoughts, "and taking Tiffany's projections into account, I found—"

Nick unexpectedly interrupted. "Just a minute, Adam."

Tiffany's heart raced; she eased her leg from Nick's.

To her surprise, he didn't notice, nor did he tell her to be a good girl. Flipping through the copy of Adam's report, Nick tapped his pen against column two. "Those aren't Tiffany's projections."

They aren't? Grabbing her data, Tiffany flipped to the page Nick was on. By God, he was right.

"Look on page eight of Tiffany's report," Nick said, turning to it.

Paper rustled as everyone turned to page eight. Given their sheepish expressions, this was the first time they had actually bothered to review this, even though it had been available for weeks.

But Nick had obviously read it. In fact, he seemed absorbed by it, until he abruptly looked up and met her gaze.

Tiffany's heart paused. Here was a man who had at least a decade more of experience in business than she had. And yet, she spoke without pause or apology. "My data's accurate."

"I know."

Her heart soared.

Nick turned to Adam with a *Well?* in his eyes.

The man frowned. "Do you want me to move on to the other parts of my report?"

"That's up to Tiffany," Nick said.

She felt so lightheaded with his approval that when Adam met her gaze, she actually smiled. "We have plenty else to get through. We'll be looking forward to hearing your full, revised report at the next meeting. Right, everyone?"

Spoons, forks, and knives stopped clacking. After a deafening silence, there were mumbles of approval.

Tiffany asked Walt Evers to report next, then leaned forward in her chair and paid very close attention to the rest of the proceedings. No one else tried to get anything past her, especially Nick.

He behaved like the perfect gentleman, treating her with the respect due an honest-to-God CEO. When the meeting finally ended, he promised to e-mail his new gaming projections to her, and then he left, joining the male execs in the hall.

It wasn't long before Tiffany heard loud laughter. A week before, she would have guessed the guys were making cruel jokes about her. Because of Nick, she knew better. After collecting her stuff, Tiffany left the conference room and walked right up to the guys.

Nick was the first to notice.

Her heart fluttered at his potent gaze, but this time she acted every inch the CEO. "Gentlemen," she said in her most gracious tone, then made eye contact with each of them before she walked past.

As the guys resumed their conversation, Nick turned. His gaze dropped to Tiffany's shapely calves, then edged right back up to her butt. There seemed to be more wiggle in it now than when she had left his penthouse in that X-rated business suit.

Who would have guessed a deadly dull executives' meeting could do that? Or make her playful enough to engage in pillow talk and run her leg up and down his. Hell, his cock had done so many push-ups during that it was still exhausted now.

She was really something. And in a week, every delicious inch of her was going to be his.

Turning back to the guys, Nick noticed two of them were also watching Tiffany. Stepping to the side to block their view, Nick listened politely to their BS, then finally excused himself and headed for the elevator.

He was just about there when someone grabbed his jacket sleeve. Nick stopped, then looked over his shoulder.

Tiffany pulled him into the service elevator and jabbed the button that closed the doors.

He pulled his other arm inside before it got crushed. "What are you doing?"

"Forgiving you."

His eyes briefly widened as she moved into him, slipped her arms around his neck, and pressed her cheek against his.

The embrace was so tender, Nick was momentarily stunned. "Are you all right?"

She breathed deeply. "Uh-huh."

Her voice was so soft, Nick's toes curled. At last, he did what came naturally and wrapped his arms around her.

Tiffany snuggled even closer. She pressed her lips to his neck, then gently suckled, her tongue flicking over his flesh in hot, wet strokes.

His balls started to ache. He pulled her closer.

Tiffany softened even more.

His voice was quickly strangled. "I'm sorry, but I just can't stand this."

Before Tiffany could ask exactly what he couldn't stand, his mouth was over hers.

Dear God. His kiss was unbelievably deep and needy, his hand suddenly beneath her jacket, covering her breast.

Without thinking or pause, Tiffany arched her back, giving Nick greater access, then returned his kiss as she had never done with another man, driving her tongue into his mouth while her hands explored.

Nick groaned as her right hand ran over his chest. When her left hand slipped over his fly and lower to cup his sac, he briefly froze as if he just couldn't believe it.

When he finally did, he quickly pulled his mouth free. "Tiffany?"

"Uh-huh?" She tried to recapture his mouth.

He wouldn't let her. "Tiffany!"

She continued to caress his sac.

"Tiffany!"

"What?"

His breathing hitched.

She breathed hard, too, then lifted her hands to his tie.

Nick's chest pumped so hard that the gold silk wiggled.

Pressing her hand over the fabric, she tugged on the knot, wanting to pull it from his collar so he could—

"Tiffany!"

"Just give me a sec, Nick."

"What for? To undress me? Do you really think we should be doing *this* in *here?*"

It was a moment before she stopped working on his tie and remembered exactly where they were. Pulling her hands away, she looked down to her own mussed clothes, then stepped back. "Sorry. I guess I got carried away."

If any other woman had said what she just did, it would have sounded like a line. Given her ragged breaths and the way she was still transfixed by his tie, he knew she meant it. And somehow that made him want her all the more.

Before he lost all control, Nick shoved his hands into his trouser pockets and stepped back.

Tiffany continued to smooth her clothing as her gaze lowered to his fly. "Can I ask you some—"

"Yes, I'm aroused. Very aroused. Fucking aroused. All right?"

"Uh-huh. But that's not what I wanted to ask."

Nick pulled his right hand out of his pocket and pressed it over his eyes. "What then?"

"Have you ever made love in an elevator?"

His hand dropped. He looked at her.

Her gaze was as blurry as her voice. ". . . I thought we could make it a part of our bet."

Any more talk like that and there wouldn't be any need for one. "Actually, I thought we'd skip all of that since it's a foregone conclusion that I *will* win."

Faster than Nick thought possible, her eyes cleared. Suddenly, she was Ms. CEO, again. "Only because you're taking unfair advantage."

He recalled her hot, wet tongue stroking his neck, and those delicate fingers fondling his balls. "Excuse me?"

"You've had more than a decade to perfect your skill. You're giving me one week."

"Well, if you think I'm going to give you a decade, then—"

"I want hours versus hours if I win a hand."

He laughed. "All it would take would be one win on your part and I'd never catch up."

"Would that be so bad?"

It might, given his demand of nothing forbidden, nothing held back.

"What's the matter?" she asked. "Are you afraid you won't—"

"Not at all."

She arched one slender brow.

Nick inhaled deeply, then sighed out his words. "Okay, forget the weeks to hours we talked about. For every hour I win of your time, you'll win two hours of mine."

"Five."

"Three."

"Fifteen."

His head fell forward. "Where in the world did you learn to negotiate?"

"What does it matter when I win?"

Hmmm. He lifted his head. "Tell you what—I'll give you ten hours of my time to your one, with the time tallied up the moment you literally lose your skirt and everything else during our game of strip poker. And that's my final offer."

Her eyes were briefly glazed. "Thanks." She smiled.

It tore his heart in two. Right now, he was ready to give her the keys to the castle, the family jewels, and his heart. "So, is that what this kamikaze attack of yours was about? Getting me to acquiesce?"

Her expression changed. She seemed honestly hurt. "Of course not—I was thanking you."

"I thought you were forgiving me, and undressing me and fondling—"

"I was also thanking you for being on my side at the meeting. I really appreciate it." She rested her left hand on his tie, then ran her right index finger over his lips.

Nick grabbed her hand before his teeth started tingling. "Tiffany, if you're talking about that stuff with Adam, then—"

"You not only caught his error, Nick, you took my work seriously. I'll never forget it."

She wasn't kidding. He cupped her hand in his palm, and softened his voice. "Your projections were sound, Tiffany. It was excellent work and deserved to be taken seriously."

She smiled. "I'm one smart babe."

He laughed.

"Which is why I'm going to win our bet," she said.

His laughter paused. "Dream on. And," he added, "no more negotiations."

Lifting her hand, he pressed his lips to her palm.

Tiffany's eyes fluttered closed; her head lolled on her shoulders.

When she curled her fingers, touching the side of his face, Nick knew she had won. Hell, with him she would always win.

Not that that would make the journey to victory any less interesting.

He slipped his tongue between each of her fingers, then kissed the tips.

While she was still moaning, he asked, "Are you wearing your gold chain now?" He ran his fingertip just below her waist to see if he could feel it, then smiled as she trembled to his touch. "Do you always have it on?"

She lifted her head and looked at him from beneath her lashes. "You'll know *if* you win."

Hmmm. Before Nick lost what little control he had regained, he turned and pressed the button that got this little box moving.

As it whooshed up, Tiffany quietly regarded him.

"Your hair's still mussed," he said.

"Your fly's open," she said.

He looked down.

As she fixed her hair, Nick zipped himself.

"Now behave," he warned when the elevator stopped.

The doors opened to a bellhop and two room service employees.

Before surprise could register on their faces, Tiffany spoke in her CEO voice, "Have maintenance check out *all* the elevators, Mr. Marlow. This is the second time this week we've had to use the ones for service. Bobbie, Frank, Richard," she said, addressing the staff.

They seemed surprised that she knew their names. There was a chorus of "Afternoon, ma'am," as they quickly moved to the side to let her pass.

As Nick exited the elevator, Tiffany turned to the left, then moved down the hall.

This time, her butt really wiggled, and not once did she give him a backward glance.

Four

When Tiffany returned to her office, there was a stack of gaming material on her desk that would have daunted the Las Vegas casino commission. Slumping against the door, she wondered if she should just let Nick win.

Like she had a choice. No matter what she did, or the handicap he offered, he was going to have her stripped bare in three seconds flat. They'd make love, he'd continue running this place, and that would be that.

Because he'd never again trust her intelligence or determination if she didn't at least try. He'd regret having supported her at today's meeting.

She'd have his body, but not his heart or respect.

"Damn." Gritting her teeth, Tiffany pushed away from the door and went to her desk.

Five hours later, blackjack and poker terms swam in her head like narration in an X-rated romance. There was *cheating, early surrender* (that one she understood), *straddle, face up, face down, double down, bottom pair* (she didn't even want to think about that), *hard hand, come hand, nuts, expectation, free roll, no limit,* and *push.*

And that didn't even begin to address the betting systems. How in the world was she ever going to learn all this?

"Ms. Taylor?"

Tiffany rubbed her temples and looked up.

Carla's smile faded. "Still not ready for the PowerPoint presentation?"

Was she kidding? Until now, Tiffany had forgotten about it. Crossing her arms over the top of her desk, she lowered her head to them.

"Ms. Taylor, are you all right?"

"No."

Carla was briefly silent. ". . . I could have the house physician sent in if you want."

What Tiffany wanted was a *Lifetime TV* movie, a drink, and more time. What she had was this chance with Nick, something she hadn't really hoped for, not even when she had slipped her note beneath his door this morning, then pounded on it to wake him.

Inhaling deeply, she finally got tough. "Please call room service and order a steak and a glass of red wine for me, whatever you want for yourself, and lots of chocolate for both of us. And have that delivered to my suite."

The chocolate and booze didn't turn Tiffany into Vegas's newest card shark, but it certainly got Carla to loosen up.

The young woman was sprawled across Tiffany's bed, affecting the same poker face she used as an executive assistant while she considered the hand she'd been dealt.

"The way I see it," she said, "your only real chance of winning is to wear something that puts Mr. Marlow off his game since you can't even beat me."

Tiffany pressed her fingers into the inside corners of her eyes. After her second glass of wine, she had taken Carla into her confidence about the eleven hopeless years she had loved Nick and how she planned to change that with this bet.

To Tiffany's surprise, the girl hadn't been appalled, but was really rooting for her, and not just because Carla was crazier than she. It seemed Carla was dating one of the junior executives and thought a strip poker game might be a cute idea for his birthday.

After this was all over, Tiffany figured she'd probably make Carla a vice president. The girl had a real knack for gaming, scheming, and seducing.

Of course, she was way off on what it took to permanently win a man's heart and love.

"I need to impress Mr. Marlow with my skill," Tiffany said.

"Uh-huh."

She frowned. "I suppose you realize that unless I shave my head, then dress like a man, Mr. Marlow is not going to be put off his game."

"I wasn't talking about clothes necessarily, but other tattoos, only these will be the kind you can peel off."

Tiffany's hand dropped away from her face. "Unless they cover me from head to toe, and I can convince him they're actually *clothing* that has to be taken off when he—wait just one minute," she said, interrupting herself.

"See?" Carla pushed her hair behind her ears. "You *can* delay the inevitable, and somehow win a few hands during it, even if it is with pure dumb luck."

Uh-huh. Despite Carla's brutal honesty, she did have a point. Of course, the means of delay didn't necessarily lie with tattoos. Tiffany pulled her laptop onto the bed, typed in a URL she had been searching earlier, then surfed until the page she wanted came up.

She turned the laptop to Carla. "How about I wear that?"

The young woman's brows arched. "Awesome. That oughta

make the game really interesting, not to mention taking him lots of wins to remove it. But for insurance you should still consider a few tattoos."

Or something a bit more enchanting, Tiffany thought, recalling the stuff she still had from Wonder Cosmetics.

Like that fake beauty mark.

You don't need it, Nick had said earlier.

Maybe not. But he might very well like the other stuff she had in mind. If nothing else, it would certainly give her the chance to win a few extra hands through pure dumb luck.

"One other thing," Carla said, as if reading her thoughts. "You really should consider playing with someone whose skills are even better than mine."

Tiffany laughed. "You never played before today."

"Yeah, I know, but I seem to have more of a knack for it than you. And I was talking about someone who can give you a few pointers. If you want, I could call Danny. He'd do it for me, and he will keep his mouth shut, I swear."

Tiffany chewed her lower lip, then grabbed her phone and handed it to Carla. "Do it."

As Carla connected with her boyfriend and went into her baby-talk mode, Tiffany headed for the living room and her cell phone.

Nick was watching the play in Piacere's ornate Baccarat room when a plainclothes security officer approached.

"Mr. Marlow, for you."

Nick took the secured phone, then covered the mouthpiece and spoke to the man in a lowered voice. "Trouble?"

"She didn't say."

She? Nick's mind raced over the recent women in his life, and those in the past, none of whom had ever called security to reach him. He wasn't a saint by any means, but he wasn't a rutting fool, either. The ladies knew he wasn't looking for love, marriage, and that baby carriage.

Lifting the phone to his ear, he offered a cautious, "Yeah?"

A sultry voice murmured, "Mr. Marlow . . . Mr. *Nick* Marlow . . . did you do as I asked?"

Right now, all Nick could do was lock his knees to keep standing. Wow, Tiffany had a luscious voice. He was so pleased to hear it he was grinning like a fool until he noticed the security officer watching.

Turning his back on the man, Nick murmured into the phone, "Ms. Taylor . . . Ms. *Tiffany* Taylor . . . what exactly did you ask me to do?"

She giggled.

Even that was throaty. Nick lowered his head to hide his loopy grin.

"Mr. Marlow," she breathed, "did you have those elevators checked out like I asked?"

Elevators?

And then he remembered. "I'm afraid not." He lowered his voice even further, and teased, "You see, Ms. Taylor, I was told Piacere's most senior execs were using them for *unspeakable* acts."

Her breathing picked up. "How shocking . . . then you're saying the moment they were alone the female exec pressed the full length of her body—her breasts, hips, *and* furry mound—to him?"

Nick's brow arched at that unexpected talk. "She did. And then she suckled his neck."

"How disgraceful . . . did he enjoy that?"

"Enough to want more."

There was a momentary pause. "And would this *more* consist of *nothing forbidden, nothing held back?*"

You bet. He told her that.

"Then you're saying he did want to strip her bare—that is, fully and completely nude—while they were in there?"

"He did."

."And would he have then used his tie to secure her hands above her head so that her breasts were uncovered and ready for his pleasure? And might his handkerchief have been used next, along with his belt, to secure her ankles, but only after her legs had been spread wide? And once she was in that position, fully opened and vulnerable to him, no part of her hidden, might he have then taken his pleasure?"

Nick's head swam with sudden images of that, while his heart hammered hard. "If she allowed it."

"And while she was naked and bound, would he have remained dressed?"

"He would. But only so that she really felt her nudity."

"While he gazed at it?"

"And tasted it with his mouth."

"And would he know where she wanted his lips and tongue to be?"

"It might be best if *you* told me."

"Licking her naked breasts, Mr. Marlow. Drawing her nipples into his mouth, Mr. Marlow. Making those hard, little tits so tight they *ached*, Mr. Marlow."

His breathing continued to pick up. "Like his balls and cock?"

"You're saying he would be *hard*, Mr. Marlow?"

"More than *stone*, Ms. Taylor. Which surely means that she would be *wet.*"

"Then his fingers would have easily slipped over her plump lips? They would have had no trouble stroking her clit before plunging into her opening?"

His nostrils flared. "I would think not."

"And after he teased her with his fingers, would he have

then moved between her legs so that he might taste that part of her with his mouth?"

God, yes. "Until she moaned in delight."

"And while she was, would he have then mounted her?"

"Again and again and yet again, driving so deep she wouldn't know where her body ended and his began."

Her sigh was very breathy as she considered that. "And this would have happened if conditions had been right?"

"If there had been time."

"How much time would he need, Mr. Marlow?"

"More than was allowed."

"So you're saying their unspeakable acts weren't long in duration?"

"Less than three minutes, I would think."

Again, she seemed to be considering that. "Then it would appear there's only one recourse left."

"And that would be?"

"We'll have to make certain not to rush ourselves the next time. Are you with me on that?"

He was, and couldn't help but laugh. "You bet."

For a moment there was only the sounds of Tiffany's sighs, and then her voice got really soft. ". . . hi."

He smiled. "Hi."

"Are you working now, Nick?"

Not if she invited him up to her suite. Suddenly, Nick couldn't imagine a nicer place to be. "Why?"

"You are, aren't you?"

"Yeah."

"Do your parents know how hard you work? Do they have any idea how *smart* you are?"

Okay, there was a question and a change of subject he hadn't anticipated. "What?"

"Your Parents," she said, slowly enunciating each word. "What is the matter with them? No, wait. That wasn't very nice. I have no right to judge them. What is the matter with them, Nick? Did they expect you to be a marine biologist?"

"Molecular," he corrected, "and yeah."

"I'm glad you're not."

He paused at that endorsement, then looked over his shoulder. The security officer was finally gone, and the players in this room were so intent on the game they wouldn't have noticed if *he* stripped *them*. Still, he lowered his voice as he asked, "Have you been drinking?"

"Because I was talking about *sex?*"

Well, that *and* his parents. "Have you been drinking, Tiff—"

"Two glasses of wine. I'm allowed. I am over twenty-one. I'm twenty-seven, by the way."

"You're a regular old lady," he said. "Why so many questions about my parents?"

She breathed into the phone, then said, "They should appreciate what you do."

"Why?"

She didn't say.

"Tiffany, *why?*"

"Because it's so damned *hard.*"

Ah. Now he got it. "Have you been studying for our bet?"

"Are you kidding? I'll never be *done* studying for it. God, this stuff isn't even in English. Who ever heard of early cheating, face up surrender, bottom pair face down, hard come hand, free roll nuts, no push—are you laughing at me?"

He couldn't help it. "Honey, you've got those terms all mixed up."

"That's what Carla keeps saying. At this rate, she's going to have to play for me and she doesn't even have any experience!"

"Carla?"

Tiffany was quickly mute.

"Carla?" Nick repeated.

"My assistant. She's allowed to help. Don't you dare bother her."

"Tiffany, I don't even know her. You're not actually trying to learn to count cards, are you?"

"You don't think I'm capable?"

Given that she sounded close to tears, Nick was afraid to tell her the truth. "What I'm trying to say is, we could just—"

"I am *not* giving up. I can do this."

"But you don't have to."

"So, now you're saying blackjack is out and you just want to strip me during *poker?*"

He suppressed a smile. "We could drop blackjack, if that's okay with you. In fact, we could drop this whole bet. We could just—"

"No. It has to be earned. You have to earn it. I have to earn it even if it's only with poker."

Nick transferred the phone from his left ear to his right and asked, "Earn what, Tiffany?"

She breathed hard, then said, "It *has* to be earned, Nick. That's just the way these things work. That's what makes it so special."

Before he could ask anything else, she hung up.

True to her word, Carla had Danny in Tiffany's suite that very night.

"I know nothing about poker," Tiffany admitted.

"Less than nothing," Carla corrected.

"It's not that I'm *stupid*," Tiffany said, then sighed. "I'm in love."

Carla nodded. "She's got it bad."

"Not to worry," Danny said, sweet as can be. "I can teach anyone this." After running his fingers through his bushy red hair, he rolled up his sleeves and started dealing.

That night they played until two A.M. The following night while they were playing, Nick called.

"Tiffany," he said.

She smiled at his deep voice, and sagged into her chair. "Yes, Nick."

Carla grabbed Danny's arm and led him from the formal dining table to the living room.

"About your e-mail," Nick said.

"Did you like it?"

His voice held a smile. "It was blank."

Tiffany stretched, then sighed, "I know. I was testing your skill."

"At reading your mind?"

Resting her head against the back of the chair, Tiffany closed her eyes. "Isn't that what every man needs to win with a woman?"

He was momentarily silent. "That would depend upon the game."

"And the woman."

"You're absolutely right. An intelligent one wouldn't be easy."

"Then we agree—she should make it hard for him."

"So hard it hurts. And you do."

She smiled. "Are you in bed?"

"The pool."

"Skinny dipping again?"

"You know me too well." He spoke above her laugh. "So what are *you* wearing?"

She spoke in a whisper, "My tattoo."

His momentary silence and increased breathing said he was picturing that. "Did I ever tell you how much I like it?"

"You did, but tell me again."

"I like it, Tiffany . . . did you get it for a boyfriend?"

Her eyes opened at the hesitation in his question, even as

her gaze turned inward to a moment three years before. That night she had seen Nick in Piacere's Baccarat Room and had given him her most adoring smile.

His gaze had momentarily touched her, then moved past to another woman who was the poster babe for female sexuality. It was in the way her hand cupped the side of Nick's face when he leaned down to speak with her. It was in her sultry laugh, and the promising kiss she placed on the side of his mouth. It was in that delicate rose tattoo she had on her wrist.

Tiffany had seen the way Nick kept stroking it.

The next day, she had gotten the one on her thigh. "Not for a boyfriend," she said, "but for a man who never once noticed me."

He was briefly silent. "Does he notice you now, Tiffany?"

"He does, Nick."

"Then he's changed?"

"We both have. I'm even beginning to understand poker."

He laughed. When he spoke again, his voice was very soft. "You sound really tired."

"I've never been better."

"Is this good-bye, Tiffany?"

"Only for a little while." As he sighed, she murmured, "Sweet dreams, Nick."

That night Nick didn't dream. In fact, he barely slept at all as he thought about Tiffany.

He was falling in love with her, of that there was no doubt. It was an unexpected surprise . . . and such a gift, because he really didn't deserve it.

She was his partner's daughter, whom he had met many years before, but never once thought of after that. He had never even bothered to notice her, until she forced him to pay attention with her starry tattoo and drop-dead good looks.

But even that kind of beauty wasn't enough.

It was Tiffany's mind and personality that was continuing to conquer. It was her voice, her mannerisms, the look in her eyes that was forcing him to his knees.

It was the abandon in her laughter and the softness of her sighs.

It was *everything* about her, none of which he had, and that sure as hell couldn't last.

In the days that followed, Nick sought her out in the executive offices and the casino, but she was never around. Hell, even the times he went to her suite, she was missing.

They only spoke by phone.

That alone made him regret their bet. Hell, they were adults; if they wanted to make love, then it should be a simple matter to hop into bed or on the service elevator, right?

Except that Tiffany knew better. She wanted more.

It has to be earned, she had said. *That's what makes it so special.*

What had started out as a bet for creative control of the gaming, with the added thrill of sex, had turned into something far more.

And he was willing to play by the rules, if only for a little while longer.

The night before their scheduled bet Nick checked his e-mail, but she hadn't sent a message. He waited for her to phone, but by 11 P.M. the call still hadn't come.

At last he dialed her.

The female who answered didn't mince words. "Who is this?"

Nick frowned. "You first."

"Mr. Marlow?"

"Yeah."

"This is Carla. Tiffany's not awake."

"Oh." He tried to hide his disappointment. "Well, if she's

already in bed—wait a sec—why are you answering her cell phone if she's already in—"

"She's not. Actually she's at the dining room table in her suite."

". . . but she's not awake?"

"Let me check." There was a brief pause, then, "Nope. She's still out."

Out? Nick frowned. "What's going on there? What did you do to—"

"I just went into the kitchen because Danny ran out of—"

"Hey!" a male voice interrupted in the background. "He's not supposed to know I'm here, remember?"

"Don't either of you dare leave," Nick said to her. "I'll be right down."

Danny Williams greeted Nick at the door. "Mr. Marlow, hi."

He put out his hand.

Carla slapped it away, pushed him aside, and pointed over her shoulder. "She's in there, Mr. Marlow."

"Asleep," Danny assured, "not unconscious."

"Then this is your lucky day," Nick said.

"We'll be leaving now," Carla said, then pushed Danny out the door.

Nick locked it and went into the dining room.

Tiffany's hair was fanned out over the table, while her head rested on her right arm. In her limp fingers were the cards she had been dealt.

Nick leaned down to look at them.

Aw, poor baby. With that hand she didn't have a snowball's chance in hell of winning.

Nick turned his face to hers and smiled at the chocolate smears at the corners of her mouth, and the way her delicate nostrils fluttered as she let out a baby snore.

He kept his voice soft. "Tiffany?"

Her brows drew together.

"Time to stop playing." He reached for her cards.

Her fingers tightened around them. One eye opened. It was as unfocused as her voice. ". . . Nick?"

"Uh-huh."

Her gaze slowly cleared, then darted to the right, the left. "What happened? Where are they?"

"Carla and Danny left."

Tiffany looked again just to be sure, then draped her left arm over her head. "*Dammit.* Nobody wants to *play* with me."

Nick suppressed a smile. "I do."

"I'm talking about *cards.*"

Yeah, well. "That, too."

She laughed, then breathed hard as if she were about to cry.

Nick gently rested his hand on her back, and his heart instantly trembled at this small intimacy. Her shirt was soft as skin, the muscles beneath it incredibly delicate and warm. "Honey, are you all right?"

"I can't move."

Nick pulled back his hand. "I didn't mean to—"

"No, I mean, I can't move. When I laughed, I pulled something in my neck. I did that yesterday, too, and had George working on—"

"You mean Mr. Massage?"

She was briefly silent. "Well, I don't know. He's about your height, but younger. Hair as full as yours, but blonder and in a current style. Eyes like yours, but—"

"A better color?"

Tiffany lowered her arm and lifted her gaze to his. "His eyes are a watery blue, and his lashes aren't nearly as long or as dark as yours, Nick."

His face felt hot.

Tiffany smiled, then quickly winced. "But he does give one hell of a ma—"

"Not tonight, he doesn't. This massage belongs to me."

Her voice grew soft. "Have I thanked you for that?"

He gave her a tender smile. "You will."

Her lids fluttered closed as he ran his forefinger over the lobe of her ear and jawline. Ever so gently, he traced her lips, the bridge of her nose, and then stroked her lashes.

As Tiffany shivered in delight, he eased the cards from her fist and tossed them to the side. "Where does it hurt?"

She inhaled deeply, luxuriously. "Between my legs and around my nipples and—"

"Tiffany."

"Sorry." She sighed. "On the left, beneath my hair."

He lifted it with such tenderness, her heart caught. When he ran his forefinger over the nape of neck, she whimpered.

"Bad?" he murmured.

God, no. It was so unbelievably good, she could barely talk. ". . . More."

"Stroking?"

"God, yes."

"And rubbing?"

"Please."

"I really should unbutton your shirt so I can pull back the—"

"Do whatever it takes. Strip me bare if you want. In fact—"

"Thank you, but no. Baring your shoulders is going to be enough to drive me nuts. But you should be sitting—"

"Aw God, no. Not that. *Please.*"

Nick leaned so close his breath warmed her cheek. "I'll help you up, all right?"

She swallowed. "Now? Can't we just stay like this?"

"If we do, *my* neck's going to hurt."

She bit her lower lip until he slipped his arm around her middle, his cheek touching hers.

Mercy. His cheek was bristly and hot, his scent all male.

Tiffany's lips parted, she breathed hard. "This is nice. How about we stay like this for the rest of the night?"

"Are you trying to kill me?"

"Sorry." She moved her face just enough so she could kiss the side of his mouth.

He trembled for just a second.

She smiled. "I'll behave."

"Sure." He moved his face and suckled her neck.

As she moaned in delight, he pulled her to a sitting position.

Her breath caught at the pain she expected. It didn't come. At last, she sighed, then sagged into the chair.

Nick's fingers circled that first button.

Tiffany bit back a moan as it slipped from the mooring. She inhaled deeply as the next one was opened, and then the next. At last, Nick's fingertips swept between her breasts as he deepened the opening.

Chilled air whispered against her skin, but his palm was incredibly hot as he brushed her hair away. It spilled over her shoulder, exposing the back of her neck. He traced the small mole at the nape.

She trembled, then whimpered as he pressed his lips to it.

His mouth was so very soft, his kisses whispery as he eased the shirt past her shoulders, then rested his hands on them after he straightened.

"Better?" he asked.

Her voice shook as he gently stroked her upper arms. "Oh, yeah."

"Good."

Actually, it was indescribable as his fingers traced her bra straps before easing that satiny material past her right shoulder, then her left.

Leaning down until his lips were brushing her ear, Nick whispered, "Now, just relax."

"I'll try, but don't be too disappointed if I also get just a little bit aroused."

His laugh was edged with a moan. "Are you going to behave?"

She moistened her lips, then swallowed. "Sorry."

Nick tenderly kissed her ear before he straightened. His long fingers dangled above the swell of her breasts as his thumbs kneaded the muscles in her shoulders.

His touch was unbelievably powerful, because it was so restrained. There was raw male need in his quickened breathing, and in the way he pressed his body against the back of her chair.

Tiffany knew Nick was hurting, possibly more than she. The man needed to bury himself in her, to feel her hot, moist flesh opening to his, giving his hardened shaft a home as he plunged deeply inside until their bodies touched, their hair mingled, and his tightened balls rested against her bare flesh.

She whimpered at the ache between her legs as his knuckles stroked her cheek. She released a long, low sigh as he gently lifted her head until the back of it was resting against his diaphragm.

Tiffany felt the impressive drumming of his heart and his heightened breathing. It matched her own as his fingers trailed down her throat to her chest, then to the swell of her breasts.

Her heart jumped. "Please!"

"Easy now," he whispered, "just relax."

"Are you joking? I can't. I want you to—I want *us* to—"

"So do I. But you're exhausted, honey."

"I've never been better." She covered his hand with her own, then pulled it over her right breast. "I want—"

"So do I."

"Then *touch* me," she begged, yanking down her bra's satin cup so that his palm touched bare flesh. *"Fill—"*

"In time," he interrupted, his voice straining for control. "It has to be earned, Tiffany."

She bit her lower lip, regretting the day she had said that. "Why? You know you're going to win."

He was briefly silent. "Then you're conceding? You're quitting without so much as a—"

"Not if you put it that way."

He leaned down to her ear and whispered, "What other way do you want me to put it, Tiffany?"

She turned her face to his. There was need in his eyes, but something else . . . something more. A challenge that demanded to be met. This was a man who wanted a strong woman—he would settle for nothing less.

Tiffany breathed hard, then said, "All right, you win. *Tonight*. But only tonight."

His gaze lowered to her mouth before returning to her eyes. "We'll see about that. Now relax," he said, speaking above her, "because I'm not stopping until you do."

Her breathing hitched. She whined, "You know you're torturing me with this, don't you?"

"I'm a regular Marquis de Massage."

She laughed, then whimpered at the brief pain in her neck.

"Still hurt?" he asked.

"All over."

"Poor baby. Let's see what I can do about that."

In the coming moments, he massaged and stroked her bare flesh until Tiffany actually relaxed. All too soon, her eyes were so heavy she could barely keep them open. When her head slumped to her shoulder, Nick's fingers paused.

"I'm fine," she said, even though he hadn't asked. "Never been . . . ah, never been . . ."

"Better?" he asked.

"It is better, thanks."

His voice held a smile. "You're welcome."

She yawned, then paused in midstretch as Nick slipped one arm around her waist and the other beneath her knees, then lifted her from the chair.

Without pause, Tiffany snuggled into his hard body. "Hmm. This is so nice. George never once gave me a massage like this."

"In that case, he's one lucky man."

Tiffany smiled at Nick marking his territory. And then she realized he was carrying her down the hall. "Where we going?"

"Time for you to go to bed."

Despite her desire, that sounded kind of nice. Despite how nice it sounded, she still had to ask, "To sleep?"

"That's the idea. I want you fresh and alert for tomorrow night."

She slipped her fingers beneath the open collar of his shirt and stroked his wiry chest hair. Her voice was drowsy as she asked, "Are you sure about that, Mr. Marlow? If I'm really alert, I'll probably beat your butt."

He alternately laughed at that and breathed hard from what her fingers were doing. "We'll see about that. This one your bedroom?"

She finished her yawn. "Uh-huh."

Nick used the back of his arm to flip on the lights.

Tiffany felt his pause. "Something wrong?"

"No."

She forced her head back to look at him. "You don't like it?"

Nick turned his face to hers. His nostrils flared with his strained breathing. "Somehow, I expected this room to be decorated in stars."

She gave him a sleepy smile. "Those are on my body, Nick."

His arms tightened around her.

"What now?" she whispered, before her head drooped to his shoulder.

Nick closed his eyes, prayed for control, then finally sighed. "Down you go."

"That sounds really nice," she said, then sagged against him after he put her on her feet.

As he held onto her, Nick pulled the comforter from her bed and paused at the provocative scent wafting up from the clean linens.

". . . something wrong?" she asked.

He looked at her. "No more talking, understand?"

She nodded. "Shouldn't I get undressed?"

Nick was torn between laughing and crying. "If you do, there might not be any tomorrow." Before she could say anything sassy to that, Nick lifted her into his arms, then gently laid her on the mattress.

She ran the back of her hand across her mouth, then forced her eyes open to look at him.

"No more talking." He rested his forefinger on her lips.

"Okay," she whispered, then drew his finger into her mouth and sucked.

Sweet Jesus. Nick's head fell forward. His voice begged, "Not now, Tiffany. Please?"

"Sorry." She released his finger, but grabbed his hand before he could take it back, and gently kissed his knuckles. "Thanks for the massage."

His voice trembled. "It was my pleasure."

She kissed his palm. Her breath was hot against his flesh as she said, "Is this good-bye?"

"Only for a little while." Nick eased back his hand, then gently pulled the comforter to her shoulders. "Sweet dreams, Tiffany."

Before he left the suite, she was soundly asleep.

Five

Tiffany wasn't even aware that she had drifted off until she stirred from a dream in which Nick was finally snuggled between her legs, filling her beyond belief. Sighing contentedly, she opened her eyes to the harsh outside light and Carla's wiggling brows.

"Naughty dream, huh?" the young woman asked.

Tiffany draped her arm over her eyes to shut out the light. "Naughty, but—" She abruptly paused, then pushed up in bed. "What are you doing here? What time is it?" Oh no, had more than twenty-four hours passed and she missed the bet?

"Early," Carla said, "and no," she added, speaking above Tiffany, "it's still the day of the bet. Now, relax." She shoved her back down.

Tiffany narrowed her eyes at the girl. "Do you mind?"

"I'm just following Mr. Marlow's orders. You're to have breakfast in bed this morning, then a massage, then—"

"With Mr. Marlow? He's going to be doing it—that is, providing it?"

Carla glanced at the handwritten note on the nightstand. "It says here, 'Carla, please call George, I know he's Ms.

Taylor's favorite.'" She looked at Tiffany. "Mr. Marlow even
underscored that. So, my guess is he was referring to—"

"Let me see that."

"I think you'd rather see this one, since it's addressed to
you."

Once that note was in her hand, Tiffany opened it and
read.

*I'll handle your calendar today. It might be my last
chance to take care of business before you beat my
butt (unless I earn yours).*

*Don't forget, my suite tonight at eight. Be. There.
Please.*

Smiling softly, Tiffany pressed the note to her chest and
sagged against her pillows. "Carla, please bring me my lip
liner and a Keno ticket."

"You're going to gamble now?"

"I'm going to write Mr. Marlow a note."

"Oh. Do you want me to deliver it?"

Tiffany closed her eyes and sighed. "Thank you, but no."
She would be delivering this message herself, and just minutes before their scheduled games began at eight.

For the first time in his life, Nick doubted his own control, specifically whether he would survive until tonight. He
tore through his schedule and Tiffany's with a speed that
had the other execs smiling.

"Atta boy, Nick," Adam said, slapping his back. "Let's
make all of our meetings this fast."

Nick returned his grin, then slapped his back. "Not if I
lose my ass."

Adam's face was still contorted from that slap. "What?"

"My ass. But would that really be so bad?"

Before the man could respond, Nick said, "It's late. Thank

God." He turned to his assistant. "No calls, no nothing until tomorrow afternoon, understand?"

The young man wrote that down. "Yes, sir."

Nick left the conference room and returned to his penthouse suite.

Housekeeping had already worked their magic, leaving everything shiny and smelling good, while room service had delivered lots of goodies just in case there was time to eat and drink.

Now, all Nick had to do was groom himself better than he ever had, and decide whether he was going to play to win or throw the bet. Not obviously, of course, since a woman of Tiffany's intelligence would clearly see through that.

But given a missed opportunity here or a foolish move there, she might very well be able to win at least once.

As Nick showered he decided he had to let her win at least that much. What would it do to her pride if she didn't? What would it do to their night . . . and their future?

That settled it. He was going to let her win at least twice. Okay, maybe three times. Just enough to lose his shirt, belt, and khakis.

By the next play, she'd be stripped bare and he'd graciously deliver his briefs and the rest of the goods.

That sure as hell should make both of them happy.

Scrubbing himself dry with a fluffy towel, Nick saw to the rest of his grooming. When he was finally dressed, he shuffled the cards while he paced.

It was fifteen minutes to eight. Then it was ten. Then it was seven. Then it was—

Nick finally stopped pacing. Glancing at his watch, he saw that it was four minutes to eight. Looking over his shoulder, he stared at the note that had just been slipped beneath his door.

His heart jumped to his throat, while his mouth went bone dry.

That note couldn't be from Tiffany. She couldn't be canceling their bet.

Nick finally went to the door and felt his heart sink. Whatever the note said, it was written in a deep red lip liner that was bleeding through the back of a Keno ticket.

Damn, damn, damn! Had he pissed her off during last night's massage? Had George given her a better one? Could George be that bold or nuts?

Nick finally grabbed the note, straightened, then forced himself to open it. The message was in Tiffany's hand and quite brief. *Let the games begin,* it said.

Nick read it again, just to be sure. When he was, he yanked open the door and stared.

She was dressed in vintage Victorian from her throat to the tips of her toes. Layer after layer of gossamer thin, antique beige fabric (and wow, there seemed to be a lot of it) fluttered over her curves for a breathtakingly feminine, but surprisingly seductive, look.

There was the faintest outline of her pebbled nipples beneath all that embroidered lace. And when Nick looked really hard, he could see the shadow of her legs. She wore soft-soled, lace-up boots that might take days to remove, but her lovely hair was swept up with just a few pins, which released wispy tendrils that trickled against her temples, cheeks, and the nape of her neck.

Her color was heightened, her eyes bright as she leaned forward, gently pressing her hand against his chest.

My God. Even that small movement delivered her musky scent.

"Hi." She kissed his cheek.

Nick's heart trembled. He covered her hand with his own, not willing to let her go. "Hi. You look amazing."

She smiled. "Thanks." Her smile paused. "You're not wearing your tie."

He gently squeezed her hand. "Don't worry. We'll just use your bra instead."

"I'm not wearing one."

He swallowed. Her smile was back as she lifted her free hand to his jawline, and gently traced it with her fingertips. "So, you better watch out."

He looked down. "I have been watching . . . exactly how many layers do you have on?"

Her cheeks pinked up. "Thirty or so."

"Then I guess we better begin. This might take me a while. At least five minutes or so."

She arched one slender brow at his bragging. "Lead the way. I'm ready for *anything.*"

Hmmm. Taking her hand, Nick shut and locked the door, then led her from the brightly lit foyer through the darkened living room to the dining room table.

Her fingers stopped playing with his as she looked at the windowed walls. Even the ceiling was glass, while floor lamps bathed the table in bright light, which made the surrounding area seem even darker.

"Isn't this kind of exposed?" She looked at him.

His eyes were hooded, his voice husky with anticipation. "Don't worry. We can see out, but no one can see in. When you're stripped bare, it will only be for me."

A flush crept up her neck. She looked back to the table. "Which do you prefer, the right side or the left? I understand in some games there's an advantage."

Releasing her hand, Nick slipped his arm around her waist, then eased her closer until her back was to his front. Dear God, she felt great—all softness and warmth wrapped in that amazing confection of clothing. Lowering his face to her neck, Nick inhaled deeply of her fragrance. "Since you're the guest, you choose."

Tiffany swallowed, then turned her face to his and murmured, "I want the one that wins."

Nick couldn't help but smile. "Of course you do." He pressed his lips to her throat until she was trembling in his arms. Satisfied with that response, he whispered in her ear. "Good luck, honey."

Her eyes fluttered open when he released her. She looked at the chair he was offering, then at him. "Good luck?"

"Uh-huh. You're gonna need it."

That same brow shot up. "Oh really? Well, for your information, Mr. Marlow, I am gonna beat your butt."

He smiled. "We'll see." Once she was seated, he leaned down and kissed her cheek. "Comfortable?"

It took her a moment to collect her thoughts before she nodded.

"Good."

"Wait." She grabbed the collar of his shirt so he couldn't move. "You wouldn't be trying to distract me, now would you?"

"Never." He ran his tongue over the lobe of her ear.

Her eyes rolled up into the back of her head.

Taking advantage of that, Nick sank into his own chair, then momentarily stopped breathing as she eased her foot between his legs to rest it on his stiffened cock.

"Are you all right?" she asked.

He swallowed, then slowly nodded. ".Never been better." He cleared the gravel from his voice. "Why don't you shuffle?" After he opened a new deck, he slapped it down in front of her.

She pulled back her foot and stared at those cards as if they might bite.

"You do know how to shuffle, don't you?" he asked.

She gave him a look that said if he made another smart crack like that, he might very well be sleeping alone tonight.

He lifted his brows. "Forgive me?"

"Maybe." At last, she took the deck and shuffled it so badly she bent several cards in the process.

"Hey, wait a minute," she said, "what are you doing?"

"Getting a new deck. Bent cards make it too easy to cheat."

She rolled her eyes.

He handed her another deck. "Now, be a good girl," he said.

"You sure you actually want that?"

He smiled. "Don't bend the cards. Me? Do whatever you want—I heal easily."

She laughed, shuffled the cards like the novice she was, then paused before dealing the hand. "We will be able to draw again if we don't like what we've been dealt, right?"

"If that's what you want. But only once."

"If that's all you need. And," she said, interrupting him, "we will be playing each hand without a lot of fancy betting, right?"

"Define *fancy.*"

"There's only one bet for each hand, even if we draw. If you win, you get an hour of my time. If I win, I get fifteen of yours. Pure and simple."

He arched one brow. "Too simple and completely wrong. I offered ten, not fifteen. And betting is what makes this a game of skill. So, we can bet as high as we want."

"Until one of us psychs the other out?"

Nick looked at the faint outline of her body beneath those gossamer duds. "That's exactly right."

"Well, if you're not going to give me a choice. But," she said, interrupting him again, "the loser still has to remove *one* article of clothing."

"In your case, that could eventually be all thirty of them."

She gave him a sweet smile. "One more thing."

Nick sighed. "Sure. I still have four minutes left before I have you stripped completely and have creative control of this place and you for the next—"

She interrupted one last time. "Whoever wins the hand

gets to pick the article of clothing the loser has to remove."

"Sure, why not?"

"And the winner also gets to tell the loser *how* to remove that article of clothing."

Okay, now she had him. "And how might that be?"

Her sweet smile turned wicked. "You'll see."

"Not if you don't deal."

She did it so quickly, three of his cards flew off the table.

When she leaned over to see what they were, Nick smiled. "Uh-uh, close your eyes or you get a penalty for cheating."

She straightened, then tapped her cards against her chin. "And what might that be?"

"We won't use any of my ties tonight."

"Then I guess I better be good."

He scooped his cards off the floor and barely looked at them before Tiffany asked, "How many do you want? I'll take six."

Nick slapped his hand over the deck. "Six? You only have five now."

"Five, then."

He looked at her hand.

She pressed it against her chest, and arched one brow.

Suddenly, he felt bad for her. He was taking advantage. No matter how book-smart she was, that certainly didn't mean she could play cards. "Take as many as you want."

"Oh, no. I don't want any special treatment."

Nick thought about his ten hours to her one. "How many would you like, Tiffany?"

She pulled her cards away from her chest, looked at them, and sighed like she was really depressed. ". . . is three too many?"

Given her voice, it probably wasn't going to be enough.

As Nick started to deliver the cards, she snatched back the ones she had laid down. "No, stop. I can do with two."

He lowered his head so she wouldn't see his smile. "You don't have to deny yourself, honey. If you want three, then—"

"Two's fine." She lowered her discards. "I want two."

"Okay." Nick dealt her the cards and took one for himself that didn't help. He still had a pair of fours and a pair of sevens.

"Since I'm the guest, do you want me to bet first?" she asked.

Nick suppressed a smile. "If you want."

"I'll bet two—no, one—no, two hours of my time." She slid one chip to the middle of the table.

Nick reached over and slid another of hers into the pot. "You bet two."

"Uh-huh."

He met that bet, then struggled with what to do next. At last he decided to treat her as an equal, knowing she deserved that. "I'll raise you three."

She stared at his chips. "Really?"

He nodded.

"And if I fold now, you win?"

He nodded again. "But look on the bright side—if you fold, you could save three of your chips and three hours of your time."

"But that would be quitting."

He laughed. "Not at all—it would be—"

"Quitting." She slid six of her own in, then wiggled her fingers. "Come on, you owe the pot three."

This was nuts. She was going to meet *and* up the bet because of a moral opposition to quitting? Nick put his cards on the table. "No way. I fold."

"You're quitting?"

"I'm *folding,* Tiffany. It's allowed. It has no bearing on—"

She interrupted, "Does this mean I win?"

He sighed. "Yeah."

"Whoa. That was easy. I should have bet higher."

Nick slung his arm over the back of the chair and watched her tally up how much of his time she had won.

"Ninety hours," she murmured. Her cheeks were pink, her eyes damned near glassy as she looked at him. "I should have bet high—"

"Tiffany, that's not the way the game's played. If you had bet higher, I would have stayed in and called." He flipped his cards to show her his two pairs. "That's a winning hand."

"Since when?" She turned her cards over and slid them to him. "Three of a kind—even three twos—beats two pairs every time."

Nick frowned at her hand, then lifted his gaze to hers. "You figured you had a winning hand all along?"

"I didn't go to Oxford for nothing."

"You *knew* all along?"

"And you didn't. That's called psyching you out."

Nick worked his mouth around so he wouldn't smile. "Deal."

"Uh-uh. You've got to remove an article of clothing."

"Fine. Nudity doesn't bother me."

She arched one slender brow, then glanced at the lights of the city below and all those stars overhead. "Well, maybe not yet." She looked at him. "Take off your shirt."

"I thought you'd never ask." He started pulling it out of his pants.

"Uh-uh," she said. "Stand up while you do it."

"Excuse me?"

"Nope. No excuses. Stand up, Nick. And take it off *slowly* until there's nothing forbidden, nothing held back."

He studied her for a long moment. "Are you certain of that, Tiffany? Remember, the same rule will apply to you."

Her belly fluttered to that promise. She nodded.

Nick pushed out of his chair and stood. As his gaze remained on her, he reached down and *slowly* pulled the tail of his shirt from his khakis.

She moistened her lips as he next freed the buttons from their moorings. She leaned forward as he then eased the shirt past his flat belly and over his heavily furred chest.

"You still with me?" he asked.

Tiffany had to clear her throat before she could speak. "Uh-huh."

Nick pulled the shirt completely off, then tossed it to the side.

"No, wait a minute," Tiffany said. "Don't sit yet."

He looked from his chair to her.

She pressed her forefinger to the top of the table, then drew lazy circles. "Turn around."

Nick watched her finger. "You do realize, don't you, that your time is going to come?"

She kept drawing those circles. "Uh-huh."

He stepped away from the table and turned his back to her.

Dear God, but he had beautiful shoulders. Broad, tan, and nicely muscular. "No," Tiffany said, as he started to face her. "Slowly. Make me *wait*. Make me *want*."

Nick stared at her, his face betraying his surprise.

"Please," she said.

He arched one brow, but did as she asked.

When he was again facing her, Tiffany said, "Now, don't move."

As he remained, her gaze drifted over his naked chest, that thick male fur covering those scrumptious muscles. *Mmmm.* Her gaze followed that hair as it narrowed to a thin line that trickled beneath the waistband of his khakis and the wonders hidden below. Unable to resist, Tiffany reached out and touched that silky hair.

Nick's breath caught. The muscles in his belly quivered as she drew lazy circles around his navel.

At last, he grabbed her hand. "Tiffany." His voice was thick with desire.

Mmmm. "Sorry." She eased her hand from his, then couldn't resist running her forefinger down his fly and very impressive erection.

He inhaled sharply. She asked, "Ready for our next game?" His eyes were still glazed; he breathed hard. ". . . sure."

Returning to his chair, Nick sank into it like a rock, shuffled and dealt the hand, asked for one new card to her four, let her bet first, then met her one-chip bet. "Call."

She looked at the chips in the pot. "Already? You don't want to raise the—"

"*Call*, Tiffany."

She didn't move. She guessed stroking his stiffened cock had been too much.

Nick tapped his foot against the floor, then fanned his cards across the table. "Can you beat a flush?"

Was he joking? She glanced at his flush, then looked back to her cards. "What's above a flush?"

"You tell me, since you already know. Now can you beat a—"

"No, all right?"

He leaned back in his chair and smiled. "It's more than all right. I win. I want your shoes."

Was he joking? "Excuse—"

"No, no, no excuses," he said, wagging his finger. "Now, you lost. So, stand up and come over here." He gestured with his finger, showing her how.

She looked over her shoulder to the windowed wall . . . all that exposure. Surprisingly, it caused her heart to race in excitement, not fear.

"Are you going to make me come and get you?" Nick asked.

She looked at him from beneath her lashes. "I'm coming, Nick." Pushing back her chair, she slowly rose from it. Leveling her gaze on his, she crossed the small space that separated them and didn't stop until she was directly in front, her right knee touching his left.

He spread his legs and patted the seat in between. "Put your foot up here."

"Which one do you want, Nick? The right or the—"

"I'm going to have both, eventually. No, no, no," he said, speaking above her while wagging that finger again. "It's a *pair* of shoes, Tiffany, which represents one article of clothing. Now, put whatever foot you want up here, because eventually they're both going to be stripped, just like the rest of you."

Warmth surged through her with that promise. She rested her left hand on the table, lifted her right foot onto his chair, and suppressed a smile at his expression as he stared at all those gauzy layers.

He gathered the first in his hand and was rewarded with her musky scent. Swallowing hard, Nick moved the fabric above her calf and thigh, resting it near her hip. He did the very same with all the others, slowly peeling them away until he saw the edge of her lacy teddy.

Dear God. Even her underwear was a Victorian's secret.

Inhaling deeply, he cupped the back of her naked right thigh in his palm.

She trembled briefly, then gasped as he ran his forefinger over her bare flesh. "What are you doing?"

He stroked even higher. "Removing your shoe."

"Okay. Do what you have to."

There was no doubt of that. As he finally unlaced her shoe with one hand, Nick continued to gently squeeze her thigh with his other before sliding his fingers to the edge of her teddy.

Tiffany gripped the table. Nick briefly closed his eyes as his fingers slipped beneath that lacy edge to touch her delicate curls, and finally her swollen lips.

Sweet Jesus. It was all he could do not to take her now. She was so opened, so vulnerable.

Her head lolled back on her shoulders, her eyes were closed, a strangled moan tore from deep within her as he stroked her damp flesh.

His own voice was strained as he said, ". . . Tiffany."

She moistened her lips and continued to breathe as hard as he. "Yes, Nick."

"Lift your foot."

She lifted her head and looked down at him.

Her eyes were blurry with passion, her gaze wanting more as she finally lifted her foot, allowing him to remove the boot.

Nick tossed it to the side. Cradling her foot in his hand, he ran his thumb over the lacy ankle sock she wore.

"No, no, no," she murmured, then paused to catch her breath. "That comes off later."

Nick couldn't help but smile. "Yes, it will. But first things first." Brushing away the gossamer fabric that had fallen back over her thigh, he leaned down and pressed his lips to her starry tattoo.

She inhaled sharply.

He just about died. Her skin was satiny, her fragrance damned near overwhelming as he licked the tattoo, then murmured, "Did I thank you for getting this for me?"

"You will."

Mmmm. "Give me your other foot."

As he unlaced that boot, his free hand slipped beneath the teddy to cup her buttocks' naked right cheek.

Her back arched. *My God*. Her breasts trembled with her ragged breathing as Nick continued stroking. "Lift your foot."

After a few attempts, she was able to comply. Once this boot was removed, Nick tossed it to the side, and gently ran his fingers down the sole of her foot.

Her toes curled. "That tickles!"

He briefly squeezed her naked buttocks, then removed his hand and murmured, "Sorry. Ready for our next game?"

It was a moment before she understood the question. Lowering her head, she saw his smug smile. "I've never been readier."

"Really? I think you're still wearing far too many clothes."

"What do you intend to do about it?"

"You'll see."

The next hand moved so fast, Tiffany saw only a blur of cards that she couldn't even begin to keep up with. Suddenly, Nick seemed hell-bent on winning. Once he did, he pushed out of his chair, lifted her into his arms, then placed her on the top of the table. As her legs dangled over the side, Nick sank to one knee and removed the socks from her feet.

She talked fast. "Nick, *don't.* I'm ticklish!"

He arched one brow to this news, then gently kissed the tips of her toes.

She smiled, and then she squealed as he held onto her foot while tickling the arch with his tongue. "*Stop!*"

He didn't until she was sprawled over the table, breathless and weak, with all of those stars staring back at her. Tiffany had never seen anything more beautiful, until Nick pushed to his feet and bent over her until their noses just about touched.

His eyes were hooded, his voice husky as all get out as he asked, "Ready for the next play?"

Her lids fluttered wildly. She slipped her hand down to his shaft. It was so stiff she could easily feel it through his clothing. "I'm ready for *anything.*" She stroked his hardened flesh. "How about—"

He interrupted with a moan.

"Is that a yes?" she asked.

He gulped air, then shook his head. "Only when you *earn* it."

Hmmm. She ran her hand from his fly to his chest. "I am going to beat your butt."

He squeezed his eyes tight, then looked down at her. "Dream on, baby."

Minutes later, he stared at her cards and said, "Uh-uh. Not so fast."

"Oh, it won't be fast," she promised, as she ran her fingertip over her winning hand. "You're going to come over here and strip off those khakis. And you're going to do it very slow—"

"You couldn't have four of a kind."

"Four jacks, actually." She tapped her cards, then glanced at his hand. "To your rags. That is what they call one lousy, losing hand, isn't it?"

He drummed his fingers against the table.

She drummed hers. "Are you doubting my win?"

"Actually, I'm amazed by it."

"Really? Well, even Carla said I might be blessed with pure dumb luck."

His expression changed. "You should consider reprimanding her."

"Actually, I'm going to promote her. As far as you're concerned, I'm not certain how to proceed."

He softened his voice. "Forgive me for doubting your skill?"

She smiled. "We'll see." She wiggled her finger. "Come here, Nick."

After quietly regarding her, he pushed out of his chair, crossed the small space that separated them, and didn't stop until he was directly in front, his right foot touching her left.

Tiffany ran her forefinger over his belt buckle. "Slowly," she said.

He obeyed, stroking that belt as if it were her naked flesh before slipping it through the buckle and releasing the small metal strip from the hole.

Tiffany tapped the dangling edges of his belt, making them dance as Nick released the waistband button from its mooring.

"Now, the fly," she said.

He lowered it more slowly than she thought possible, or actually wanted.

At last he was ready to shove those khakis down.

Before he could, she said, "Just a moment." Her voice was surprisingly soft despite the thrumming of her heart. "Put your hands behind yourself."

"Behind my back? But how—"

"I'll remove the khakis from you."

Nick's chest pumped hard. And then he did as she asked, leaving himself vulnerable to her gaze and touch.

Moistening her lips, Tiffany drew her fingers across the navy waistband of his briefs.

The muscles in his belly coiled.

She trailed her fingers still lower, to the brief's soft fabric and his shaft's hard flesh.

Nick talked between strained breaths. "Do you have *any* idea what you're doing to me?"

"Teaching you patience," she whispered, her mouth to his navel. She circled it with her tongue, dampening those short, dark hairs surrounding it. She pleasured him beyond reason, earning his response.

Nick's body shuddered; he struggled to catch his breath as she pressed her cheek to his belly. It was hot, bearing a male scent, the muscles quivering as she slipped her fingers beneath the waistband of his khakis, then lowered them over his briefs and lean hips until they sagged to his ankles.

Cupping his buttocks in her hands, squeezing that firm flesh, Tiffany licked the silky line of hair below his navel. She marked him again and again with her mouth and scent, before glancing up.

He looked like a man about to concede. He looked entranced, and quite possibly in love.

"Are you ready for the next hand?" she asked.

Nick nodded since he was momentarily unable to speak.

He never knew a woman could be so seductive. He had never wanted or loved one more.

He made quick work of the next hands, playing as he never had. If Tiffany had doubted his skill or his determination to have her, she didn't anymore.

At last those gossamer layers were strewn across the floor. She was lovelier than Nick ever imagined, and continued to surprise. She had pasted five tiny rhinestones on her right shoulder. Beneath the light, they glittered like diamonds.

Nick honestly liked them.

Other than that and her gold waist chain, she wore only that beige antique teddy. Its embroidered silk was the last thing that separated him from her delectable flesh.

Nick stared at her tightened nipples as they pressed against the wispy fabric. His gaze lowered to the faint outline of the chain hanging low on her waist.

His cock strained against his briefs as she neared him, ready to be stripped bare.

He had won this moment and the bet, but not enough hours of her time to last.

He needed this to last. Resting one hand on her waist, he placed his other over her left breast. She inhaled sharply at his touch; her nipple tightened beneath his palm.

Nick savored the moment as he gently squeezed that warm globe of flesh.

She inhaled deeply, then arched her back, delivering herself to him.

It made Nick dizzy. Breathing hard, he ran his fingers over the nipple, causing it to tighten even more. He fondled her right breast in the same manner, then ran his forefinger down that teddy and up the leg to her delicate curls.

They were damp with wanting, her hidden lips plump and moist. She wanted him, but this had to last.

"Turn around," he said.

She blinked slowly before she looked at him, her expression saying she didn't understand the question.

Nick lifted his finger, then moved it in a small circle to show her what he meant.

She moistened her lips. "You want my back to you?"

"Please," he said. "And spread your legs."

Her cheeks got pink, but she did as he wanted, then briefly flinched as Nick unsnapped the crotch of her teddy.

"You okay?" he asked.

"Uh-huh." Her voice was beyond throaty.

"Take the pins from your hair," he said. "I want it to hang loose. And keep your legs parted."

Tiffany took several deep breaths, then lifted her hands to her hair. As she did, Nick lifted the back of her teddy until her buttocks were naked, exposed.

A hairpin fell from her hand. There was a small pinging noise as it hit the table. Another soon followed as Nick pressed his lips to the small of her back, just above her buttocks, then ran his fingers over that plump, satiny flesh.

Tiffany's head fell forward, her hair spilled over her shoulders. She gripped the edge of the table as Nick's gaze and touch explored. He circled the small mole on her right cheek, and ran his hand between her legs so that his fingers could stroke her damp curls.

After a moment, he pulled back his hand, then lifted his fingers, inhaling deeply of her female scent. It was better than he had ever imagined, but still he wanted more, he wanted it all, and so he dropped to one knee.

Before Tiffany could ask what he was doing, Nick lowered his mouth to the back of her thigh and leisurely suckled.

Tiffany whimpered; she moaned. Her breathing hitched as if she were about to cry.

Nick finally lifted his head. "You all right?"

"I can't take any more, *please.*"

"I don't want to rush, we have all—"

"I can't wait all night. You won, I concede—now, dammit, you *have* to make love to me!"

He smiled at her reasoning, but said, "Not yet."

She lowered her head to the table, unaware of the provocative view that gave him of her naked ass.

"*Not yet?*" she moaned. "*Why?*"

"I want you stripped bare." Before she could think to respond, Nick pushed to his feet and said, "Stand up and face me, Tiffany. I want to see all of you. I waited a very long time for this."

She lifted her head from the table and looked over her shoulder to him. "Eleven years, by my count."

His voice was soft and filled with tenderness. "Right now, it seems far longer."

Her cheeks flushed. She pushed away from the table and faced him. "Do what you have to."

Nick smiled at her sass. "It's what I *need* to do, Tiffany."

She smiled as he carefully slipped the teddy's right strap past those glittering rhinestones, then off her shoulder before doing the same with the left. The fabric briefly billowed away from her body, then whispered back, falling just above the crest of her nipples.

Nick's gaze touched hers before he returned to the task at hand. Slipping his fingers beneath those straps, he eased them down her arms until her breasts were bared.

He looked at her again, seeing need in her eyes. But that didn't begin to describe the love behind it—nor the trust that allowed for *nothing forbidden, nothing held back.*

Nick's gaze returned to her breasts. Each time she breathed, that flesh quivered as if inviting him to touch.

Not yet, he warned himself. *Patience.*

For the moment, he allowed the cool air to pebble her

nipples, along with his unashamed gaze. He deliberately stepped back and quietly regarded her as his cock grew even harder. He stepped to the side and felt his balls tighten at the beauty of her firm breasts. Those upturned nipples seemed to be waiting for that moment when he would draw them into his mouth, touch them with his tongue, and suckle until they couldn't get any harder.

Not yet, he ordered himself. *Patience.*

Stepping closer, he eased those straps until they were free of her arms. The teddy finally slipped over her hips and floated to her feet.

At last, Tiffany was naked and vulnerable to his gaze and touch, wearing only that glittering shoulder jewelry and the delicate waist chain.

Nick slipped his finger beneath it. Until this moment, he wouldn't have guessed something so small could stir him so deeply. "Do you always wear this?"

"I can take it off if you want."

He slowly shook his head and stepped back.

Minutes passed as he regarded her nudity at his leisure, his gaze moving from her naked breasts to that dark blond triangle of hair between her legs.

Tiffany's skin flushed—never had she felt so exposed. It was the look in his eyes, and all these windows. She was surrounded by them and the city below. When she listened closely, she could detect the faint hum of traffic. Overhead, she briefly heard a jet.

In here, water splashed into the pool, the air-conditioning hummed, her breathing quickened to Nick's continued silence and gaze.

When he moved around to the back of her, Tiffany's first reaction was to look over her shoulder. She fought it. She allowed herself to be as vulnerable to his gaze as she would soon be to his touch.

She didn't have to wait long as Nick moved into her, his

front to her back. Resting his hand on her flat belly, he splayed his fingers, using them to push her even closer. She felt his stiffened shaft against her buttocks; she sighed at his trail of kisses on her shoulder and neck.

"I want you," he said.

Cupping the side of his face in her palm, Tiffany turned her face to his and spoke without thinking or pause, "I've wanted you from the moment we met."

His gaze never left hers. "I didn't mean to make light of this."

"I know."

"I don't think you do." His voice quickly knelt as he said, "I love you, Tiffany. My God, I really love you."

He seemed so stunned by his own admission, Tiffany had to smile. She had waited eleven endless years to hear those words. She had imagined when they were finally spoken, rockets might burst or angels would sing. At the very least, she had expected to be surprised, but she wasn't. "I know." She turned until she was facing him. "I guess I've always known."

"How could you when I didn't?"

"I just did." Cupping his face in her hands, she kissed him. *Really* kissed him, like the man had never been kissed before. Love gave her the courage—it gave her that *right*.

Nick floundered in surprise, until passion took over. Wrapping his arms around her, he used her mouth completely and well until Tiffany's lips were bruised.

When he finally pulled free of her, he said, "I've waited long enough. No more patience, understand?"

It was a moment before she could catch her breath. "Whatever you say."

Smiling, Nick cupped her naked breasts in his hands, then drew his thumb over the taut left nipple, while circling the right with his lips.

As he drew it into his mouth, Tiffany's head fell back against her shoulders to the intense pleasure and heat. She eased her fingers through his thick, silky hair keeping him to her as he suckled. She refused to release him until he had fully tasted both of her breasts.

His eyes were hooded as he finally straightened. "It's time," he said, then took her hand to lead her from this room, presumably to the bedroom.

She held back. "Wait a minute."

He looked at her. "Wait? *Now?*"

"Just for a sec. I know you won," she quickly said, "but can I have at least one request?"

He seemed quickly cautious. ". . . okay. What?"

"I want to make love out here." She pointed to the table.

"*On* the table?"

Her smile was downright wicked. "Not exactly."

"Then what exact—"

"Once I'm bent over it with my legs spread apart and my back arched, I'll let you know."

Nick swallowed; he whispered, "Don't let me miss anything, all right?"

"Have it your way." She ran her finger over his briefs' elastic band.

Without pause, he pulled off his briefs, straightened, and let her have a look.

Her lips parted, releasing all of her breath in a wanton sigh.

Nick was so aroused, the head of his penis was nearly purple. Tiffany reached out and held this amazing part of him in her palm. "Does it hurt?"

His voice was really strained. "You can't imagine."

Tiffany thought she could, but didn't say. There were just some things a woman couldn't say to a man. "It's really beautiful."

"It's yours."

"Not yet, but it will be." Giving him a smile that was

more adoring than all the others, she went to the table and was surprised to see a faint reflection of herself within all those city lights. She saw Nick, too, as he moved behind her.

It *was* time.

Bending over the table, Tiffany spread her legs widely apart and arched her back. Her voice trembled with anticipation. "Is this all right?"

Nick quietly regarded her until she felt more naked than she ever had in her life. Seemingly satisfied, he eased her legs a bit wider, then leaned down to her ear. "It is now. I want full access to you."

Her heart raced. She whispered, "Do whatever it takes."

"Don't you worry, honey—I will." He gave her his baddest grin, and then a tender kiss on the shoulder.

Her eyes fluttered closed, her head sank to the table.

Nick moved between her legs and her breathing instantly picked up. As he skimmed her damp curls, then separated her plump lips, she wiggled.

"Now, be still," he said, then rested his left hand on her hip to make certain she was.

Thus held, Nick explored her with his fingers.

Tiffany's heart raced as he drove one, then two into her opening, stretching her, preparing her for his hard rod.

It pressed against the back of her thigh. It was hot. Insistent.

At last he lifted it, then bathed the blunt head in her moisture and heat. Her moan was lusty, and then it was loud as he entered her with one powerful thrust, working her flesh until she took all of him inside and their bodies touched.

Never before had Tiffany felt so deliciously filled, unbelievably stretched, and so very ready for pleasure.

Nick did not disappoint.

His hands were heavy on her hips as he slowly pulled out, then plunged into her once more. Again and again, over and over, he took what he needed, what had been his all along, while also promising the ultimate pleasure.

With all the skill he owned, Nick tempted her body, he teased, not allowing Tiffany immediate relief. He stroked, he plunged until she thought her body would burst. At that moment, he paused.

She lifted her head and moaned in protest. And then she cried out in delight as he unexpectedly continued, bringing her to orgasm.

The contractions were strong, sending wave after wave of pleasure. During this, Nick continued pumping, finally allowing his own release. His roar of delight was primal and so very male Tiffany climaxed again.

After this, the only sounds were their ragged breathing.

At last, Nick swallowed, then gently kissed her back.

"Mmm—*oh.*"

He had just pulled her to a standing position. As he remained inside, with both of them still breathing hard in pleasure, he lowered his right hand to her clit.

Dear God. Tiffany wiggled, she moaned, then wrapped her hands around his. "Nick, it's too much, I don't think I can stand—"

"Don't think. Just enjoy. Let me give you this pleasure."

She breathed hard.

He murmured. "Tiffany, just—"

"Aw God, do whatever it takes!"

"Don't you worry, honey, I will."

By God, he did. As he grabbed both of her hands in one of his and held them to her body, he used his foot to ease her legs even farther apart. When she was completely exposed and vulnerable, Nick *slowly* stroked her vaginal lips and clit.

Tiffany's head fell against his shoulder. Her muscles coiled, her eyes glazed. The feeling was unbelievably intense, but each time she came close to release, Nick's fingers slowed, then paused, making her wait. Making her want.

She thought she'd go nuts. At first, she tried to bring her legs together to stop this delicious torture, but his feet blocked hers. When she tried to release her hands, his embrace tightened.

Again he stroked. Slow, maddening, wonderful strokes that finally caused the room to spin and her vision to blur.

At last, she was so lost in pleasure, nothing else existed except the feel of his body against hers and his fingers skillfully stroking, then pausing, stroking, then—

The climax came so unexpectedly Tiffany shuddered, she whimpered her release. When it was finally finished, she went limp as a rag doll, releasing all of her weight into him.

He continued stroking, teasing. "Want to go for double or nothing?"

She gasped. "*. . . nooooo.*" She got even limper. "I want to pleasure you, Nick. You earned it."

His chest thrummed with her words. "I'm all yours."

Indeed, he was. After all those years.

They melted into the past while Tiffany pleasured him as no other woman ever had in a place that was simply magic.

The stars were above them, the lights of the city below. And the future stretched endlessly ahead. Which finally begged a question.

"How are we ever going to top this?" she asked.

It was near dawn, but neither of them felt sleepy.

"We'll perfect it," Nick said, snuggling his face against her neck.

She giggled as he licked that flesh. "How?"

"Well, there's always our weekly executive meetings. We could—"

"No, we couldn't. That's for business. What kind of a SCEO are you anyway?"

"Well, I don't know. What in the hell is a SCE—"

"Second Chief Executive Officer. You're still under me, you know."

He gave her a wicked grin. "I really liked when you did all the work."

"You know what I mean. I'm going to continue letting you run the show."

"That's awfully sweet of you, honey, since I won the bet."

She arched one brow. "So, how are we going to top this?"

"There's always the service elevator."

Indeed, there was. "And your gold silk tie?"

He kissed her shoulder. "I have several ties." His gaze lifted. "After the way you behaved last night, I figure I might need quite a few."

Her nostrils flared at the thought. "And you'll wear your dark blue suit?"

"Only if you wear your tattoo."

She moistened her lips. "And after you use your ties to secure me, will you remained dressed while you take your pleasure?"

"It could be arranged."

"Is that your final offer?"

"It is."

"Well then, Mr. Marlow, I believe these negotiations are—"

"Over," Nick said, pulling her close for the next round of pleasure.

Not Another Fairytale

Jen Nicholas

Prologue

July 2003

Tap. Tap. Pause. *Tap.*
   Tap. Tap. Pause. *Tap.*
   Allison Dare gripped the arms of the unyielding metal chair as if her life depended on it. In actuality, though, it wasn't her life hanging in the balance. Mrs. Halverson, of the drumming fingers, was about to die. Allison gave her thirty more seconds to quit that goddamn tapping before she reached over and broke her fingers, one by one, painfully, at the knuckles.
   She wasn't usually a violent person. Okay, sometimes. But not often. However, that persistent, irritating tapping on the desk was driving her quickly toward insanity. As she looked at the woman across the wide expanse of slate-gray metal desk, she wondered what type of tic made the woman do it. And then Allison wondered if the old bat would even notice if she stood up and began screaming like a banshee.
   Tap. Tap. Pause. *Ta* . . .
   Allison cleared her throat, loudly. Mrs. Halverson looked up, her long, pink fingernails pausing in midtap.

"Yes?"

"Oh, nothing, ma'am, excuse me," Allison said. She was trying to rein in the urge to check and see if the woman's pale pink nails were real or acrylic. The color was probably something totally vomit-inducing, like "Sensuous Seashell" or "Baby's Butt." But if they were acrylic, she could rip them off—quite gleefully, in fact. "Just something in my throat."

"Hmmph, yes, well," Mrs. Halverson replied, bringing her hands, thank God, to her lap. "I've read over your application and credentials. And although you seem to be quite qualified, I'm not sure that we have anything that would really, well, *mesh* with you."

Allison stared at the woman, green eyes at a slit.

Please tell me you didn't just say mesh, she thought to herself.

"And what exactly does that mean, Mrs. Halverson, if you don't mind my asking?"

Mrs. Halverson at least had the decency to look away.

Allison gritted her teeth. The bitch did, indeed, mind her asking, but knew that she couldn't avoid the question. And oh yes, Allison knew what was coming. She was too *extreme,* too *out there,* and Mrs. Halverson didn't think that she would be a good fit with Riley & McNault.

"Well, Ms. Dare, the thing is, this company was founded over sixty years ago. And we still like to do things the old-fashioned way, the way that our founding fathers did them. And although your skills are impeccable, I just don't know that you'd be comfortable with the way that we do things."

Allison had had enough.

"I see. What you're basically saying is that although I'm overqualified for this position and would make an excellent addition to your team, because I have a brain and would undoubtedly use it there's too much risk involved." Allison stood up and grabbed her purse. "I'd thank you for your time, ma'am, but I'd be lying."

She couldn't resist giving the door a satisfying slam on her way out. Even though it didn't end up being all that satisfying after all.

One

September 2003

Do you remember those stories you heard when you were little? Those great romances that your parents would read to you as you lay in bed, edging toward sleep? You know the ones I mean. They always started out with "Once upon a time" or "Long, long ago." And, of course, they always ended with "They lived happily ever after" or "And all was well in the land of Eternal Happiness." I'm sure you remember them, just as I do. Just as I'm sure that, by now, you also know they're a load of crap.

Allison looked over what she'd just written and frowned. It wasn't a very romantic beginning to an article that was supposed to be highlighting the joys of living and loving with your soulmate.

"Dammit. How am I supposed to write something decent when I don't believe in fairytales anymore?" She wasn't really looking for a response, although Bella did give a rather loud purr in agreement.

"You're no help at all," Allison muttered.

This assignment was important. More like a matter of survival. She'd been struggling for months to find a job that would showcase her writing talents, but openings, especially for freelance writers in New York, were slim to none. Too many applicants, too few openings. Even when she'd applied for other jobs, when she'd attempted to put aside her love of writing and fall back on her secretarial skills, she still hadn't been able to find a job.

Then the position with *Loveswept* had practically fallen into her lap. She had a friend, who had a friend, who knew someone who worked for the premiere romance magazine in the nation. They were looking for a freelancer, and Allison had been lucky enough to have her name passed along to someone who mattered. So here she was, working on her first assignment on a job that she desperately needed, and all she could write were horror stories.

She knew it was her own fault. She hadn't been in a relationship in over a year. She hadn't felt any stirrings of desire in a very long time. How could she write about the joys of love, laughter, and devotion with a man when she couldn't even find one for herself?

Allison straightened her spine against the rough material of her computer chair and rolled her shoulders. Tossed her mane of long, dark hair to one side and took three deep breaths, in and out. Flexed her fingers over the keyboard, working on remembering those tai chi moves that were supposed to bring her mind, body, and soul into alignment.

Now, I know you're saying to yourself that this sounds rather harsh. But face it, ladies, life stinks. There is no knight in shining armor who's going to come charging in on his white horse to whisk you away into the sunset. There is no man-god with a warrior's body, soul-searching eyes, and Einstein-esque intelligence. There

is also no Playgirl *centerfold who's going to come to
your apartment and offer to do your housework. These,
ladies, are what we call myths. Or, as I call them, bald-
faced lies.*

"This is not working out. This is supposed to be a light,
airy piece on love." She practically growled it, and had to
restrain herself from kicking something. Preferably, something with a penis. Instead of flowers and rainbows, this
was turning into the bitter last stand of a pissed off, totally
rejected, life-without-a-lover single woman with severe
PMS. Where was the God of Love when you needed him?

The knock on her door didn't improve her mood. Unless
it was a forgotten pizza order or the reps from Ben & Jerry's
telling her she'd won a lifetime supply of Chocolate Chip
Cookie Dough ice cream, she didn't want to talk to anyone.

She threw open the door with a distinctly unfriendly,
"What?"

Holy hell, I asked for God and the Devil answered.

Naked chest, ripped button-fly jeans *unbuttoned*. A lump
the size of a golf ball at the hairline of a head of thick blond
hair. Glazed blue eyes the color of the Arctic. A trail of blood
followed a path down one sharply chiseled cheek. He looked
like a giant sequoia ready to fall.

Allison's belly quivered with immediate, unadulterated
lust.

His voice was scratchy and he was definitely dazed. His
eyes didn't quite focus on her as he propped one hand on
her doorframe for support.

"I think," he started, then stopped to raise his free hand
to his temple. "I think some woman just tried to rape me."

Oh yes, there was a God, but He had a sick sense of
humor.

Allison just stared at him for a moment, this man who looked
like death warmed over and yet still somehow managed to

have her breath hitching and her insides quivering with lust. *Real* lust. The kind of take-me-now-you-stud lust that she hadn't felt in a long, long time. In that case, she didn't think she'd ever felt this kind of lust before. She wasn't sure whether to laugh or slam the door in his pretty face.

Then she realized that Mr. Lust-Master was swaying. Swooning. *Falling*.

"Oh, shit," she said, and moved out of the way just in time to avoid his lumbering frame. He hit the floor with a resounding crash, and although Allison had had a fleeting thought of trying to catch him, she was glad that she hadn't tried. Very likely she would have now been a human pancake.

"Great. This is just great. Now what do I do?" Bella had come to investigate, sniffing the stranger and pausing to rub seductively against his still torso. Allison had a brief moment of wondering what rubbing up against this man would feel like.

"You're sick, Allison, totally sick. The man is undoubtedly hurt. Could even be a psycho, for all you know." She stood staring at him another moment and then groaned. "Ah, hell," she spat out, and stomped over to push his feet inside the doorway. Task accomplished, she closed the door and wondered what to do with him.

She couldn't move him; of that she had no doubt. The man looked to be around six-three and probably weighed over two hundred pounds. There was no way she could move him. Allison might be smart, but she knew her physical abilities. In technical terms, that meant she was a wimp.

Bella was still rubbing against the man, causing Allison's belly to do that same tapdance of lust every time she thought about doing the same. Now, how bad was that? She had a half-naked stranger passed out in her living room, an unfinished article blinking at her from her computer monitor, and her legs were shaking in time with the shivers of desire making their way up and down her spine. This was bad. This was very, very bad.

"Okay, think. Think, think." Allison walked around the fallen man, trying to decide what to do first. She should probably check him for any other injuries and take care of that head wound. It had looked pretty nasty, from what she could see of it. That is, when she was looking at the lump on his head and not the way his pectoral muscles bunched and flexed when he leaned in her doorway.

"Oh, dear Lord. I am so pathetic." She stooped down beside him, pushing Bella away so she could look him over. His back was smooth, tanned skin stretched tight over muscles that were heavenly to look at, even in his unconscious state. A trim waist led down into the waistband of his jeans. His legs ended in a pair of high-tops, obviously broken in. They looked like they'd seen a lot of use.

On his back was a tattoo. Strange. Lady Liberty, torch and all, next to a pair of scales. Scales like the ones that they had on law office buildings, or the ones she'd seen on those lawyer shows on TV. Underneath were the initials J.T.F. That was definitely very interesting.

Allison moved her way to his head. It was hard to tell if his wound was still bleeding, especially since his face was now smashed into her carpet. She needed to roll him over.

"All right, buddy, I'm going to have to move you. I apologize in advance for any more injury that I might cause." She wedged herself into the space between the man's body and her couch, hoping that between the two she'd get some leverage.

She put her hands on his side, one up by his shoulder and one on his waist. His heat was like a furnace, pouring into her hands. Damn, the man was hot, and in more ways than one. She wedged her back into the cushions of the couch and watched as Bella moved a safe distance away. The cat had seen a few instances of Allison's lack of coordination in the past. It was actually a wise move for her to back up.

"Okay, guy, here goes. One, two, three." Allison gave a giant push and the man flopped over, much like a dead fish. Or a two-ton beached whale. Damn, but the man was built like a stone pillar.

"Well, that's done," she said, moving up from her crouch to hover over him. Now that she was staring at his face, she had to admit he looked pretty bad. Nasty lump at his hairline, dried blood on the side of his face. Her eyes moved lower, taking a mental inventory. He was clean-shaven and had what looked like the beginnings of a pretty nasty black eye.

Moving lower, his chest looked fine, though. Really fine. Really *damn* fine.

"Crap, Allison, get a grip on yourself." Bella meowed in agreement. "Oh, what the hell do you know, cat? You wouldn't know a fine male specimen if you saw one. Now let me get back to the one I can see clear as day."

He did have a nasty bruise by his rib cage, but it didn't look too serious. His jeans were beyond hope. They had a huge tear on the right side, which afforded her a great view of his hairy, muscular thigh. But it was a fine display of flesh, even with the jagged gash cutting across it.

"Mmmmm." Allison knelt down beside him, assuring herself that it was only to get a better look at his injuries, and not that glimpse of skin.

His jeans were unbuttoned, riding low on his hips. Allison could see a few coarse, curly hairs sticking out of the gap, and ripped her gaze away. But she at least had the grace to admit that it was only because her head was spinning too fast to fully concentrate on more than one thing at a time.

The jeans were ripped, stained, and badly torn. But other than that nasty lump on his head, he didn't seem to be too badly injured after all. And then she remembered what he'd said. A woman had tried to rape him. Was that even possible? Well, damn, she hoped that he wasn't seriously injured. She wasn't sure what she should do. The urge to kick someone with a penis had passed, but now it was replaced with indecision. And oh, don't forget about that lust. Lust had replaced the kicking urge with a loud, obnoxious entrance.

Allison sighed, weary and wary and still fighting that sense of unwarranted sexual longing that this stranger stirred up in her. She'd get him cleaned up first and then decide what to do. Call the police, maybe, or an ambulance.

"Mister, just stay right there and I'll get something to wash you up with. I need to put a bandage on that bump and make sure to stop the bleeding. I'll be right back."

She wasn't sure why she was talking to him, since he was out like a boxer after ten rounds, but it focused her. If she was talking to him, she wasn't thinking about touching him. And if she wasn't thinking about touching him, then she could put his hard body out of her mind. Really. Yes, of course. And she was the fricking Tooth Fairy.

Allison entered the bathroom and flipped on the light, catching a glimpse of herself in the mirror over the sink. Flushed cheeks and huge green eyes with her hair in a long, sweat-stained mess.

"Gorgeous," she said with a snort.

She rummaged through her medicine cabinet and found some peroxide and Band-Aids. The yield under the sink was better, where she got a sponge, some sterile bandages, and medical tape.

Allison brought them back into the living room, seeing that her charge hadn't moved. She dropped the stuff on the couch and went to the kitchen to get some warm water.

She grabbed a bowl from the cabinet and turned on the tap. She heard rain outside the windows and caught a look outside one as a bolt of lightning tore across the New York skyline. Or what she assumed was the skyline, since she couldn't actually see it due to the high-rise four feet away from her.

Bowl of water in hand, she made her way back to the mysterious Mr. Brick. She had decided that's what she'd call him, at least until he was coherent enough to tell her his real name. But anyway, Brick fit. He was built like one and weighed like a whole ton of them. Mr. Brick it would be.

And there he was, right where she'd left him. She hoped he would wake up soon, and yet part of her secretly wished that he'd just stay as he was. If he was unconscious, she wouldn't have to look him in the eye. Because if she looked him in the eye, she was sure that he'd instantly know all of the thoughts she'd been having. About him. About his chest. His thighs. His body. His, well, everything. God, just thinking the word *everything* had her wanting to rub up against something hard and hot. Like the man on the floor.

Allison growled low in her throat and forcefully shoved away the mental images of her body sinuously wrapped around the stranger's. She definitely had a problem. Some type of mental imbalance, or maybe a chemical deficiency. Maybe even low blood sugar.

She put the bowl of water on the floor beside him and lowered herself to his side. His breathing, thank God, was nice and regular. And his head wound seemed to have stopped bleeding. She soaked the sponge and wrung it out, then gently placed it on his forehead. She carefully wiped his brow, his cheeks, and then pushed aside his long hair to see the actual wound.

It was big but not gaping. She didn't think he needed stitches. She cleaned it out as best she could, then opened the bottle of peroxide.

"This might sting a little," she said, and poured some directly onto him. He didn't move a muscle and she quickly applied a bandage. That done, she figured she'd better check out the rest of him and see what she could do to help.

Bella meowed, and she looked up to see the cat jumping onto the couch. And then she saw the paw prints. Red paw prints. Her eyes shot fire as she followed them back to Mr. Brick, who had bled onto her carpet.

The cat meowed again and settled against the cushions. Allison scrambled up for a towel and kicked over the still-warm bowl of water. As light pink water grew in a pool on her once-pristine carpet, spots danced behind her eyes and she snapped.

"Belllllllllllllaaaaaaaaaa."

It came out as a half-scream, half-yodel, like a bad scene from her own version of *A Streetcar Named Desire.*

Bella burrowed farther into the couch and closed her eyes. Allison counted slowly to ten, and when that didn't work, added twenty more. Still pissed, she stomped into the kitchen with the now-empty bowl. Slamming it into the sink, she grabbed a towel from a drawer.

"Goddammit. All I wanted to do today was write. Finish my job, then maybe have a quick dinner. Who knows, maybe even watch a movie later. But did it work out?" She turned on the faucet and wet her towel, then stomped back to Mr. Brick's side.

"Of course it didn't. Why would the gods of fate want to smile upon little ole Allison Dare today?"

She scrubbed until the carpet and couch were almost back to their original light gray color. Bella had disappeared, which was probably a good thing. That just left the man who was the reason behind her ever-growing crappy day.

Allison needed to get his pants off and check his body for any other injuries. She'd already looked for a wallet and hadn't found one. The thought of undressing him made her slightly queasy. She hoped it was from being worried about him, and not because she was afraid that her self-control would desert her when she saw him naked. Yep, definitely a chemical imbalance.

She took off his shoes and socks and set them aside. Reaching down, she grabbed the waistband of his jeans, intending to slowly peel them down until she got them to his feet. Those asshole gods of fate, though, had other ideas.

The doorbell rang just as she crouched between his legs, the fingers of both hands looped under his waistband. Allison had just realized that he wasn't wearing anything under them, and as the spit dried in her throat and her airway mysteriously tightened up, she wondered what in the world was happening to her.

The doorbell rang again, this time accompanied by sharp, quick knocks.

Allison sighed and removed her hands from Mr. Brick's pants. Would this day ever get any better?

She opened the door to find Cissy, the last person in the world she wanted to see at the moment. Well, besides her mother. Mom showing up right now would not be a good thing. Then again, her mother suffered from an even bigger chemical imbalance than she obviously did, so she'd probably get a kick out of the whole sordid mess.

"Cissy. Hi, but I'm kind of busy right now. What's up?" Allison stood with the door cracked open, subtly blocking the entry, but Cissy wasn't one for taking a hint.

"Hi, Allison," she said, pushing into the room. "I was just wondering if I could borrow some . . . oh my *God!*" she squeaked.

Allison turned to follow her gaze, already knowing what Cissy was looking at. Or rather, who she was looking at.

She cleared her throat. "Well, like I said, now's not really a good time."

Cissy was still staring, and Allison swore that there was now a string of drool hanging from her open mouth. *Pervert.*

Cissy turned to look at her, blue eyes wide. "Why is J.T. on the floor?"

"J.T.?"

Cissy frowned. "Yes, J.T. You know, the guy from 17D." It was Allison's turn to frown. "He lives here?"

"What do you mean, he lives here? Of course he lives here. In 17D. But why is he on your floor? Oh . . . *ohhhh*."

Allison had to think for a minute. If Mr. Brick lived in 17D, that meant he lived right across the hall from her. She frowned. She'd lived in 17C for almost two years now and never remembered seeing him before. And she was sure she would remember. Come on, how could she see that body and not remember it?

She glanced out the hallway, and seeing no one, shut the door. "No, Cissy, not *ohhh*. But I really can't explain right now. I'll tell you all about it later, I promise. So what did you want to borrow?"

Cissy wasn't taking the hint. Then again, Cissy probably didn't even realize it *was* a hint. "He looks hurt, like he's had an accident or something." She'd stepped closer to Mr. Brick, or J.T., and was staring down at his prone form.

Allison felt her eyes rolling back into her head and tried to contain herself.

"Yes, Cissy, he's hurt. But like I said, I don't know what happened. I'm trying to find out. So tell me what you want to borrow so I can get back to it." She was sounding snippy and didn't care. Cissy was the epitome of the dumb blonde, and dumb blonde was one thing she couldn't handle, especially on a day like today.

"Huh?"

Allison sighed out loud. Another hint. Another blank look from Cissy. "Borrow, Cissy. What did you want to borrow? Oh, Cissy, I'm over here," she snapped.

Cissy slowly turned away from the guy on the floor and looked at Allison with glazed eyes. "Laundry soap. I went to put a load in the washer and the soap dispenser is broken. Can I borrow some?"

"Sure. Stay right here. Right here, Cissy," she said, grabbing onto the woman's arm to get her full attention. "I'll be right back."

Allison practically ran to the pantry and grabbed a bottle of laundry detergent. Rushing back into the living room, she saw that Cissy hadn't moved. Neither, thank God and all his helpers, had the stranger. She sure as hell hoped God was listening. She'd done more "thank-you's" today than she usually did in a year.

"Here you go," she said, shoving the bottle into Cissy's hands. "You can keep it. I've got more." She none too gently turned Cissy around and herded her to the door. "I'll talk to you soon, okay?" she told her, and then shut the door as Cissy continued to stare over her shoulder at her floor.

"Good God almighty." Allison rested for a moment with her back to the door. This day was going to kill her. Forget tai chi—she needed a damn Valium.

She made her way back to Mr. Brick and before she could argue herself out of it, she reached down and pulled his pants off as fast as she could.

Holy ape shit, but the man was built. Gorgeous, really. Well-toned muscles and hair in all the right places. Strong arms and legs, toned thighs, great-looking calves. His face wasn't anything to frown at, either, even with the stark white bandage against his tanned skin. And his . . . oh man, she really, really shouldn't be looking at that. The man was unconscious and couldn't defend himself. He claimed that he'd almost been raped.

Allison hitched in another lungful of air and forcefully released it. She grabbed her hair in two fists and gave a nice little yank, hoping to knock some sense back into her sex-deprived soul. The man was totally defenseless and had suffered who-knew-what type of trauma.

The thought hit her that she could see why the woman in question had jumped him. Allison gave up then and simply slid down until her butt hit the floor.

He was unconscious. Hurt. Defenseless. Hard as a rock. Mr. Brick might be out like a light, but Mr. Brick, Jr. was alive and well.

Two

J.T. had died and been sent to Hell.

When he'd first opened his eyes a few minutes ago, he was sure that he was in Heaven. He was lying on his back, and there was a woman straddling his lap. He couldn't see anything but the back of her head and a curtain of long, dark hair. She had beautiful hair, falling like liquid silk almost to the small of her back. Then he felt water on his thigh and realized she was washing him. Her touch was gentle, and amazingly enough, it was nearing his dick. This had to be Heaven.

Until he realized that although her voice was pretty, even seductive and slightly familiar, she was using it to spit out some of the most imaginative words he'd ever heard. He wasn't exactly sure what a crack monkey was or why it was a son of a bitch biscuit, but he had a feeling that it wasn't a good thing. Even that alone wasn't enough to convince him he wasn't in Heaven, though. That came when he happened to glance up and saw the face of the Devil staring him in the eyes.

The cat was huge. Yellow eyes bored into his with what he knew was evil intent. Total maliciousness. He knew as soon as he looked at it that it wanted to rip him apart from end to end. After all, cats always hated J.T., but that was usually all right since the feeling was mutual. He couldn't stand cats. To tell the truth, the damn furry mice-eaters freaked him out.

This one, though, was totally frying his mind. He was definitely in Hell, and the furball was its gatekeeper.

He tried to move, to speak, to get the cursing beauty's attention. But he didn't want to take his eyes off the cat. Who knew what it would do when he dared to look away? Better to keep his eye on the damn thing.

And then the demon smiled. He watched in horrified silence as its whiskers twitched. Then its big, ugly thin lips stretched even wider, and he saw the tips of several sharp, pointy teeth. Beelzebub was here in New York and had taken the form of a cat.

"You're Satan," he whispered, and rushed headlong into the darkness that swallowed him whole.

Allison heard Mr. Brick mutter something, and all of a sudden three things happened simultaneously.

She caught movement from the corner of her eye as Bella hissed and ran headlong into the coffee table, stopping only to shake herself once and then take off down the hallway. Allison turned around quickly, hoping to catch J.T. before he passed out again, but the man had already sunk back into unconsciousness.

And then her hand landed on his crotch and she froze. Her blood turned to molten lava and her muscles atrophied as she felt him grow hard and hot under her hand. Her cheeks flushed, and she felt something tight and needy unfurl in her belly.

Allison shuddered out a breath and forced her gaze to J.T.'s face. His eyes were closed, his breathing once again regular and even. He was unconscious, and her hand was suddenly glued to his most private part. What was even worse was the fact that she liked it. The man felt good. Hot and hard, yet smooth like satin. Unyielding, yet pliant. Her hand wanted to learn its shape, wanted to mold itself around him and feel the weight of him.

She tore her hand away as if she had burned it. Allison brought her hands to her face and covered her eyes, dark hair moving to cover her like a curtain. She was a cretin. A sex-starved, wannabe-rapist, no better than the fool woman who had injured this poor man earlier. And here she was, still straddling his lap like an animal.

Allison jumped up and onto the couch in one quick movement. She couldn't look at him, couldn't even think. What to do? What should she do?

It was nearly nine o'clock. She'd forgotten all about dinner and the TV movie she'd been thinking of watching. All she could think of now was J.T. All she could watch now was J.T.

Allison snuck another peek at him. He looked better now that she had cleaned him up and bandaged the two cuts. His ribs were turning a strange purplish color and the ring around his left eye was going to be one hell of a bruiser tomorrow. But rather than detract from his good looks, all they did was add an edge to him, a hardness that turned her insides to jelly.

Allison pushed her hands against her belly, hoping to quell that quivering, swirling mass of sensation that just wouldn't go away. She didn't know where it had come from, didn't know why it was happening now, with this stranger, but it felt good. Gratifying. She wasn't dead after all. She'd just needed a gentle push in the libido department, and holy kamoley but Mr. J.T. Brick had given her one hell of a jump-start.

"I guess I better cover you up, huh?" she asked him. "Although I have to admit there's nothing wrong with the view, and you're obviously not cold—it's probably the most humane thing to do." As she realized how that sounded, she hoped once again that he couldn't hear her.

Allison went to the hall closet and retrieved a blanket and pillow. When she returned, she gently lifted his head and placed the pillow underneath it and laid him back down. She couldn't resist running a hand through his golden mane. It was a little sticky—from sweat and shock, no doubt—but full and gorgeous nonetheless. She brought her hand to his closed eyelids, down the bridge of his nose, across his cheek to his lips.

His lips, even at rest in sleep, were full. He had a dimple in the cleft of his chin. She rested her index finger there lightly for a moment, then impulsively leaned down and placed a light kiss upon his lips.

She stood up and carefully draped the blanket over his naked frame. It barely reached his feet, but that could be due to the extra fabric sticking up like a tent over a certain area of his anatomy.

Allison sighed. She turned on the small side table lamp, turned off the overhead lights, and headed for the hallway and the soon-to-be-soothing salvation of sleep and her own room.

"Sweet dreams, J.T."

First, she went to her computer, saved her current fiasco-in-progress to disk, and shut it down for the night. Then she went to the kitchen and refilled Bella's water bowl and emptied the old cat food from earlier in the day. Finally, she filled the coffeepot and set the timer for seven A.M., and when she ran out of mundane tasks, she turned off the light and headed for bed.

Once safely ensconced in her room with Bella in her cat bed in the corner and her fake silk pj's buttoned up to her chin, Allison realized that she wasn't the least bit tired. Well, all right, she was exhausted, but mentally her mind was still racing a mile a minute. And how could she be expected to sleep with the mysterious hunka-hunka strewn out on her living room floor?

Allison stared at the ceiling and worked on thinking about anything but J.T. She should be thinking about her article for *Loveswept*. She needed to make a conscious decision to take the article in a different direction. So far, it had sounded nothing like what it needed to be. And she didn't even understand how it had ended up the way it had.

She wasn't the bitter, dried-up old maid that the piece was making her out to be. Allison was twenty-eight, hardly old maid material. Plus, up until a year and a half ago, she'd had an active, healthy sex life. Maybe it hadn't been fulfilling, but Troy had been, well, enthusiastic if nothing else. So she didn't always have an orgasm. So she didn't always feel in the mood. So she didn't always . . . hell, she didn't always even like the guy. But it was the first semiserious, totally monogamous relationship she'd been in, so she'd thrown herself into it the only way she knew how.

In the end, it was her sassy mouth that had ended it. That and the fact that Troy stopped looking like a dark-haired Roman soldier and more like a green-scaled, wet fish.

Allison had finally told him, in no uncertain terms, that it had to end. She wasn't attracted to him anymore, and although he was a nice guy and usually unselfish, he turned into Mr. Gimme-Gimme in the bedroom. And that just didn't cut it.

Thankfully, there had been no hard feelings. Turns out old Troy had thought of her as the ice princess with the mouth of a navy sailor, so it had all worked out in the end.

Allison readily admitted that her mouth got her in trouble. It was one of the main reasons that she hadn't been able to find a job earlier in the summer. She was smart—she knew that—but the bad habit of always saying what was on her mind had been her downfall. A downfall that she wholeheartedly blamed on her mother. Damn DNA. Add to that the fact that her New Year's resolution to curb her cursing had flown out the window the same day she'd made it, and she knew that she was her own worst enemy.

So she'd been on a dry stretch, thankful to have the new job and Bella's company. She'd worked hard to convince herself that it was enough, that she didn't need a body attached to any male equipment to keep her company. If she could take care of herself in other ways, Allison figured she could take care of herself in this one, as well. After all, if there were no single, male-less women out there, the vibrator-making companies would have gone out of business a long time ago.

She turned over, hugging her pillow and molding it to her body. What the hell was it about the man in the other room that had her rethinking her stance? It couldn't be his witty banter, ha ha, since the man hadn't said anything but a garbled mumble the entire time she'd known him.

And although he was hot, a gorgeous body, that was just a shell. She'd learned a long time ago not to judge a book by its cover, and that went for the good-looking covers as well as the ugly ones. Actually, chances were that J.T. would turn out to be the world's biggest prick. But damn, he'd be the hottest-looking prick she knew, wouldn't he?

What did it really matter anyway? She'd obviously lived across the hall from the man for quite some time and done just fine without his acquaintance. And he probably had a girlfriend, or at least someone to keep his bed warm at night. How could a guy who looked like he did not have someone? So it didn't matter what she thought of him. It didn't matter that she wanted to tiptoe back into the living room and find another excuse to straddle his lap.

It didn't matter, not one iota, that she wanted to lift the blanket off of him and see if his cock was still hard and huge, ready to fill something, or someone, to capacity.

Allison groaned, long and low, and pushed herself farther into the comforts of her pillow. Her body was warm and demanding, with an ache and a wetness down below that she could feel even through her panties. She needed to stop tormenting herself like this, thinking of things that didn't need to be thought about.

It was a very, very long time before she fell asleep.

"Come here," he said, and she obeyed. She stood before him, wearing nothing but her skin for protection from his ice-blue gaze. He looked her up and down, from her long, straight hair to her unpainted toenails. Her body burned, ached, wherever his eyes landed. Her breath came faster as her breasts heaved, her nipples having already hardened under the scrutiny of those eyes.

"You're absolutely gorgeous, Allison. I am so glad that you were my rescuer, that you saved me from those horrid women who want me only for my body." He paused as he walked behind her, and she shivered as she felt his breath upon her neck. "You, though, you see inside me. You know there's more to me than a pretty face and a hard body." His voice was melodic, soothing, and her entire body, her every nerve ending, throbbed in time with his words.

His hands gently caressed her shoulder blades, moving down her sides in a tickle that was both soothing and erotic. He skimmed her trim waist, then brought the pads of his fingers around to her belly. Up they went, up to the tips of her hardened nipples, stopping to lightly pinch one, then the other, between his skillful fingers.

"You want to be with me. You want me to be with you. You want me to fill you, to own you, to take you. Isn't that right, Allison?" he asked, as those same fingers suddenly delved into the cleft of curls between her legs.

Allison's breath rushed out on a moan of pleasure as one

*finger made entry into her pussy. Her legs went limp and
her thoughts scattered as he expertly worked her toward
orgasm.*

*"Say it, Allison. You always have something to say. Tell
me that you want me. Tell me that you want this." His fingers moved faster upon her as his free hand came up to
grasp her nipple. His tongue scorched a path of fire on her
neck, and Allison gladly leaned her head back onto his.*

*"Do you want this, Allison? Do you want what I can
give you? Tell me what you want."*

*Allison felt the climax coming, felt her entire body tight-
ening in response. She arched harder against his fingers as
her hips bucked. As he pinched her nipple and bit the lobe
of her ear, as he pushed and prodded and rubbed against all of
her sensitive places, she cried out with the force of her release.*

*"I want you, Mr. Brick. I want you hard and hot and
wanting like I am, spread out on the floor, defenseless, with
your cock buried inside of me to the hilt."*

*She felt his laughter against her cheek as the waves of her
pleasure ebbed and flowed.*

"You are one sexy, perverted woman, Allison Dare."

Allison bolted upright in bed, her hands fumbling to turn
on the bedside light. Her hands were shaking, along with
the rest of her. The horrible thing was, her clit was throbbing and full, and as she realized that she'd just had an orgasm, *from a dream,* she didn't know whether to laugh or
cry.

Or be sick.

She'd just dreamed about a mysterious stranger, a man
she didn't know from Adam, who was at this moment lying
unconscious in her living room. A man who'd been injured,
beaten. A man who'd had attempted rape committed upon
him hours earlier. A man who'd brought her to orgasm in

minutes, while she was sleeping. A man who thought she was a pervert. Maybe.

She was convinced this day was never going to end. Or that if it did, it would only be because she couldn't take it anymore and threw herself in front of the first available mass-transit bus she could find.

Three

J.T. awoke with a headache from hell, a sore back, and the belief that the last twenty-four hours had to be a product of his imagination.

Please, God, if you like me at all, let all this have been just my imagination.

The light shining through the windows was a good sign. The fact that he was lying on the floor, naked except for a blanket that wasn't his own, was not. Reality had failed him once again. Plus the fact that he'd never had a good imagination.

He moaned, trying to stretch out, to work out the kinks that seemed to be embedded in every body part. His ribs were killing him. His head throbbed, the echoes of his heartbeat reverberating through his brain like the very loud engine of an eighteen-wheeler.

J.T. grabbed the edge of the couch and painfully, slowly, pulled himself into a sitting position.

And then he remembered the cat, that damn gatekeeper to the depths of Hades.

He whipped his head around, trying to catch a look to see where the thing could be hiding. He had no doubt it was there, somewhere, staring out at him from some hiding place. Biding its time until it could pounce and rip him limb from limb.

J.T. didn't see the cat, but he could see the black dots that danced in front of his eyes caused by his quick movements.

"Shit, better not do that again," he said, holding onto his head with both hands. Okay, okay, he needed to regroup. Since he was on a floor that wasn't his own and in the company of a feline that had been sent to torture him and steal his soul, he obviously wasn't in his own place.

That meant he was somewhere else. The trick was figuring out where exactly that somewhere else was.

"Okay, J.T., time to go over the facts. Get the facts, be rational, and you'll figure this out," he muttered.

Fact one: He was naked. Usually, naked was a good thing. However, the fact that his nakedness didn't include that great after-sex glow, coupled instead with the glow of getting his ass kicked, said that this time being naked wasn't necessarily in his best interest.

Fact two: That same ass-kicking suggested that he'd been involved in something that had him on the losing end. Kind of like a one-armed fight, except that they hadn't even let him use the one arm.

Fact three: Whoever lived here, they liked bold colors and sharp lines. Not to mention shitty carpet. Damn, but the least they could have done was buy a carpet that had *padding*.

Fact four: Last but not least, it all added up to him being in a shitpile of trouble.

J.T. sighed and painfully dragged himself up to his feet, keeping the blanket wrapped around his private parts like a toga.

"Great, now I look like an ass-kicked prisoner of war wearing sackcloth."

He made his way carefully to the hallway, holding on to

the walls and whatever furniture was handy for balance. He needed the bathroom and clothes.

He found a door he assumed was the bathroom and cracked it open, guessing that since he wasn't in his own apartment, that someone else lived here. Undoubtedly, that someone else was still here, and maybe was already making use of the facilities.

J.T. stuck his head around the corner. Then yanked it back so fast that he caught his ear on the door and almost shut his toe in it.

"Fuck," he said, and this time he wasn't referring to the pain. "Oh, this is bad, J.T. This is really, really clusterfuck bad."

He hadn't found the bathroom. What he had found was one Miss Allison Dare, his neighbor. The woman with the foul mouth. The woman who owned the demon cat. The woman who haunted his dreams and way too many waking moments with images of sex and depravity.

"Oh yeah, big clusterfuck here," he muttered, turning across the hall and entering the open bathroom door.

J.T. shut the door behind him, then flipped on the light and grimaced at his reflection in the mirror. As his mama would say, he looked like shit. Worse than death warmed over. More like a pile of bat dung, or something equally disgusting.

His golden-blond hair looked almost brown from sweat. It was stuck to his scalp like a helmet, except for the three or four spots sticking up like homing beacons for any interested UFOs. His eyes, usually a clear, bright blue, were still blue. At least the parts of them he could see around the red. The purple-yellow bruise around his left eye didn't add to his sex appeal, but what the hell.

He had a huge white bandage at his temple. He assumed that accounted for his raging headache. His bare chest was unscathed, still tanned, with nice muscles and a light sprinkling of hair. At least he knew that no one had held him down and buffed him while he was out.

J.T. dropped the blanket, continuing his inventory. His legs seemed to be in the right positions. He had a bandage on his thigh, up high near his groin. J.T. seemed to remember someone washing him there, but it seemed like a lifetime ago.

Holy moley, Allison had touched his thigh.

The thought had his tongue sticking to the roof of his mouth and his dick rising to attention.

"Well, that's just lovely."

The rest of him looked the same as always. Calf muscles bunching and flexing, legs ending in size thirteen feet. Everything seemed to be in working order.

Now, he just needed to find some clothes and he could slink out of here with his tail between his legs. There was no way, *no way,* he could face Allison Dare looking like this. The woman had already seen him beat up and passed out, but he hadn't been able to help that. He hadn't been in control. He'd been *unconscious.* Now, though, oh yeah, now he was awake and kicking. And there was no way he was letting the woman he dreamed about on a nightly basis see him looking like this.

J.T. reached into the shower stall and turned the water on hot. He needed to clear the last of the cobwebs from his brain, quickly, before he could make his escape. No way he could even make it across the hall if his head kept pounding like a runaway steam engine.

He stepped under the spray and sighed. He washed his hair, then his body, doing it all with quick, precise movements.

Get it done and get out.

Get it done and get out.

It was his new mantra. Wash, dry, and escape. He was Houdini. He was David Blaine. He was screwed.

J.T. removed the bandage from his thigh, then winced when the tape of the one at his temple stuck a little. He reached up, probing it gently, and was glad when his fingers came away without blood. That was a good sign.

He turned off the water and opened the glass door. When he stepped out, he reached over and dropped the bandages into the garbage can. He could at least clean up after himself. Now he just needed to borrow a towel to make the dash across the hall to his own apartment.

J.T. turned around, his left hand attempting to keep his long hair out of his eyes, and reached for the linen closet.

And saw Allison Dare standing on the other side of the toilet, holding the cat, staring at his naked body with her emerald-green eyes wide and a look of sheer horror on her face.

Allison couldn't speak. She could, however, squeeze Bella a little tighter than the cat preferred. Bella made a sound halfway between a growl and a wheeze and began clawing her way down Allison's leg. Startled, she dropped the cat, who made a beeline for J.T. The same J.T. who, in response, jumped backward into the shower and slammed the door shut.

Bella made a loud exit through the open bathroom door. Allison stood in stunned silence, unable to tear her eyes away from the shadowy figure of J.T.'s naked body behind etched glass.

Now would be a good time for the Black Hole to make an appearance and swallow me up.

When it didn't, she cleared her throat.

"Umm, well, umm, good morning." Brilliant. Her English degree had been a sham. Obviously, Professor Talbert had only given her that "A" based on her looks, not on her use of the English language.

Silence came from the shower.

"I'm sorry," Allison said, reaching behind her to grab a towel from the closet. "I didn't realize you were in here. Not until, well, you know, not until I saw you. I was going to go check on you once I, umm, took a shower."

Now her mind was filled to the brim of herself in the shower. With J.T. Naked. Wet. This day was not shaping up to be any better than yesterday.

"Are you feeling better?" she asked him, tossing the towel up to the top of the stall. "Well, I mean, obviously you're feeling better, or you'd still be passed out on the living room floor. But, well, I mean, how's your head? Does that cut on your thigh look any better? Do you need some aspirin?" She was rambling like a goddamn idiot. A moron. A lunatic. A . . .

"Much better, thanks," came the voice from the shower. Like the man behind the curtain in *The Wizard of Oz*, Allison thought, then had to hold back a snort of maniacal laughter.

"Good, good, that's great. Umm, so, well. I guess I should let you get back to it, huh?" She stepped to the door but paused on her way out. "I'll make some coffee. Would you like some coffee? Because I'm going to make some, so if you'd like some, I could make you a cup."

She now had the linguistics of a three-year-old. Something had happened to her in twenty-four hours. Was there such a thing as intelligence regression?

"Coffee would be great, thanks. But, well, I was wondering if you had a robe or something. I don't seem to have any clothes."

Allison's bubble of laughter spilled out. She saw J.T.'s head turn her way through the glass and cut it off in midspurt.

"I'm guessing I'm missing something. Is the way I lost my clothes something that's really funny? If it is, please tell me, because I seem to have misplaced what the hell happened to me last night."

"No, no, I'm sorry. I'm just nervous, I guess. But no, no, in answer to your question, it's nothing funny." Allison gripped the doorknob for dear life. "I'm sorry. There's actually a big terrycloth robe on the third shelf in the closet. I'll be in the kitchen," she said, and slammed the door behind her.

Allison leaned against the door for a moment, attempting to rein in her heaving breaths and racing heart. Dear Lord, she'd seen him naked. *While he was awake.* And somehow, it had fried her mind until her brain was now silly putty.

She was a goner. She didn't want a man, wasn't looking for a relationship, and didn't need something with a dick to take care of her.

But she wanted J.T., the mysterious man from next door. The man who'd collapsed on her floor. The man who was now conscious and naked in all his glory in her bathroom.

She'd gone crazy. But damn, it felt good. It felt really, really good.

Allison raced into the kitchen to start the coffee. She got a filter from the cabinet and reached into the freezer to take out the coffee beans. Her mother had taught her that trick a long time ago. To keep coffee fresh, store it in the freezer.

She took filter and coffee to the coffeepot and froze. The coffee was already made.

Of course it's already made, you dummy. You set the timer last night.

Oh, hell. Was forgetfulness another sign of that chemical imbalance? Allison sighed and put the coffee back into the freezer, then threw the filter in the trash. She took two mugs from their hooks and filled them, then placed them on the breakfast bar. She filled her creamer and sugar bowl and laid them out neatly on the top of the bar, along with two spoons.

She then stood with indecision as she wondered what to do next. Then she squeaked in horror as she realized she was still wearing her ratty pj's and had yet to brush her hair.

She took off at a run down the hallway, around the corner, and straight into Mr. Brick's brick wall of a chest. His arms came out to catch her and she swallowed her breath, her tongue, and her brain, all in one big gulp.

"Fire? God, I hope not. I'm in no shape to help you put it out."

Allison just stared at him, feeling the heat of his hands melt the polyurethane fabric of her pajamas. She was melting. Oh yeah, there was a fire. A big one. And if he looked down at her bra-less breasts or dared to venture his hands lower, he'd be burned to a crisp.

"Yes. No. No. Of course not," she stammered. Her upper arms were clasped hard between his large hands. Her face was only a millimeter away from his. God, she wanted to kiss him.

J.T. smiled at her. "Good. Is everything all right?"

He hadn't let go of her arms. Allison saw that he'd put on the robe, but it did little to hide his nakedness. The front gaped over the sash, and his chest was just as scrumptious as she remembered it. And, someone help her, but the erection he'd had last night was still there, pressing tightly against her belly. She was going to pass out.

Allison wrenched away from him and reached behind her until she felt the wall at her back. Plastering herself against it in defiance of plastering herself against him, she tried to smile and failed miserably. "Yes, everything's A-okay. There's coffee in the kitchen. I just need to, umm, get dressed. I'll be right there, but help yourself."

He gave her another smile, but this one was more like a sexy grin. "Why bother getting dressed? I'm not."

Allison tried to think of a brilliant response, but her brain cells weren't firing on all cylinders this morning.

"Yes, yes, I'm really sorry about that. Really. But I've got clothes, see, in the other room. So I think I'll just go put some on."

She ran past him, hugging the wall, and shut her bedroom door behind her, flicking the lock. Then simply melted into a burning heap of hormones onto the floor.

Four

J.T. sat at the bar in the kitchen, drinking his coffee and wondering what the hell was going on. Allison was either totally repulsed by him or totally turned on, and he couldn't decide which. Before, in the close confines of her bathroom, she'd looked at his naked body with a look of horrified fascination. And just now, in the hallway, she'd all but plastered herself against him and used her eyes to beg him to kiss her. Then she'd taken off like the Devil was at her heels. Or maybe it had just been the cat.

He'd dreamed of this day, of being alone with her. Of being naked with her. Of having her look at him with that same look of wantonness and lust. God, just knowing she was a couple of hundred feet away, getting dressed, had his dick bobbing up and down like a buoy adrift in the ocean.

J.T. had long had fantasies of Allison. He'd first seen her about five months ago as she'd entered her apartment. He'd been looking through the peephole, waiting impatiently for his Chinese food to arrive. He'd watched as she'd dug through her purse, obviously searching for her keys. He'd seen her throw the thing to the floor, too, and stomp on it a couple of times before bending over to pick it back up. Damn, but he could still picture her bending over in that skirt. The thought alone made his mouth water.

That had been the start of it. He'd seen her a few more times, sometimes through the little hole in his door, sometimes as he'd grabbed his paper as she was leaving the building. J.T. had seen her outside a few times, too, getting into or out of a cab or walking down to Miller's, the market on the corner.

Not that he'd made a point to look for her. And not like he'd been watching her without her knowing or anything. Okay, maybe he had, a few times. But hey, he wasn't a sicko, he was just interested. And too damn chicken to approach her and ask her out. After all, he might have been watching her, but the lady didn't even know that J.T. Freedom existed on the planet Earth.

But really, it had started off innocently enough. He'd be on the job, sitting in his car like he was on most workdays, waiting to snap a picture of a cheating spouse or a supposedly disabled office worker. And then his mind would just drift off, to thoughts of . . .

Holy shit in a handbasket to hell.

It all came rushing back to him. The job he was on yesterday. Sitting in his car and then seeing the two women. Then seeing the one woman who had turned out to be something else entirely. Getting the crap beat out of him and trying to stagger home. He remembered knocking on Allison's door, thinking it was his own and trying to beat his way in without his keys, but nothing after that. He must have some lump on his head.

This was just great. J.T. finally got the chance to meet the woman of his wet dreams, and he did it by ending up at her doorstep, looking like a giant pile of pureed hamburger.

He heard her enter the kitchen behind him. Her steps were hesitant, and she didn't look directly at him as she took the stool across from his.

"Hi," he said, giving her his best Cary Grant signature smile.

Allison didn't seem fazed. "Hi."

J.T. cleared his throat and took a sip of coffee. "Well, this is actually kind of embarrassing. I'm J.T. Freedom, and I sincerely want to apologize for showing up at your door yesterday and probably ruining your day."

"Oh no, it's not a problem. You were hurt. And I'm Allison Dare, by the way."

"Oh yeah, I know."

"You know me?"

J.T. knew that his cheeks were slightly flushed as he looked at her over his coffee cup. "Umm, yes, I've actually seen you around a few times. Here in the building, I mean."

Allison's eyebrows scrunched together and she bit her lower lip, but then she leaned over the counter to shake his hand in greeting, giving him a nice view of her tits.

All that did was make him want to drag her over the top of said breakfast bar and then bend her back over it. His mind drifted off in that pleasant direction until he realized she was still talking.

"Well, anyway, do you want to talk about it? Or maybe not," she stammered, sitting back down and pouring cream into her coffee. "I would understand if it was traumatic."

"Traumatic?"

Allison looked at him. "Yes, you know, with the woman trying to rape you and all."

J.T. froze. "Rape me?" He watched as Allison frowned.

"Well, that's what you said, when I opened the door yesterday. That some woman had just tried to rape you."

He burst out laughing. Allison stared at him with wide green eyes, her hand trembling visibly on the handle of her coffee cup. J.T. had to work hard to cut it off.

"I'm sorry, I'm sorry. Wow. I really said that?"

"Yes. You really said that."

"Then I'm doubly sorry for all the trouble I've caused you." He got up from the stool and made his way to the counter, refilling his cup. "No, I don't think a woman tried to rape me. Someone that I *thought* was a woman beat the living daylights out of me while another woman watched, but no, I don't think there was any rape involved."

Allison had turned around, following his path to the coffeepot. J.T. leaned against the countertop and took another fortifying gulp of black, liquid caffeine.

"That really doesn't make a whole lot of sense," she said.

"You're right. Okay, this is really, really embarrassing, and I won't hold it against you if you bust a gut laughing. But since you let me sleep on your floor last night, I'm sure I owe you an explanation."

"Actually," Allison said, "you don't owe me anything. I was happy to do it, really."

J.T. tried to decipher if that happiness gave him permission to take her to bed and act out some of his favorite fantasies, then decided it was a subject best not pursued at this moment in time.

"Thank you. I really appreciate all that you did, whatever it was. But I still owe you an explanation. If nothing else, for saying something totally crazy like that rape thing. I must have been a little more brain-damaged than I originally thought."

Her laughter was a finger of desire that licked its way from the base of his spine, up to his neck, and down around, directly into his dick. He walked back around to his seat and sat down fast, hoping the top of the bar would be enough to cover his ever-growing hard-on.

"Well, okay, here goes. Like I said, my name is J.T. Freedom. I work as a P.I., own my own business, actually. *Freedom Investigations*. Yesterday, I was on a routine stakeout that turned out to be anything but routine."

J.T. watched as Allison propped her elbows on the bar and placed her chin in her hands. She was an attentive audience. And she had great lips. Kissable lips. Suckable lips. Very, very . . .

He cleared his throat and gave his head a little shake. "Anyway, yesterday I was tailing a man named Rod Stoller. His wife has suspected him for months of having an affair. I finally caught up with him—at an apartment complex, amazingly enough, only three blocks south of here."

"Wow. Your job sounds really exciting."

"It has its moments. Some good, some, like yesterday, not so good."

She smiled at him, and it was brilliant. Just her smile had his headache lessening and his body feeling more relaxed. Allison Dare was one potent woman.

"So anyway, Rod goes into an apartment, and about twenty minutes later, two women go up to the same one. They're on the third floor, street side, right across from the alley where I'm parked. I couldn't see too much after the ladies showed up. I'm guessing they either went into another room for their tryst or were below window level."

J.T. watched as Allison blushed. God, she was hot.

"So anyway, about forty-five minutes later, Rod leaves, and I get an entire roll of film of him giving a very, well, let's just say a very *involved* good-bye to the women. He drives off, and five minutes later the women leave the apartment. And then it all got shot to hell."

She leaned toward him over their coffee cups and grabbed his hand. "Oh, tell me, tell me! What happened?"

Her excitement had put a glow in her eyes, and now her breasts were heaving, threatening to spill over the top of her vee-neck T-shirt.

J.T. took a deep breath and tried to finish the story before he came in his . . . robe.

"To make a long story short, one of the ladies in question saw me taking pictures and didn't take too kindly to it. So before I could drive away, they were at the car. One beat the crap out of me while the other one egged her on. Punching, biting, kicking. I don't remember everything that happened, but I know it hurt. I also know why they weren't too happy about the pictures."

"Why's that?"

"One of the ladies, the one who did the punching, biting, and kicking, wasn't a lady."

He watched as Allison frowned, and then as her eyes widened and her mouth dropped open. "She was a *guy?*"

"Yep. Guess she, or he, didn't want that getting out. I'm guessing old Rod won't be too happy about it, either, once his wife finds out what's been going on."

"But your camera. You didn't have a camera when you came to my door."

J.T. smiled. "I tossed my camera in the glove compartment with my wallet before they got to me. It has a key, and I don't carry it with me. For just that reason."

"Hmm, very smart. So, do you have women kicking your ass every day?" She was laughing as she asked it, and J.T. couldn't help but laugh with her.

"Not usually, no. Actually, I don't usually have much interaction with people at all. Most of the work I do is from afar—taking pictures, making notes, stuff like that. This is the first time I've been seriously ambushed, and hopefully the last."

Allison smiled at him, and all was right with the world.

"I mean it, though. Thanks for putting those bandages on me and letting me crash here last night. And for not killing me for being a psycho when I said that thing about the rape."

She was shooing away his comments even as he made them. "There's nothing you need to thank me for. Any respectable citizen would have done the same. And I'm just glad that you weren't really hurt by those women, rape or not."

"Me, too."

"And I didn't think you were a psycho, not really, especially after Cissy vouched for you. Or kind of vouched for you. She told me that you were my neighbor, which made me look like an idiot, since I had no clue."

"Ah, yes, Cissy."

"You know Cissy?"

J.T. gave a bark of laughter. "At last count, I've turned down Cissy's invitation for a date twenty-two times. She doesn't quite seem to get the hint."

Allison laughed with him. "Cissy is a really nice person. But when it comes to getting the hint, she's a little slow."

J.T. smiled at her. "But anyway, Allison, back to our discussion. When I look at you, the last thing I see is an idiot."

He loved watching her blush. Her green eyes would get even brighter, even greener, and that slightly pink hue would come over her cheeks. Add to that her sexy mane of hair, her even sexier body, and the fact that he couldn't stop thinking about her on the breakfast bar, and it was a killer combination.

J.T. glanced at the clock on the wall. "Well, Allison, I think I've probably taken up enough of your time."

She smiled at him and rose from her stool along with him. "I keep telling you, it hasn't been any trouble. A little nerve-wracking maybe, but no trouble."

He made his way through the living room and stopped at the door. "I forgot to ask. Where's the demon?"

"Are you delirious again?"

J.T. laughed. "No. I promise. I meant your cat. Cats and I don't really bond well. I think it wants to kill me."

Allison laughed, and laughed, and laughed some more. She bent over, holding her hands to her stomach, as J.T. watched.

She finally stopped, and had to wipe the tears from her eyes before she could answer him.

"Bella? Holy hell, that is just too funny. The only thing Bella ever hurts is herself. She's almost as uncoordinated as I am. And I can't imagine," she said, raising an eyebrow at him, "that a big, strong stud like yourself could possibly be scared of a little bitty ball of fur."

J.T. wasn't sure whether to be thrilled that she thought he was a stud or insulted that she thought he was scared.

"Not scared. Exactly. Just wary. The thing looks vicious."

"She's harmless, I promise. Me, on the other hand, you have to watch out for." Allison's mouth dropped open as soon as she finished the sentence. J.T. supposed she was shocked that she'd just said what she had.

He couldn't help but grin. "Really. And what, precisely, should I watch out for?"

"Never mind. Oh God, I can't believe I said that." She moved to turn away but he grabbed her arm and pulled her back. Now she was almost nose to nose with him.

"Really, Allison, are you *dangerous?*"

J.T. watched her throat work as she swallowed, and lowered his gaze to her full, plump breasts, which were rising and falling as if she'd just run a marathon.

She didn't answer him. But her eyes, God, her eyes bored into his until he felt like they were connected somehow. Here he was, in nothing but a robe, having done nothing but embarrass himself before her for the past twenty-four hours. But she was looking at him like he was . . . well, a stud, and he'd be damned if he'd let this opportunity pass by unnoticed.

J.T. pulled her closer, until he could see the gold specks in her pupils and feel her raspy breath against his face.

"How dangerous are you, Allison?"

She swallowed hard but refused to lower her gaze. "I've been known to cause national disasters."

J.T. chuckled. "Well, is that right. That's interesting. Because I've been trained in cleaning them up."

He bent down to kiss her before he could change his mind. Just one little taste, that's all he needed to get the enigma that was Allison Dare out of his mind. Just one touch, that one taste, and he could go home in his borrowed robe and never again wonder what kissing her would be like.

Yep, and pigs flew south in the summer to avoid the acid rain.

He was kissing her before she even realized it. His lips were firm and smooth, and although they moved expertly over her own, J.T. wasn't demanding. Allison felt his tongue at the corner of her lips and couldn't suppress a smile. The man was definitely talented.

Quick little kisses at the corners of her mouth, across her cheek, back down to her neck. And then that wonderful mouth was back upon hers, and she eagerly opened her mouth to let him inside.

The first rasp of his tongue against her own had her sighing. The light pull as he gently sucked on her tongue had her groaning. And the deep, thrusting motions of that same tongue against her own had her pushing him back against the door.

God, he could kiss her all day. She moved her head slightly to the right, trying to find an angle that would let her get even closer. Allison moved her hands to his long hair and tangled her fingers in it, then held on as his own hands grabbed her ass through her thin jogging shorts.

Her mouth met his thrust for thrust. Holy shit, she was burning up, starving, drinking in his kisses as if her life depended on it. She pushed harder against him, aligning her throbbing pussy as close to his dick as possible. It still wasn't enough.

"Allison." She heard him say her name, but it was like

listening to sound echo through a tunnel. "Allison, stop. God, you're killing me here."

She didn't stop, just wiggled closer, ever closer. More, she needed more.

"Does your head hurt? Am I bruising your ribs even more?" At the confused shake of his head, she laughed. "Mmmm, then I don't want to stop."

J.T.'s groan was loud in her ear as his hands continued their exploration of her ass. Allison continued to kiss whatever parts of him she could reach. God, she was so hot for this man. It was an embarrassment to humankind, really, but screw it. She wanted him, and she'd have him.

"Allison," J.T. said again, "for God's sake. If you don't stop kissing me like that this is going to go a lot further than you probably want."

Allison pulled back a little and looked at him, at the desire that filled his eyes and mirrored what she was feeling.

"I should probably tell you, J.T., that I have a terminal disease."

His jaw dropped and the grip on her ass became almost painful. "Oh my God, you're dying? What? What is it?"

She bit down on her lip to hold in her laugh. "No, I'm not dying. But I have terminal foot-in-mouth disease." She licked his bottom lip, then nipped it with her teeth. "I have a really bad habit of always saying what I'm thinking. I have a horrible impulse thing where I act before I think. And right now I'm feeling all of the symptoms of a foot-in-mouth attack."

J.T. continued to stare at her, eyebrow raised and a look of puzzlement on his face. "I'm not sure exactly what that means. Do I want to know what that means?"

Allison laughed and let her hands drift down the open front of his robe, her fingers dragging through his chest hair until they reached the knot where he'd tied it. She let one hand drag lower, down to the hem, and then back up until just her fingertips touched his dick. He was hard and pulsing, and he jerked under that one light touch.

"I'm guessing that you'll like it."

J.T.'s sharp, indrawn breath ended on a moan. "Spit it out already, Allison."

"What I'm trying to say is that I'm really, really attracted to you. Actually, truth be told, you make me hot. It's been a long time since I've been hot, J.T." She glanced up to see if she had his attention. He was staring at her with rapt fascination, and his cock was bobbing against the fingers that she held pressed against it. Oh yeah, the man was certainly paying attention.

"Anyway, I usually say things that either piss people off or shock them into a coma. I hope you won't do either. But J.T., I don't know how to be delicate, how to say what I feel and what I think in flowery speech. The truth is, I want you. I want to have sex with you." Her hand uncurled and reached up to grasp his erection. It filled her hand, overflowed it, and her clit gave an answering pull in response.

"I want you to fuck me."

She heard him swallow, saw his Adam's apple bob as she traced his lips with one hand and explored his ever-growing cock with the other.

"You mean it?"

Allison laughed. "I mean it. So what do you say? Are you ready to go home, or would you like to stay awhile? It's kind of like *Let's Make a Deal.*"

J.T.'s hands moved from her ass to tangle themselves in her silky hair. His fingers tightened there as he ground himself against her and brought his lips to within a hairsbreadth of her own.

"I'm not an idiot. I'll take door number two. I might have been unconscious before, Allison Dare, but I'm wide awake now. Besides, no man in his right mind would say no to an invitation like that. I'll fuck you, honey, if you fuck me back."

"This is the part where I say you've got a deal."

J.T.'s mouth wasn't gentle on hers this time, and that was good. His tongue was voracious, demanding, plunging into her mouth and dueling with her own as his body pushed against hers insistently.

She moved her hands around to his ass, which was hard and hot like the rest of him. When his mouth moved from her own, she took the opportunity to kiss his neck, to lick a path of fire down the hollow of his throat to his chest.

J.T.'s hands were busy, moving to her breasts through her thin T-shirt, tormenting her nipples into hard peaks. Her body was liquid silver, heavy and hot and full. She needed to lie down, and she needed him to fill her.

"Come here," she said, and let go of his ass long enough to take him by the hand. She felt J.T walking behind her, his searching hands touching everywhere they could reach. His fingernail flicked over a sensitive nipple and she stopped in the hallway to turn around and take his mouth once again.

The kiss wasn't gentle, too much pent-up emotions and anxiety zinging around for them to worry about taking their time. As she felt him push her back against the wall, she couldn't stop herself from speaking.

"Tell me you're not married." She pushed aside his robe and licked one brown nipple. "Tell me you don't have a girl-friend sleeping in your apartment right now." Allison heard him groan as she moved to his other nipple and sucked it into her mouth. "Tell me this is okay."

"It's okay, Allison." His hand moved down between her legs, rubbing her through her shorts. At her sharp intake of breath, his teeth settled at her throat as his fingers teased her through her already wet panties. "It's more than okay. As long as you have condoms somewhere, don't plan on biting off my head like a preying mantis when we're done, and will let me make love to you to my heart's content, it is way more than okay."

Allison pushed against his hand, cursing the fabric that separated that aching center from his long, talented fingers.

"I've got condoms. I'm not going to kill you. And we can do this as much as you want. Come to bed with me, J.T."

Five

She led him to the bedroom, this time not stopping. Allison felt him tense when he saw Bella asleep in her cat bed.

"I'll let her out," she laughed at him. "I can't do it with her watching anyway."

She picked up the cat, who wasn't thrilled with being disturbed in the middle of her nap, then flipped the lock on the door. When she turned around, J.T. was naked, eyeing her with a look of lust and desire as he stood by the foot of the bed.

Now that she had him here, in her bedroom, ready and willing, she wasn't sure what to do with him. Allison wasn't the type to pick up the first man she saw. She wasn't the type to succumb to a man's charms or his cheesy come-ons. She *definitely* wasn't the type to tell a man, one she didn't even really know, that she wanted to fuck him. Contrary to popular belief, her outward personality was more a shell than the real her. She used that shell for protection, but the truth was, she could be embarrassed. She could be scared and lonely and hurt. Her mouth was her way of keeping people at bay.

She had a feeling that she wouldn't be able to keep J.T. Freedom at arm's length for any amount of time.

"Why are you looking at me like that?" His voice held humor and a strong dose of desire.

Allison shrugged and moved closer to him, reaching for the hem of her T-shirt. "You're good to look at," she said, and watched as his hand reached out to stop hers from taking off her shirt.

"Let me do it. I want to look at you, all of you. I've waited for this moment for a long time."

"Say that again?"

The man actually blushed, color rising from his neck to the roots of his hair. "Well, see, it's like this. I told you that I've seen you around the building. What I didn't mention was the fact that seeing you tends to turn my dreams into teenage come-fests."

She actually felt her mouth drop down to her toes. For the first time that she could remember, she was speechless. Allison Marie Dare was never speechless.

J.T. laughed as he pulled her T-shirt over her head and threw it into the corner. His laugh died in his throat as he stared at her breasts, bare for the world with nipples already hardened into sharp points.

Allison was still trying to think of something to say. Never, not once in her whole life, had a man told her that she was the basis for his dreams, never mind the types of dreams that had men leaving streaks on their sheets. This was new territory. This was serious.

Her mind clicked back into gear and her mouth along with it. "I guess I should say thank you, but I'm at a loss for words. Do you know how miraculous that is?"

J.T. laughed again as he slipped his fingers under the waistband of her shorts. "I can guess that it's something new. I like you, Allison. You're funny, you're feisty, and you have no problem saying what's on your mind." He pulled her shorts down her legs and she automatically stepped out. "Contrary to popular belief, a lot of men like women who can speak their mind."

"Really. That's interesting, because I've never found one."

"I think you've been looking in all the wrong places. Now come here so I can act out my fantasies before you change your mind."

Allison went to him willingly, and it was if they'd never stopped the foreplay from ten minutes earlier. She seamlessly went into his arms and wound her own around his neck. His mouth came down on hers, slow and sensual, and she sighed a breath of relief. He still wanted her. She hadn't imagined it. J.T. Freedom desired her, mouth and all.

Their kiss went from slow and soft to hard and fast in a heartbeat. His hands were everywhere: on her breasts, around to her back, down to her ass. His mouth was hungry on hers and Allison fought to catch her breath.

She pushed him down until he fell to the bed, and she pounced.

"God, woman, if you're not careful, this could be over before it even gets started."

"Then we'd just have to start all over again," she said, and she knew her smile was wicked.

J.T. laughed. "Good point."

She leaned down to kiss him, letting her mouth wander to his chest. She placed a quick kiss on each of his nipples and continued the exploration that she'd wanted to make ever since seeing him in her doorway.

As her lips neared his dick, she heard him gasp. Allison let her tongue lash out to take one quick taste, just a fast swipe of her tongue to taste the length and breadth of him. His salty, slightly spicy taste was heavenly. She pulled him into her mouth and took one long, hard pull, and released him at his harsh, in-drawn breath.

"Do you always have to be in control?" he asked, as he used her hair to bring her face back up to his own.

"Usually. I like being in control. I know what to expect that way."

"Not this time. Get the condoms, Allison, and get your pretty little ass back in bed."

She stared at him, wondering how to reply. Then she simply jumped up and ran to the bathroom, returning seconds later with an unopened box of extra-large condoms.

"I always think big," she said in response to his quirked eyebrows.

They laughed together. She opened the box and pulled one out, lying it on the bed beside him for quick access. And then froze, because she wasn't sure what to do next.

J.T. took the choice away from her, and for once in her life she was glad.

He prayed to anyone who might be listening that he wasn't dreaming. Allison Dare was finally in his bed. Well, technically she was in *her* bed, but the fact remained that she was in a bed that included him. He couldn't blow this. He couldn't mess it up.

J.T. looked up at the woman who was now straddling his lap while he was conscious and coherent.

"You're so beautiful," he said, and he meant it. Gorgeous, nearly black hair that hung like a shroud surrounding her face. Her green eyes were as brilliant as perfectly cut emeralds, and they were drinking him in, swallowing him whole. She had a pert little nose, and full lips that were made for kissing.

Her tits were full, plump, and a hefty handful. J.T. had never been a breast man, but he was sincerely rethinking the idea. If he could look at Allison's all day, he knew he was a reformed man.

She had a trim waist and a not-quite-flat belly that had his entire body quivering with barely restrained lust. Her legs were long and limber, with well-defined calf muscles. The woman even had pretty feet.

J.T. held her in place with one hand at her waist as he used the other to trace a path from the pulse pounding at her throat, down around one nipple and then the other, and on down until he came to her belly button. He gave it a teasing swirl with his finger and thought about putting his mouth there. The thought had his dick straining against her, searching for fulfillment.

Allison's hips were subtly moving against his own, and she'd closed her eyes on a groan of either arousal or frustration. J.T. suddenly flipped her over, so that their positions were now reversed.

"You know that you have to open your eyes, Allison. I want to watch you when I make you come, over and over again."

Her eyes flew open and a blush stained its way over her breasts and up into her cheeks. God, the woman was so beautiful, especially when she was turned on.

"Watch what I can do to you."

J.T. brought his lips down to hers to plant a feather-light kiss. He moved on, to that same throbbing pulse in her neck, and licked a streak of fire from it to her breasts. He whirled his tongue around one nipple and smiled against her as her hands grabbed onto his hair to push herself more tightly against him. The sounds coming from her throat were half moans, half sobs, as he teased her until her hips were flailing on the bed.

Slowly, he licked his way to her other breast, teasing that tit with lazy strokes that were just out of reach of her aching nipple. Allison groaned and planted her hands more firmly in his hair, causing his pleasure to border on pain that had him wanting to forego the foreplay and ram himself into her.

"Shh, baby, it's okay. We'll get there, I promise." He licked his way to her belly and used his tongue to circle her belly button. "I've waited too long for this to take the easy way out now."

"J.T., please," she said, and her plea almost did him in.

"I know, Allison. I know what you want. Hold on, babe, and I'll give it to you."

His tongue continued its journey, down over her belly and over one thigh. Then the other, all the while feeling her resistance as she tried to push her straining pussy toward his face. The woman had been telling the truth. She knew what she wanted, and she wasn't shy about letting him know.

J.T. pushed her legs apart, then pushed until her knees bent and her feet were planted firmly on the mattress. She was beautiful everywhere, with dark curls protectively guarding her most special place, that place that had caused him innumerable nights of suffering. He'd be damned if he'd suffer any more.

He brought his mouth to within a hairsbreadth of her entryway and breathed out a stream of hot breath. Allison's hands had left his hair to grip the sheet that they lay on, and he watched as the blast of air had her fingers curling into it.

J.T. used one finger to tenderly probe her, testing her readiness. Allison was already wet, her juices raining down to drip onto his finger. He glanced up and noticed that her eyes were once again shut against the maelstrom of her emotions.

"Open your eyes, sunshine, and watch me."

"I can't," she moaned, and turned her head away from

him. "Oh God, I want you so bad, and yet I'm so embarrassed."

J.T. stroked her once more with his finger, avoiding her clit as he slowly worked his finger up and down in a dizzyingly slow dance. "You can, Allison. You can watch me, and tell me what you want, or I'll stop."

Allison's eyes flew open and sparred with his. "You wouldn't."

He smiled. "Oh, but I would. See, I can be wicked, too. I've dreamed of hearing you scream out my name in pleasure, Allison, and that's what's going to happen. But I'm not going to give you what you want unless you beg for it."

J.T. watched as her eyes took on the fiery glow of determination. "Fine. Then give me what I want."

"And what is that?"

"You know damn well what that is."

He nodded. "Uh-huh, I do. But I told you you'd have to beg for it." His smile was wicked.

Allison sighed and brought her hands up over her breasts, down her belly, and rested them lightly at the juncture of her thighs.

She smiled at him. "J.T., if you don't put your mouth on me in the next five seconds, I'm going to have to hurt you."

J.T. smiled again and did as she said. After all, who was he to argue with the unstoppable Allison Dare?

He used his tongue like a power torch. He made lazy circle-eights around her clit, which he knew had to be hard and throbbing for release. His tongue was his weapon, his sword, and he wielded it with all the might that he possessed.

J.T. felt her hanging on to the edge, felt her fighting to get closer to his teasing tongue. He refused to touch that most sensitive spot, though, until she asked. Begged. Power trip or no power trip, they'd see who was in control of this situation. This was one time where only her fierce tongue and mighty mouth could save her. Literally.

He heard her groan with frustration and removed his mouth to glance up at her. "What's the matter? You need something?"

"Damn you, J.T. You're a, a, a thug. An evil, meanie thug."

"Yep. So what are you going to do about it?"

Allison's hands pulled his head back to her mound as she pushed against him. "Suck it, J.T. Suck my clit and put me out of my misery. You wanted me to beg, but I'm telling you. Do it now. Please," she added, and her voice shook with emotion and frustration.

J.T. opened his mouth and placed his lips gently around her. He flicked her most sensitive spot with his tongue and shuddered along with her. He licked her hard and fast, and then slowed down to soft, feather-light jabs that barely touched her skin.

Allison's groans were coming quick and ragged, and her hips were bucking like a barroom electronic stallion.

J.T. took pity on her, or on himself, and sucked her clit into his mouth between his teeth.

Her yell of satisfaction took him by surprise, as did the orgasm that raged through her and had her juices pouring into his mouth. He sucked her until she was done, and held on to his self-control for dear life.

Six

"I'm dead. I died and you killed me." She was lying on her back, trying for all the world to catch her breath and a little piece of sanity. It seemed to be a lost cause.

J.T.'s snort of laughter sounded more like a plea of desperation. "I sincerely hope you're joking. If you're dead, we can't finish this the way I'd like. And if we don't finish it, I'm going to drop dead of the world's most painful erection that's ever been recorded."

Allison looked at him in disbelief. This guy's mind worked along the same lines as her own. That was very, very scary, and yet somehow comforting.

"Don't worry, we'll finish it," she laughed, and moved over to straddle him once again. "We're not done yet, and anyway, I couldn't let this painful erection be your parting thought of me." She smiled as she said it, and opened the foil packet on the bed beside her. She slowly slipped it over him, loving the feel of him, like crushed flower petals or smooth velvet.

J.T. raised a hand to push her hair back over one ear. "I don't want any parting thoughts of you."

She stared at him, not quite understanding. "I'd say 'huh?' but that would make me sound pretty stupid, wouldn't it?"

J.T. sighed a sigh of infinite patience. "This isn't going to end here, Allison. One quick fuck and then we're through is not going to be par for the course." He moved his hips until his dick was poised at the opening of her pussy. "I don't play mind games. I don't sleep with a woman and then disappear." He rubbed himself against her, once, twice, barely touching her. "I'm a one-woman man who's completely devoted to long-term, monogamous relationships." He placed the tip of himself inside her and heard her breath catch.

"This is going to last as long as we can make it, Allison," he said, and thrust up until she was impaled upon him.

Allison shook, with desire, with need, and with the thought that she'd finally found a man who could match her, step for step. She leaned back and rode him hard, taking all of him. Harder, deeper, faster, more. She needed everything that he could give her, and that still wasn't enough. Finally, *finally*, she'd found a man who, if he wasn't that perfect fairytale lover, he was as close as you could find on solid terra firma.

She opened her eyes to meet his gaze as his hands reached up to knead her breasts. His fingers teasingly pinched her nipples as she locked her thighs, pushing him toward a release that would hopefully match the power of her own.

Allison saw his pupils widen and heard his breath become harsher. She felt his hands, rough and callused, against the pale, smooth skin of her waist as he pushed himself harder and faster inside of her.

She felt her orgasm approaching and fought to find the words, the right words, to tell J.T. what she was feeling. He seemed to understand, though, as he reached to entangle his fingers with her own. Allison rushed toward that outcropping of desire and threw herself over it headfirst. She heard her name upon his lips as she felt him jerk inside of her, spilling himself into the protective sheath of the condom.

She came back into her body slowly, and slid down with him still planted firmly inside of her, until she could lay her head on his shoulder. It took a while for their breathing to get back to normal, and she realized with amusement that she felt comfortable with him even without talking. For her, that was a first.

When she woke up, he wasn't beside her. But he'd left a note, and the terrycloth robe, folded neatly on the bed beside her.

Allison,
*   By no means is this good-bye. I need to get to the office and set up an appointment with the soon-to-be-ex-Mrs. Stoller. I have to get my car from where I left it, and get my film developed. You need to feed the devil cat and finish whatever work I interrupted yesterday. I'll be back at seven for dinner, and I'll even bring the wine.*

J.T.

P.S. I'm so positive that I've been waiting for you for a lifetime that I'm even going to tell you what the J.T. stands for. So feel privileged. You're the only one besides my parents who will know the truth. Just think, Allison, I'm giving you free blackmail material.

She had to laugh. The man was crazy, just like she was. And sexy, and funny, and smart, and had the body of a modern-day Hercules. And here she'd thought that fairytales were idiotic lies spun by people with nothing else to do on a Saturday night.

Then she froze. What the hell was she thinking? Things like this, where everything just fell into her lap like manna from Heaven, did not happen in the real world. They especially didn't happen to people like her. Was she nuts? Thinking about happily-ever-after with a man she'd just met, what, six hours ago? Since she couldn't exactly count the time that he was knocked out flat on his back as intimate moments, she'd barely just met him.

"Get a grip, Allison. Don't set yourself up for another fall." She got out of bed and began to gather the things she'd need for a long overdue shower. "You should know better than anyone that there's no such thing as love at first sight."

The shower did nothing except give her more time to talk herself out of even harboring the idea that J.T. could be more than a casual lay. How could there be a future with a man she didn't even know? Sure, the sex had been out of this world, but at twenty-eight she needed something more than just good sex. If she ever wanted that storybook life of a marriage and a family, she needed to get her ass in gear and get started. And picking up the first guy who passed out on her floor was not the way to go.

Allison fixed a sandwich and made a fresh pot of coffee. She felt a little more human, and still had the aftereffects of some of the best sex she'd ever had racing through her bloodstream.

She booted up the computer and brought up her *Loveswept* folder. She reread what she'd written the day before and was thoroughly frustrated.

New direction, remember? You have to take this piece in a new direction, or you're going to screw up this job, too, before it even gets started.

Allison took another fortifying sip of coffee and began to type.

Now that we've established how the world of love doesn't work, we need to concentrate on how it does. How do you know, for example, that a person you've met is "the one"? Obviously, they're not going to be wearing a sign that says, "Here I am, your soulmate. Take it or be screwed forever." So how do you tell if your internal bullshit meter is being honest or going haywire from overactive hormones and sexual longings? Good question.

Let's use an example. Say you meet a guy who seems to be, at first glance and several glances after that, everything you've ever looked for in a lover. He's kind, he's funny, and he seems to have an IQ over 20. He's quirky, like you; he doesn't run at the first sign of your raging hormonal imbalance, and he even laughs at your stupid jokes. He doesn't find you obnoxious, but instead seems to be genuinely interested in what you have to say. He knows how to listen and how to make you speechless. And as if that weren't enough, he's also sexier than any man you've met in the past year. Or two. Or ever. Not to mention the fact that the sparks flying between the two of you are enough to start another California wildfire.

Well, she had the facts. But where did she take it from there? How *did* you know when you'd found your soulmate? Or even just a man who was planning on sticking around longer than a double-header played on a perfect summer afternoon?

Allison sighed and propped her chin in one hand. That was the kicker. There were no guarantees. Not in life, and especially not in love. Besides, she shouldn't even be thinking about love and J.T. in the same sentence. For God's sake, she'd just met the man. And the sex, although it had been totally mind-blowing, could have been a fluke. The result of a severe lack, a bad dry spell, an overactive libido.

But even being the cynical, hard-core, mouthy woman that she was, she recognized something in J.T. Freedom that she'd never seen in anyone else she'd dated. A sincerity, maybe. Or maybe just a basic goodness. Whatever it was, she was starting to believe that he was serious when he'd said that he wasn't going anywhere anytime soon. And what could it hurt, really, to give this go-round a chance?

She'd always planned to settle down eventually, and maybe, just maybe, *eventually* was knocking at her front door. So if she could just keep her damn mouth shut, or at least edit what came out of it, she and J.T. might have a chance to see where this could go. It couldn't hurt to give it a shot.

Allison grinned. J.T. was sure better than any other prospects she'd had, and was a lot better to look at than most. And now that she knew her mouth hadn't scared him off at their first meeting, they just might have a chance.

J.T. spent the morning setting up an appointment with Mrs. Stoller, who unfortunately couldn't meet him until Monday morning. He took his two rolls of film to a one-hour photo joint, and when they were developed he sealed them in an envelope and stashed them back in his glove compartment.

He grabbed a quick bite to eat at a deli, then wondered what to do with himself until seven. He could go home and watch some TV, but that would just allow him more time to replay his night with Allison. And if he replayed his night with Allison, he'd get hard and hot all over again, with no way to put out the fire.

J.T. settled behind the wheel of his car and headed toward home. He'd behave himself, watch a movie or take a nap before it was time to take the three steps across the hall to meet Allison for dinner. Damn, but the woman was the epitome of hot. He'd known there was something about her that appealed to him. Just catching glimpses of her, even knowing she didn't know he existed, had made him want to get to know her. But now that he'd met her and had enjoyed some of the best sex in his life with her, he *had* to get to know her.

Allison Dare might not know it yet, but J.T. was here to stay. Sticking like glue, or like a fly stuck on some really nasty flypaper. Either way, she'd just have to get used to the idea. After all, he planned on telling her his name, which he never told *anyone*. Never, ever. So this had to be serious.

J.T. stood outside her apartment, ear pressed to the door, feeling like an idiot but doing it nonetheless. He didn't hear a thing, which meant she was either asleep or being very, very quiet. He sighed and entered his own apartment, casting one last look over at her closed door. It was two in the afternoon, and he had five more hours to kill.

This was going to be one hell of a day.

Allison told herself she hadn't really been watching for J.T. through the peephole. But when she saw him start down the hallway toward her door, she was too stunned to look away. She saw him press his ear to her door and had to suppress a laugh.

The look he cast toward her apartment before he closed his own door was one of longing and expectation. Not to mention lust. Can't forget that lust.

She went back to her desk and stroked Bella a few times, wondering what she should do. Five hours until their "date" ... five hours, at the least, before she could get her hands on him again. Unless she took action. And wasn't Allison Dare a woman of action?

She smiled to herself as she saved her article and gently lowered Bella to the floor. Time to see exactly what sort of stuff she was made of. And what J.T. Freedom was made of, as well.

Seven

It took her twenty minutes to decide what to wear. She wanted to look sexy without looking trashy, wanted to exude sex appeal without looking like she was hunting him down to have sex. For a woman with the fashion sense of a breeding mare, it wasn't an easy task.

In the end she decided on simple. You couldn't go wrong with simple. She chose a black skirt that was neither too long nor too short. It hit right above the knee, with a sexy little flounce that was about as romantic as she was willing to go. The top was tight, to showcase her best assets. A vee-neck front that showed a hint of cleavage, and open in the back. She thought the bright psychedelic colors made her eyes seem greener.

Allison hated shoes. She could never understand those women who had pairs upon pairs of shoes. She owned about ten pairs, total, four of which were different versions of the same brand of sneakers. Then she had three pairs of black shoes, none of which were appropriately sexy enough to go with her outfit. She finally dug up a pair of strappy sandals from the back of her closet, in a box that had never been opened. She guessed that they were a forgotten Christmas present from her mother, a self-proclaimed shoe goddess.

She spent fifteen minutes in the bathroom, arranging and rearranging her hair. Allison had read somewhere that men loved long, loose, flowing hair, but it kept getting in her way. After several tries, she decided to do it in an upsweep, and held it all together with two wildly colored clips. Makeup was easy, since she usually didn't wear any. A touch of mascara and a hint of bronze lipstick, and she was ready.

Now that she was ready, she wondered if she was about to make an ass out of herself. Here she was, about to go and seduce a man who was practically a stranger. Allison had to insert the *practically*, because a man who'd spent the morning giving you orgasms couldn't be a total stranger.

Now that she was finished, that old nemesis called *doubt* came charging in, rearing its ugly head. Did she really want to do this? Did she even have the guts to do it?

What would she do if she showed up at his door and he said he was busy, or was otherwise engaged? Oh shit, what if there was someone else over there? Granted, she hadn't seen anyone, especially a woman, enter his apartment, but for the past hour she hadn't been staring at the door across the hall.

But hadn't J.T. said himself that he didn't have a girl-friend? Allison scrunched up her face and thought hard. No, he'd said he wasn't married, but he'd never said anything about a girlfriend. He had said, though, that he wanted to get to know her, and that he wasn't going anywhere. Did that constitute a no-girlfriend arrangement?

Dammit, why did she always do this to herself? Time after time, she worked herself up into a frenzy about something, and then talked herself right back down into depression by analyzing every little nuance. God, she was irritating.

She'd never know what could happen if she didn't walk her ass over there and knock on his door.

Allison stomped to the kitchen as well as she could in the unaccustomed heels and grabbed a bottle of merlot she'd been saving for who-knew-what reason out of the fridge. She double-checked to make sure Bella had food and water, then turned out all of the lights except for the lamp in the living room. She didn't need a purse, and after considerable thought, locked her apartment door behind her and placed her spare key under the welcome mat. She was only going next door, after all.

She stood in the hall for a minute, staring at J.T.'s door, willing herself to imbibe through osmosis what he was doing. Allison didn't hear anything, but then again the walls were a little thicker than paperboard.

She took two long, deep breaths and raised her hand to knock.

And stared into those same two gorgeous blue eyes as the door opened before her knuckles even hit solid wood.

"Oh, umm, hi. You're going out? Sorry," she said, and took two steps backward toward her own door. "It was pretty presumptuous of me to assume you'd just be sitting over here doing nothing." She gave a nervous laugh that came out more like a choked yelp. "I'll, umm, just see you at seven."

Allison turned around and bent to grab the key back out from under the mat. And froze as she felt J.T.'s hard frame come up behind her. Something was pushing against her ass, and she had a feeling it wasn't a fire poker.

"Allison." That's all he said, and just the sound of his voice sent shivers cascading down her spine, all the way to her toes, which were now curled like talons inside of her stupid, sexy sandals.

She stood up slowly but didn't turn around. "Yes?"

J.T. planted his hands on the door, effectively trapping her between two solid hard places. "Sometimes you talk too much."

She couldn't turn around, couldn't look at him. God, she was a complete, utter moron. "Hmm, yes, well, I warned you of that."

He chuckled, and the sound of it reverberated in his chest and transferred to her back, around to her breasts, and straight down under her skirt.

"Yes, I guess you did warn me. But you know what?"

When she still didn't move, just stood still as a statue with her apartment key in one hand and the bottle of wine in the other, he moved one hand from the door to gently turn her around to face him. He lifted her chin until their eyes clashed.

"I hate rules. I don't do well with warnings. And sometimes, Allison, you just need to shut that beautiful mouth of yours."

It wasn't shut now. Actually, Allison was pretty sure it was hanging down somewhere around floor fifteen. Was he telling her to shut up? No one told her to shut up. No one told her to . . .

"Hmmph." That's all she got out before his mouth took hers in a kiss that was unlike anything she'd experienced with him before. J.T.'s mouth was hot and hungry on hers, not letting her get away or get a word, or breath, in edgewise.

She wanted to fight him. Who did he think he was, this virtual stranger who had somehow wiggled his way into her life? The nerve. To actually have the gall to tell her . . . and then she lost her train of thought, and her mind, as his hands were everywhere. She felt the bottle of wine slip from her fingers, but couldn't hear the sound it made as it hit the floor for the roaring in her ears.

Allison felt his hands upon her breasts, and then her ass, and then her knees and her thighs and oh God, he was edging his fingers teasingly toward that part of her that was already wet and ready for him. His mouth was still devouring hers—huge, hungry bites that swallowed her up. J.T.'s tongue was like a whirlwind, here, there, everywhere, and Allison was sure she was going to slink to the floor like the wine bottle if she didn't find something to hold on to, and fast.

J.T. read her mind. His mouth still firmly attached to hers, he placed his hands on her waist and lifted her three inches off the ground. He stepped backward through his doorway and used her body to shut the door. The next thing she knew, she was plastered to this door the same way as she had been in the hallway.

God, she was burning up, floating away, drifting off somewhere that she'd never been before. Allison planted her fingers in his hair as his tongue continued to light streaks of fire down her throat, to her earlobes, light nips up and down her neck. When that wasn't enough, she lowered her hands until she could lift the hem of his polo shirt, and sighed when her fingernails scraped across curly hair and flat nipples.

But it still wasn't enough. She needed something, needed *more.* She was greedy, wanton, pent-up with something that she couldn't name. This was more than lust. More than sex, more than desire. This was passion, the likes of which she'd never before felt. Allison wanted this man in the worst way, and she wanted him for more than just today.

"J.T.—oh God, J.T., what have you done to me?"

"Nothing more than what you've done to me," he said, aligning his erection with her opening. Even through her skirt she could feel every ridge, every smooth, hard curve, and it made her so hot she was amazed that she didn't just combust on the spot.

Allison wiggled against him, trying to get ever closer. Pretty soon she'd be crawling up his chest. Actually, that idea had merit.

"Something," she started, and took his mouth again. "Something's happening to me, J.T. Something about you is under my skin, making me act all crazy. Crazier than usual, even."

She used her tongue to tease the cleft in his chin, then brought a hand down to enclose him through his jeans.

"I know, Allison, I know. I feel the same way. You've screwed me up for other women, you know." He rubbed her ass with his hands and moved to take a nipple into his mouth, right through her shirt. "God, everything about you turns me on. Even that mouth of yours."

Allison couldn't help but laugh. "That's a first. Oh, J.T., take me to bed already."

"Yes, ma'am."

He wanted to take it slow and easy this time, prolong it so that it was everything they'd both ever wanted. As soon as he saw her in his bed, though, all hope of taking it slow was shot to hell.

J.T. knew, from the minute he saw her standing outside his door, with that vulnerable, uncertain look on her face, that he'd finally found the woman he wanted to spend the rest of his life with. Sure, she had a big mouth, and frequently used it to get herself in a shitpile of trouble. But like him, underneath all the bravado, underneath the tough-as-nails exterior, was a woman with the same basic needs and desires that he had.

And right now, as he watched her squirming under his touch, in his bed, in his apartment, he knew that her desires matched those of his own.

He couldn't keep his hands, or his mouth, to himself. Her kisses were like an aphrodisiac to his soul. Her mouth burned him wherever it touched, and her hands on him— on his chest, in his hair, on his dick—was like a branding iron that marked him as hers and hers alone.

J.T. waited until he knew Allison was on the edge before he brought himself between her legs. He rubbed against her, just a little, until she gasped and moaned in frustration.

"You remember that I said I'd tell you what the J.T. stood for?" he asked, reaching over to grab the condom from the top of the bedside table. He expertly opened it and rolled it on, watching her warily out of the corner of his eye.

He brought himself back to her as she stared at him through glazed eyes, pushing herself against him, trying to make him insert himself into her hot, slick passage.

Her breath came in great, heaving gulps. "You can talk at a time like this?"

J.T. used his dick to stroke her, up and down, up and down, loving the way she wiggled and moaned. The sounds she made, deep in the back of her throat, had him wanting to give up this charade and bring himself home inside of her.

"Not really," he answered, giving an answering swivel of his hips. "But this is serious enough that I thought I'd better wait until you weren't in any position to laugh."

She brought her hand to his erection and pushed the tip of him inside. "Then hurry up and tell me, mister, so we can finish this before I pass out."

J.T. gasped as his chuckle died in his throat at her hand pumping away at the base of his penis.

"Okay, here goes. You know that tattoo on my back?"

The thrust of her hips against him, causing him to slide in another couple of inches, was his only answer.

He hissed at the feeling being inside of her caused him.

"You already know my last name is Freedom, hence the Statue of Liberty." J.T. moaned as she lifted her hips and he slid in farther. "The scales are for my first name."

Allison purred as he sank himself fully into her, as his thumb came around to tease her clit. "Mmm-hmm. The scales," she mumbled, arching her back against the mattress.

"Yes, the scales." What was he saying? Oh yeah, the damn scales. "My mother was big into politics when she was pregnant with me." He hissed out another curse as she did some sort of wiggle-squirm-swivel that had the head of his dick almost touching her womb. "Anyway, she thought Freedom was a perfect last name to go with Justice Truman. Hence the scales of justice."

Allison's hips stopped in midswing, and she raised her head up off of the pillow. "Your name is Justice Truman Freedom?"

J.T. was on the verge of a climax to beat all climaxes, and the woman wanted to dissect his name. But shit, he'd brought it up, so it was his own damn fault.

He started a new rhythm, hard and fast, and watched as her head fell back. He couldn't resist taking one plump nipple into his mouth, suckling hard and then biting the tip. At her gasp of pleasure, he smiled against her skin.

"Yes. Justice Truman Freedom. Is that going to be a problem?"

He felt her muscles contract around him, heard her breath grow even faster and shallower, and held her as her orgasm stormed through her. When the shivers had stopped and she lay pliant beneath him, she smiled that sexy, saucy smile at him.

"No. Now you shut up, J.T. Freedom, and finish what you started."

It wasn't in him to deny her.

J.T. took as much time as he could, bringing Allison

again and again to that pinnacle of desire and then bringing her slowly back down. She was begging him at the end, begging him to make love to her and bring them both to completion.

One last thrust, one last look into her brilliant green eyes, and he took them both over the edge. This time, they came together. It was, J.T. decided, the way it should be.

Hours later, they watched through the peephole in J.T.'s door as Cissy knocked for five straight minutes outside Allison's apartment. The fit of giggles almost had Allison doubled over, and J.T. was finally so overcome that he had to leave the room for fear of Cissy hearing him.

She finally took pity on her friend and opened the door.

"I'm over here, Cissy," she said, and couldn't suppress a grin at Cissy's squeak of surprise.

"Man, Allison, you scared me to death. What are you doing over ther . . . *ohhh*," she stuttered, as J.T., naked except for a pair of shorts, came up behind Allison in the doorway.

Allison had to laugh. "Yes, Cissy, this time it's *ohhh*."

Cissy's eyes were almost larger than her head. "Well, never mind. I was going to see if you wanted to go catch a movie, but I guess not."

This time, the blonde obviously got the hint.

"Maybe next time, Cissy, Okay?"

"Sure, sure," she sputtered, moving off down the hall. "Next time."

Allison and J.T. dissolved in a fit of laughter at her look of pure bewilderment.

They'd spent hours talking about everything and nothing. About J.T.'s family, about his mother and late father and two brothers, all of whom he spoke of fondly. About Allison's family, which included a mother that was even more of a loudmouth than she was and a father who pretended never to hear her mother when she talked. Allison was an only child, and loved listening to the stories of mischief and mayhem that J.T. and his brothers had gotten themselves into.

Allison left around midnight, because she didn't think she was ready to spend a full night in his apartment yet. Tomorrow, though, might be a different story.

So what does all of this tell us, ladies? In general, that life offers no guarantees. There is no warranty that comes with life, no "satisfaction guaranteed or your money back." You just have to hope that one day, you'll get it right. One day, after all the losers and rejects and the bad ones that you've tossed back into the sea, the one you've been waiting for will finally take your bait. One day, you really will find that knight in shining armor, but this time you'll be able to not only recognize the dings and the dents and the scratches in the metal, but you'll be able to accept them, too.

*Your soulmate is out there. The trick isn't in finding him, but in recognizing him for what he is when he shows up at your door. Fairytales might not exist, but who wants a cardboard cutout of a man, anyway? Love, ladies, is not just another fairytale. It's **the** fairytale. Love, in all its ups, downs, and sideways, is the one thing that makes life what it is.*

Allison smiled and sighed in delight. She'd finally finished it. The article had finally gone in a new direction, and she thought it was one both she and the editors at *Loveswept* could live with. Truthful without being cheesy. Romantic without wanting to make her gag. Perfect.

Now, if she could just put some stock in it. Let go of her inhibitions, her worries, and all her doubts, and for once take life by the horns and ride the ride for all it was worth. She smiled. J.T. seemed worth it. What could it hurt? If it didn't work out, she'd do what she said in her article. She'd dust herself off and just keep looking.

After a quick dinner and a long, hot bath, Allison decided to call her mother. It had been almost two weeks since she'd last talked to her, and her mom wasn't one for long separations. Besides, Allison was one of the few people who could actually listen to her ramblings for any length of time.

Her mom answered on the first ring, almost as if she'd known who would be on the other end of the line.

"Helllllo," she said in that Midwestern twang that still brought a smile to Allison's lips.

"Hi, Mom, how are you?"

She listened with half an ear as her mother went on to list her numerous aches and pains. The daily battles with getting her father to pay attention to her, the horrors of having to work for a huge insurance company who only knew her as a number, not a name. On and on, with Allison half-listening.

"How's Daddy?" she asked when her mom paused for breath.

"Hmmph, well, you know your father. He's sitting in his chair in front of the boob-tube, watching some show that's nothing but tits and ass."

Allison's snort of laughter echoed down the line. "Mom, that's not a very nice thing to say." She bent down to pet Bella, who was feeling a little left out.

"Since when am I nice? And anyway, enough about me. When are you finally going to find a nice guy and give me some grandchildren, Allison Marie?"

Allison sighed. She should have known this would come

up eventually. It always did. Should she tell her mom about J.T.? Why not? She had a feeling that he was one guy who would get along perfectly with her wild, zany mother.

"Actually, I did meet someone."

She heard her mother's sharp intake of breath from a thousand miles away. "A man? You met a *man?* Hallelujah and blessed be and all that happy crap. How long have you known him?"

"Uhmm, well, about forty-eight hours, actually."

"Has he taken you to bed yet?"

"Motherrrrrr." She knew she was blushing, and they weren't even in the same room together.

Her mom's laugh could only be described as wicked. "I'll take that as a yes. And since you've obviously let him poke you once or twice already, I'm guessing that you really like him. Right?" she asked, when Allison could do nothing but hold the phone out in front of her face and stare at it.

Her mother had just said *poke*. And used it as a sexual term. She was crazy. Insane. The woman talked like a heathen and never stopped to think how the words coming out of her mouth might sound to other people. She sounded like, like . . . oh dear Lord, her mother sounded exactly like she did. The laughter that poured out had tears streaming down her face and her mother screaming into the phone.

"Allison? Allison Marie Dare, what the hell is so funny? Allison, answer me."

Allison sucked in a breath and wiped her eyes on her sleeve. "I'm sorry, Mom, but I just had an epiphany." She sighed and tucked her legs up under her on the couch, stroking Bella and thankful that she had this wonderful, crazy lady to share her life with. "And yes, Mom, I do like him. And the funny thing is, he seems to like me, too. A lot. He doesn't even mind my mouth."

Her mother's laughter this time was hearty and full of

love. "He sounds like a keeper, baby girl, and like a man that I could really get along with. Just be sure to let me know when to show up for the wedding, okay?"

They laughed together, and when Allison hung up the phone a half an hour later, she felt relief. Her mother, for all her faults, was a great woman. She hoped that she'd be able to grow up and be just like her.

Epilogue

Amazingly enough, the powers that be at *Loveswept* ended up loving her first editorial piece even more than she did. It seems that they received so many letters—from people who loved her, from people who despised her, from people she inspired, from people she pissed off—that they decided she needed to be a permanent feature of the magazine. Allison was hired on as a staff member, got the go-ahead to write an article for each biweekly issue of the best-selling magazine, and they even paid her to do it. Life was finally falling into place.

It took Bella and J.T. four months to become comfortable enough with each other for Allison to broach the subject of them moving in together. It caused their first argument, where J.T. suggested that Bella should be taken to the animal shelter and Allison advised that J.T.'s camera should be shoved up his ass.

In the end, the cat and the camera both stayed where they were.

Six months later, J.T. proposed.

He showed up at her door in full armor. Literally. Helmet, chain mail, the whole kit and caboodle. Allison stood there in total amazement as he took a step through the door and promptly fell face-first onto her floor. Again. Christ, but the man sure had a way of making an entrance.

"Are you all right?" She could barely choke it out, she was laughing so hard. After she helped him roll over and removed his helmet, the thought hit her that she had no idea where he was going with this.

"Fine. Except for looking like an ass, I'm perfectly okay." J.T. sucked in a breath and reached for her hand. "This isn't the way I wanted to do this, but will you do me a favor?"

Allison nodded, still too unsure of what was happening to speak.

"There's a chain around my neck. Can you undo the clasp in the back?"

She lifted his mane of hair and silently undid the chain, and gasped with disbelief as a ring slid off of it and into her hand. Allison brought it closer, staring with utter shock at the single, pear-shaped diamond solitaire in a platinum setting.

"I'd get down on one knee," J.T. said, "but right now I can't even move. I'm your knight in shining armor, Allison Dare, with all the dings and dents that we've talked about. I don't promise to be perfect, but I promise to always listen. I love you, have loved you almost from the first moment I saw you. So what do you say? Wanna get married and try out that happily-ever-after thing together?"

Her tears were silent, but she hoped that her brilliant smile showed him just how much he meant to her.

She waited until she'd said yes before she told him that Bella, after escaping from the apartment one day several weeks ago, was now expecting her first litter of kittens.

PRIVATE INVESTIGATIONS

Jordan Summers

One

She had to be the worst thief he'd ever seen.

Brandon Walker propped his large frame against the door-jamb, watching the hypnotic movements of the woman's perfect ass as she fiddled with the filing cabinet, oblivious to his presence.

Dressed in black slacks and an iridescent sweater that cupped her full breasts, she bobbed and shimmied before his eyes like an exotic dancer, tempting, luring him into the room.

Brandon tipped his glass of champagne, wetting his suddenly parched throat, too constricted by the starched shirt and bow tie these occasions demanded. The sweet, dry bubbles felt good going down. He gazed at her, transfixed. Damn, it had been too long since he'd felt the rush of excitement that accompanied instant attraction.

He drained his glass, placing the crystal flute on the oak side table just inside the door. Her bottom wiggled again, drawing his eye. A man of many appetites, Brandon could truly appreciate the view.

Hunkered down on her knees and bent forward at the waist, the woman continued to work, a flashlight in one hand

and a jangling collection of tools in the other, utterly oblivious to the noise she created.

Hell, a Salvation Army bell ringer would've been quieter. What in the world was she after in the filing cabinet?

She grunted with the effort that it took to force the lock, sending red curls falling into her face. She didn't stop to push them out of the way, like most women he'd known would've done. Her sole focus remained on the lock thwarting her from reaching the files.

He hadn't gotten a good look at her face when she'd slipped past him in the hallway earlier. Nor had she noticed him sitting in the alcove. She'd seemed too preoccupied, and now he knew why.

One glimpse had been enough to let him know he didn't recognize her from the usual crowd downstairs. There was no way he would have missed that long red hair, turned-up nose, and heart-shaped bottom sashaying past.

No way. He may be bored, but he wasn't dead. An inkling of familiarity washed through him, settling into his gut.

"Open, damn it!" She groaned, shaking the lock in frustration. The movement sent her full breasts quivering beneath her sweater and she grunted again.

Brandon's attention locked to the front of her shirt, his previous thoughts forgotten. Her soft voice brushed over him like a caress, despite the tension of the moment.

With little effort, he could imagine hearing those groans in his ear as he slid inside her. Brandon held back a growl as he eyed her tantalizing ass and her submissive position once more.

He could certainly think of a lot better ways to put that position to use than breaking and entering. His cock stirred behind the cover of his dress pants. Brandon reminded himself he was dealing with a criminal, no matter how inept or tempting she may be.

But that knowledge couldn't deter his gaze from lazily

flicking over her body, cataloging, assessing, imagining. If sheer will alone could remove her clothes, she'd be naked by now.

The cabinet rattled again. He marveled that she still had no idea he was in the room with her. The tool in her hand dropping to the floor was followed by a very unladylike curse. She quickly retrieved her tools, and then went back to work.

Brandon's lips twitched in amusement. She'd definitely livened up an otherwise tedious office party.

He pushed from the doorway and stepped deeper into the room. It was time to put a stop to this commotion, before she drew more official attention to her activities. His fingers slid along the wall until he'd located the silent alarm button. Brandon hesitated, then stopped, casually crossing his arms over his broad chest.

His gaze refused to leave her, as he imagined taking the woman right there on the carpeted floor, until her curses turned to moans. He cleared his throat.

"You'd do better with less force and more finesse."

The muscles in the woman's body froze a moment before she leapt to her feet and spun around with flashlight in hand to face him. Her tools clattered to the floor behind her.

She quickly doused the light, leaving her face in shadow. The dim light from the hallway only afforded him an unobstructed view of her rosy lips. The pout forming there was enough to capture and hold him.

Damn. She had a mouth made for kissing and a whole lot of other things he wasn't going to think about right now. Brandon swallowed hard, ignoring the urge to close the distance and taste the tempting bud.

"You have to be the worst thief I've ever seen."

She made a move for the door.

"Tsk . . . tsk . . . tsk." His hand flew out toward the silent alarm.

Her gaze followed his actions. The moment she locked onto the alarm, she froze. The woman's mouth gaped a second before she recovered. "I-I'm no thief," she replied, sounding indignant as she gathered the items at her feet and shoved them in her purse.

Brandon arched his brow. "You're not a thief, eh? Then why, may I ask, are you in Bill Cavanaugh's home office, making a miserable attempt to break into his filing cabinet?"

The woman's chin tilted up a notch, hinting at a stubborn streak that under different circumstances would have turned him on. He still couldn't see her eyes or make out her features clearly, but he could tell she was looking at him. Brandon realized he wanted her to step forward into the light and reveal herself.

"You wouldn't believe me if I told you." She sighed. "How did you know where to find Cavanaugh's silent alarm?"

He grinned. "Some of us have actually been invited into this room."

Was it his imagination or had she just tensed at his words?

His fingers stroked the alarm button, drawing her attention to the movement.

"What do you want?" she asked, her voice tight, apprehensive, her gaze shifting from his fingers to his face.

From you . . . —he allowed his gaze to rake her—*a lot of things,* he thought. "For the moment, let's start with what you're doing here."

He could see her pulse fluttering beneath the long column of her neck. She may not be visibly shaking, but she was scared. Smart woman.

Her steady voice held a hint of challenge when she spoke again. "It won't matter what I tell you, so you might as well press that button instead of playing with it."

He smiled, as his fingers circled the button like he longed

to caress her nipples. Brandon shook his head, trying to dispel the image of rose-colored areolas puckering at his touch. She was a thief, a long-legged, shapely-assed thief, who obviously hadn't learned her lesson yet.

"I don't think you're in a position to be making demands." He glanced to the floor, remembering the sexual position she'd been in earlier, before returning his gaze to her.

The woman's nostrils flared, as if she'd thought of the exact same thing. Her tongue dipped out to wet her bottom lip. The innocent move had his cock leaping to attention.

Brandon shoved one hand in his pocket to disguise his current state of arousal, leaving the other casually resting on the alarm. He wasn't the type of man who'd ever had to deal with sexual frustration. He didn't like it one bit. He also didn't like the fact that this woman had managed to get him hot and bothered without even trying.

The last thing he needed was for her to realize how much being near her affected him. She was a criminal, and he'd do well to remember that.

Hell, *she'd* do well to remember that. Didn't she realize he could turn her in and she'd go to jail? Better yet, throw her down on that carpet and ravage her seven ways to Sunday.

That simple act of defiance fired Brandon's blood, raising his need two notches higher—to inferno. He wanted this woman, thief or no, naked and writhing under his body as he fucked her senseless. The thought pissed him off.

Time to call her bluff. "I'm sick of this! You haven't answered a single question. I'm giving you one last chance to save your pretty ass. You've got five words to convince me that I shouldn't turn you in."

She shoved the flashlight into her pocket, leaving her hands to rest on her hips. Well-manicured fingertips tapped impatiently as she seemed to debate his request. She opened her mouth and closed it again. Her breathing grew shallow. He could tell she'd finally realized he was serious.

"You heard me. The clock is ticking." He tapped the alarm lightly for emphasis.

She stiffened, a moment before a cool smile spread across her face. That devilish grin had the hair at the nape of his neck standing on end. His body jumped to high alert.

"You . . . know . . . who . . . I . . . am."

Those five words slapped Brandon across the face, challenging him to remember—daring him to recall. His eyes tried to penetrate the darkness and get a good look at her face. Did he know her?

He couldn't recall anyone with flame-red hair, but then again, he'd gone through a plethora of women during his wilder days. Her voice penetrated his memory, fragmenting his thoughts.

"I'm almost disappointed in you, Brandon," she said softly, a teasing familiarity tinging her words. "The man I used to know wouldn't have hesitated to act. The man I used to know would've jumped at the opportunity to be on top of a thief."

"Cara?" Realization crashed down upon him like ice water, as the years rushed by, tossing and turning him until he landed firmly in the past.

He opened his mouth to say more, when footsteps heralded someone's approach. Damn it! Not now! Brandon covered the distance separating him from Cara Martin and grabbed her by the elbow. He let her gather her purse, then hurried her toward the closet.

He threw the door open and pushed her inside, before stepping in behind her. For a second, they stood, pressed together, his aching sex nestled firmly against her lush bottom. Cara's spicy perfume assailed him in the confined space, curling around his instincts, tugging at the leash of his desire.

Brandon fought the urge to grab her, pull her into his

arms, and kiss her senseless, until she spilled all of her secrets. Equally as strong was the urge to shake her silly for being so careless.

Unfortunately, given her identity, neither was an option.

Instead, he stepped back and pulled the door closed, leaving a slight crack so he'd be able to hear if anyone entered the room. Of all the people his mystery woman could've turned out to be, why did she have to be the one person he could never have?

Cara's heart pounded so hard she thought it might explode in her chest. She reached for her flashlight and flicked on the beam.

Two things became abundantly apparent: she'd been caught, and Brandon Walker had no idea who she was until seconds ago. She wasn't sure which one aggravated her more.

"Take your clothes off."

"Excuse me?" Cara swung her flashlight around, her gaze bulleting to Brandon's face. He couldn't be serious. Under the beam, his chiseled features were hard, unyielding.

Brandon loosened his tie. "We don't have time to argue," he growled in frustration. "Do as I say—Cavanaugh will be here any second."

"How do you know it's him?"

He looked at her as if she were dense. "Who else would it be? The party is downstairs, or hadn't you noticed?"

The click of a switch sent light streaking in through the crack of the door. They both stilled instantly, listening. *He was here.* Cara shoved her flashlight into a nearby jacket pocket, before once again facing Brandon.

She leaned close and whispered, "It wasn't my idea to hide in the closet."

"No, it was your idea to break into his office the night of

the corporate Christmas party," he hissed. "What were you thinking?"

"Oh, shut up—he's going to hear us."

Footsteps padded across the carpeted floor, drawing nearer to their hiding place. Papers shuffled. He must have stopped at his desk, which meant he hadn't noticed the open closet door yet.

"Take your clothes off now." Brandon's teeth clenched and his green eyes narrowed in warning.

"No!" She shook her head. "There has to be another way." Cara stepped back, her hand brushing against the Italian silk jackets hanging in the cedar-scented closet. She set her purse down on a shelved ledge.

With speed that contradicted his large size, Brandon moved, reaching for her cashmere sweater. A quick flick of the wrist and he'd managed to pull the material over her head, before tossing it onto the floor.

Cara gasped in disbelief. "I said no."

Deft fingers reached behind her. She heard a faint click a second before her bra straps slid from her shoulders, spilling her full breasts into the charged air.

"You assh—" Before the curse could leave her lips, Brandon swept her into his arms, crushing her against his hard chest, his mouth crashing down upon hers in a punishing kiss.

The second their mouths impacted, Cara's world tilted. Hard met soft, wet melded with dry. Her lids fell as warmth spread throughout her body like a wildfire left unchecked, singeing her senses, scoring her mind. Her nipples beaded against the scrape of his dress shirt, leaving her wanting.

Brandon's tongue dipped, teasing, drawing her to him. Before she could stop her response, Cara wound her arms around his neck, sinking her fingers into his thick, whiskey-colored hair.

Masculine spice mixed with the sweet champagne he'd been

drinking earlier, intoxicating her. Making her forget where they were, why they were there, and who she was with. Their bodies pressed together as muscles locked.

The closet door wrenched open, sending glaring light into the small space. Cara's eyes flew open, the bright light blinding her for a second. Brandon stepped back from the embrace just enough to look at the intruder, but not leave Cara exposed, his ragged breathing as uncontrolled as her own.

"What the hell are you doing in here, Walker?" Cavanaugh's surprise colored his words.

Brandon's brow arched as he lazily caressed Cara's bare back with his callused fingertips. The rough pads sent delicious shivers racing along her spine. Her breathing hitched. Brandon's voice was husky when he finally spoke. "We were searching for a little privacy."

Cavanaugh stared, his gaze scanning the entire closet area before reaching the clothing strewn on the floor. He snorted. "The Hyatt is down the street. I suggest you book a room."

"No problem." Brandon shrugged his broad shoulders, a languid smile flitting on his lips.

In the next instant, the closet door slammed shut, shrouding them in darkness. Cavanaugh's laughter shattered the silence.

Cara couldn't seem to catch her breath, and from the sounds of things, neither could the man standing beside her. Stunned, and more than a little shaken, she slipped from his embrace.

Brandon Walker had kissed her. Cara's lips quivered and her heart continued to race a marathon in her chest. Her breasts throbbed, her nipples aching to the point of pain. She crouched down, groping for her clothing in the dark.

To his credit, Brandon didn't open the door. He didn't move or even flinch as Cara brushed past his legs while searching for the items he'd discarded earlier. In fact, although she couldn't see him, he seemed to be rooted in place.

It was just a kiss, she reminded herself again. A ruse Brandon came up with at the last second, so she wouldn't get caught breaking into William Cavanaugh's filing cabinet. Cara's fingers trembled as she found her clothes and dressed in haste.

So why did it feel like more?

Two

As soon as she'd slipped the sweater back over her head, Brandon pushed the closet door wide. Cara opened her mouth to explain why she'd been in Cavanaugh's office, but didn't get a chance.

"Don't say a word," he hissed between clenched teeth. He grabbed her by the elbow and propelled her from the room. His body vibrated in unreleased anger as they descended to the first floor and into the crowd.

The party was still in full swing with Christmas music playing in the background. Designer clothes draped the attendees, wrapping them in luxury, cocooning them from reality. There were more rhinestones and diamonds in the room than at a Dolly Parton concert.

Cara took a deep breath. Her head itched, her feet hurt, and she couldn't stand the people around her. Present company excluded.

She knew the second they got outside, Brandon would let her have it, so she slowed her pace. It only delayed the inevitable, but the delay would buy her some time to come up with an explanation he'd accept.

She glanced around the massive great room. Cara was no

stranger to wealth, but she'd never been inside a house this size. Twinkling multicolored lights lay strewn over the adobe-inspired mantel and around all the window frames, while fake snow decorated the panes.

A crackling fire raged in the fireplace, giving off a warm glow, all the while fighting the blast of arctic air coming from the air-conditioning unit. Through open French doors, the crowd spilled out into the desert landscape overlooking Phoenix. Cara could see cacti draped in lights dotting the backyard. The smell of piñón blended with pine in an olfactory symphony.

A twenty-foot Christmas tree stood majestically in the center of the vaulted-ceilinged room, parting the crowd like water. Champagne flutes clinked as toasts were raised. The sound of laughter and chatter peppered the air, grating on Cara's nerves like fingernails scraping Styrofoam.

She frowned at the ostentatious display.

Brandon's firm grip slid from her elbow to her hand; the shift in warmth sent a delicious tremor zinging up her arm and over her spine. He interlaced his fingers with hers, and then led her deeper into the crowd, threading them through the revelers as Bing Crosby's "White Christmas" came pouring from the speakers.

The revelers pressed in, temporarily halting their progress. Cara turned her attention to an older couple beside them.

"Can you believe the size of Bill's home?" the woman murmured. "You could practically fit a football field in here."

"He's certainly done very well for himself recently," the man observed. "Business must be booming." The couple nodded in agreement at their assessment of their colleague's wealth.

Cara made a mental note, filing the conversation away for later use.

A woman's voice trilled over the crowd. "Brandon, honey, where are you going?"

They both froze, turning as one to face the woman approaching them. She had blond hair the color of honeyed wheat. Her dress, a lilac silk, hung from her lithe body like the perfect mannequin that she was.

Cara glanced at Brandon's face, hoping to catch his reaction to the willowy form. Familiarity flitted over his features a second before he closed off his expression. Cara looked back to the woman, who was now slowing to join them.

The woman slipped her hand around Brandon's elbow. He stiffened for a second before relaxing. His firm lips quirked at the corner as if he found the whole situation amusing. Cara stared at the exchange, wondering just how well Brandon knew this human celery stick.

"Hello, Vivica."

"Sorry to hear about you and Julie," the woman drawled, then spared Cara a glance. "Who's she?"

With that southern accent, she obviously wasn't from Phoenix. Cara straightened beside her, resisting the urge to adjust her own clothing. She knew she was probably a wrinkled mess, having spent most of the evening on her hands and knees.

Brandon pulled his arm free from the woman's possessive grasp. "She's an *old* friend."

"Speaking of friendship." Cara reached out and rubbed a smudge of lipstick from the corner of his mouth. "I don't think it's your color." She laughed, holding up her finger for him to see.

For an instant, something sparked in Brandon's eyes, before they once again became unreadable.

The woman's attention turned to Cara, her gaze starting at Cara's shoes and slowly working its way up until they were staring eye to eye. She didn't say a word, but arched a finely sculpted brow in disapproval, before turning to face Brandon once more.

"Are we on for later, sugar?" Vivica asked, paying no attention to the fact that Brandon was holding Cara's hand.

Cara wanted to scream. She wanted to hold up their joined hands and shove them in the woman's perfectly made-up face. Not that there was anything going on between her and Brandon, but Vivica didn't know that.

Brandon beat her to it. "Now, Viv, you know that we weren't planning to meet tonight."

The woman's face flushed slightly. "But I thought you wanted to discuss the court case."

Brandon smiled. "We can do that at the office."

"But we've got court in three weeks."

Brandon shrugged nonchalantly. "It'll wait until after the holiday."

"But Ted said you worked with him night and day until his case went to trial."

"It was a different kind of case."

Not to be deterred, she reached into her clutch purse and pulled out a sprig of mistletoe, which she jiggled in front of his face. Brandon's jaw clenched, but he didn't say anything. Fascinated by the woman's daring, Cara watched as Vivica boldly moved in and captured Brandon's mouth. The whole thing seemed to occur in slow motion. Brandon didn't pull away, but he didn't participate, either.

The kiss seemed to go on forever. Cara felt her cheeks start to color. A level of awkwardness she hadn't felt since her teen years settled over her, tightening like invisible thumbscrews, adding physical discomfort to her current state of embarrassment. This was worse than the day she was pantsed in third-period gym class.

What had happened to the Brandon Walker she'd known? He'd grown up, that's what. His round face from boyhood had thinned, giving definition to his tanned, warrior-like features. His lips were savage—not too thin, not too full.

He'd lost much of the soft padding that had come from

his football days. He was now solid muscle, his body chiseled and hard, daring her to touch. With one hand, he gently detached himself from the embrace. Cara stared at Brandon. Other than a slight flush to his cheeks, he seemed unaffected by the kiss. The unexpected pleasure from that realization startled Cara.

"Merry Christmas, Vivica. I'll see you on Monday."

He didn't wait for her to respond, before he started walking. Cara had no choice but to follow.

"Brandon! Sorry to hear about you and Ann. Good gal," a man in a blue suit slurred as they passed by, a martini dangling in his hand. He gave Brandon a sympathetic look, before his eyes lit upon Cara and a smile spread across his weasely face. "But it looks like you're not letting the grass grow under your heels, eh?" He waggled his eyebrows and moved on.

Just how many women was Brandon seeing? Cara wondered, then just as quickly realized she didn't want to know. She'd heard enough.

Brandon didn't think they'd ever reach the front door. His coworkers seemed to be taking great pride in accosting him over his love life this evening. He'd never been shy about the fact that he enjoyed the company of the opposite sex. He'd gone through a bevy of transitory beauties over the past few years, and it had never once occurred to him that the number should embarrass him, until now. For some reason, with Cara here, it made him decidedly uncomfortable.

He was beyond grateful that he'd managed to elude Bill Cavanaugh. The last thing he needed was to have to explain what he was doing in the man's home office closet. Hell, he didn't even know himself. Never mind the wild-haired idea that had him pulling Cara Martin into his arms.

What had he been thinking?

He'd told her to remove her clothes initially to make the scene more believable for Cavanaugh, but once her sweater came off, something shifted inside of him, changed.

He'd reached out and undone her bra clasp, with a skill that came from years of experience, knowing full well he wanted to hold her naked in his arms—not just convince a colleague they were playing grab-ass in the closet.

Brandon reminded himself again that she was unquestionably off-limits. There may be only a few unspoken rules regarding women, but this was one: keep your hands off your best friend's sister. There would be no more touching her firm breasts, kissing her soft lips, or thinking about the feel of her supple skin beneath his fingertips.

The spicy smell that lingered in the air whenever they stopped had to go, too. The mix, a subtle combination of perfume and sexually aroused woman, had given him a raging hard-on. Hell, he'd been hard since he'd first laid eyes on her, but that was before he'd known who she was. Brandon didn't want to think about how finding out hadn't made any difference to his stubborn male body.

Double-damn.

He pushed the front door open and stepped out into the warm desert night. It may very well be December, but it felt more like April. He took a deep breath, hoping to clear his lungs of Cara's intoxicating scent.

She took a step forward until they stood side by side. He glanced at the face he'd known for years. Her blue eyes met his and his gut clenched in reaction.

He'd been so mad earlier and so turned on that he'd come close to turning Cara over his knee and paddling her pretty ass. If he hadn't been worried he'd enjoy it too much, he would have.

She had no business here, sashaying back into his life looking like sex incarnate. When had she moved back to

Phoenix? Why hadn't Granger mentioned it? All good questions. He'd get answers later.

It was time to find out what was going on. "How did you get here?" He scanned the sweeping driveway for the banana-colored Camaro she used to drive.

Cara hesitated, glancing sideways at the eight-foot privacy fence. "I scaled the wall."

Brandon jerked her around to face him. "You *what*?" He released her arm, his hands fisting at his hips. "I'm surprised you didn't break your neck."

"Nobody saw me. I'm competent at my job."

"Job? Competent?" Brandon laughed. "You've got to be kidding me." He shook his head in disbelief. "From what I just witnessed a few minutes ago upstairs, honey, your competency rates right up there with the winners of the Darwin award."

Her blue eyes narrowed to icy slits. "You know nothing about me, Don Juan." She poked him in the chest to punctuate her words. "We haven't seen each other in over ten years, so I suggest you back off and mind your own business."

Brandon couldn't stop the smile from spreading across his face. Cara was as fiery as he remembered, except now she had the backbone and confidence of a grown woman.

Without thought, he stepped forward, closing the distance between them. An urge to dominate swept through him so powerfully he had to act. He reached out and gripped her by the chin, tilting her face up until they were mere inches apart.

"Now you listen to me, *little girl*. You *are* my business, always have been, always will be."

Cara arched a brow in challenge.

He released her as his own words penetrated his mind. What was he saying? She really wasn't his business, hadn't been for a very long time. Brandon rubbed his hands together, trying to dispel the feel of her warm, soft skin.

Her pearl-like complexion glowed in the starlight. A single freckle dotted her face, near her eye. He'd always thought the lone spot added character. Cara's deep blue eyes remained fathomless, refusing to give away any secrets.

Her mouth was lush, fuller than he recalled, her smile outshining Julia Roberts any day. The only change he could note was the outrageous red hair. Where the hell had that come from? She wasn't the same girl he'd treated like a kid sister. She'd grown up.

Cara had filled out since the last time he saw her. Her breasts were rounded and firm, while her hips flared, nipping into a slender waist. Brandon's mouth practically watered at the sight of her.

At twenty-eight, she was a woman now, something far more dangerous to his sensibilities than she'd been back when they were no more than kids. All in all, he liked what he saw, which was a very bad thing.

Her gaze narrowed on him, but she said nothing.

He stared at her curly red hair, remembering how black and luxuriously straight it had been at one time, before frowning. "I don't like what you've done to your hair. It doesn't suit you."

Cara snorted. "What I do with my hair—and my life, for that matter—is not your concern."

Brandon's jaw clamped shut as he tried to rein in his temper. Cara was beautiful without having to change her hair color. For some reason, it bothered him that he hadn't known.

"Where did you park?" he snapped out, aggravated at himself for his loss of control. His gaze flicked to her body. There was nothing brotherly about his thoughts.

Cara's return disturbed him on many levels. He never lost control, not when it came to women. Unfortunately, Cara wasn't just any woman. She knew him better than anyone did, because she was the only one who'd ever managed to get close to him.

Cara crossed her arms over her chest and glared at him. The slight action shoved her breasts higher until they peeked out of the top of her sweater, unknowingly taunting him.

"Now's not the time to be stubborn," he pressed. "Just answer the question. Where did you park?" his voice sounded as if he were gargling gravel. So much for keeping his cool.

She blew out a frustrated breath. "A few blocks over, outside the gated community."

"Good."

Brandon grabbed her arm and pulled her along toward his platinum-colored Jaguar. He reached into his pocket and thumbed the remote to unlock the doors. The lights came on as they approached, highlighting the car's cream leather interior. He shoved Cara into the passenger seat, before slipping behind the wheel.

If her family knew what she'd been up to tonight, they'd tan her hide. The thought brought a smile to Brandon's face. He started the car and pulled out into the street.

Night blanketed the desert city as he wound his way through the wealthy neighborhoods of Paradise Valley until he reached the Interstate.

He entered the ramp and punched the gas pedal, taking his frustrations out on the high-powered machine. The Jaguar glided into the lanes, its speed increasing by the second.

"You better slow down, Mario, or would you rather I call you Romeo? I had no idea you'd turned into a male slut."

Brandon glanced at Cara, then focused back on the road. "Considering your lack of experience in the dating field, I wouldn't be too quick to judge."

Her mouth gaped. "My lack of experience . . ." Cara sounded incensed. "Just because I don't fall into bed with every guy I meet doesn't mean I'm inexperienced."

He reached down to the console without looking and flipped a switch. A dial tone buzzed from the tiny, semiconcealed speakers in the car's interior.

"What are you doing?"

He glanced at his rearview mirror. "What does it look like?" From his peripheral, Brandon saw Cara flinch. "Call Granger." He sent the command to his voice recognition phone system, all the while fighting the urge to smile.

She sighed. "You don't need to do this."

"Oh yes, I do." His grip on the steering wheel tightened.

"Yo," a gruff male voice answered, cutting off their conversation. The connection crackled and spit.

"Granger, this is Brandon. Where are you?"

"I'm on . . . pop . . . my houseboat . . . hiss . . . at Lake Pleasant."

Brandon laughed. "That explains the connection. Can you hear me okay?"

"Loud and clear."

"Great. Guess who I'm sitting next to?"

There was a pause on the end of the line. The tension in the cab of the car rose exponentially. "Some leggy blonde with a nice set of—"

"Your little sister," Brandon cut in, before his best friend put his foot in it.

"What has she done now?" The voice on the line was deadly calm, too calm for Granger. His passions ran hot or cold. There was no in-between, which meant he was pissed. Brandon almost felt sorry for Cara . . . almost.

He nudged her elbow. "Now's no time to be shy—say hello to your big brother, Cara."

The line crackled.

"Hello, Granger."

"What the f—. No, don't tell me."

Cara took a deep breath. "It's not what you think, Granger."

"Oh yes, it is," Brandon piped in.

"Shut up—you're not helping the situation." She glared at the strong profile of the man beside her.

Her brother growled on the other end of the line. "You have no idea what I'm thinking, little sister."

"We're on our way now. I'm sure Cara will explain everything once she gets there." Brandon spared her a glance, easily weaving his way in and out of traffic. There were no wrong moves. Brandon drove like he did everything else: flawlessly.

Granger hung up the phone, a curse slipping from his lips.

Cara sighed. "Since you're so gung ho about me telling Granger the whole story, I'm just curious—does that include the incident in the closet?"

Brandon made a choking sound. "There's no need to go into that kind of detail."

"Why not? You want him to know what happened." Cara crossed her arms over her chest. When Brandon didn't answer right away, she continued. "We're both adults here. I'm sure Granger would understand that unplanned things happen when you're working a case."

"What exactly do you do for a living, Cara?"

"I'm surprised Granger didn't tell you. I'm a private investigator at the family firm."

"Since when?"

She shifted until she could face him. "It's been about two years now."

"Two years!" Brandon looked at her for a couple of beats as if to gauge if she was serious or not. His jaw suddenly firmed, and he stared back at the road before shifting into a higher gear.

"Yep, two years." She nodded.

"No, Granger didn't mention it."

"Oh well, it probably got lost in all the girl talk you guys do."

He shrugged uneasily. "It doesn't matter. Listen, Granger may be an understanding guy, but he's not going to appreciate his best friend getting hot and heavy with his kid sister."

Cara realized she'd finally managed to strike a chord. *It's about time.* She watched as Brandon sped north on the Interstate. They'd reach the Lake Pleasant exit within fifteen minutes.

She recalled the first time she'd seen Brandon Walker. He'd waltzed into her family's kitchen behind her older brother Granger. She'd had her nose shoved in a book, which was her norm at age fourteen. One glance and her mind had ceased to function.

She'd stood there gaping at him like the goofy adolescent she was at the time, her heart firmly emblazoned on her sleeve. Brandon's hazel gaze had locked with hers for what had felt like an eternity, before Granger slapped him on the shoulder and proclaimed him his new best friend to the whole family.

After that, Brandon went out of his way to treat her exactly like Granger did. She was, for all intents and purposes, his little sister. Someone to protect, look out for, tease and torment, but never, under any circumstances, touch.

Unfortunately, his decision had done nothing to deter her raging hormones. She'd fallen in love with him at first sight. Cara glanced at Brandon's broad chest and firm thighs. She hated the fact the jerk still made her heart race, made her believe in fairytales and happily-ever-afters.

For years, she'd imagined what kissing Brandon Walker would feel like. Would his lips be hard or soft, wet or dry? Would he be all tongue or coaxing in his approach to a kiss? She'd played every possible scenario in her mind and now, fourteen years later, she'd finally found out.

The kiss had quite simply been . . . wow! Her toes refused to uncurl. She could still feel the silky texture of his whiskey-colored hair on her fingertips, as if the strands had been branded into her skin.

The worst part was her body had somehow picked up the imprint of his, leaving her achy and more than a little horny. God help her, she wanted this man more than she'd ever wanted anyone.

Cara inhaled, trying to calm her jangled nerves. Big mistake. Brandon's male musk clung to her pores, surrounding, seeping into her senses, triggering a craving that no amount of chocolate would ease. Damn him!

Considering his level of experience with women, he'd probably done it on purpose. Cara ran her hand over the leather side panel, trying to discharge her nervous energy. The car smelled of rich leather and Brandon, a potent aphrodisiac to her senses.

The twinkling lights of the houseboats on Lake Pleasant shone in the distance. Cara knew Granger wouldn't be at the dock waiting for them. He was probably moored in his favorite cove, seething. She'd have to do some pretty fast talking once they reached her brother.

Brandon pulled into the parking lot at the top of the hill. "We're going to have to take the speedboat out to Granger. I doubt he'll be parked in the slip."

Cara nodded in agreement. "He won't be."

They made their way from the car down toward the marina and over to the slip holding Brandon's black speedboat. Two cream-colored bucket seats flanked the controls, while padded benches lined the stern. Cara watched as Brandon began untying the lines.

"Why are you doing this?" she asked.

He paused. "I guess I haven't gotten out of the habit of looking after you."

"I'm not exactly a baby anymore, if you hadn't noticed." Cara held her arms wide for emphasis.

* * *

Brandon's muscles refused to unlock. He'd noticed, all right. It had been impossible to ignore after his hands had felt the soft swell of her breasts. His mind had thought of little else. What had happened to the innocent little girl he'd known years ago? He certainly couldn't see her in this siren standing before him.

Why in the hell had he kissed her after he'd realized who she was? The question returned time and again, niggling at him like a loose tooth refusing to fall out. He knew better.

Brandon swallowed hard. He could still taste her honeyed sweetness on his lips. He cleared his throat to keep from groaning aloud as he bent down to release another tether holding the boat. If his cock got any harder, it would split the seams of his pants.

He took a deep breath, letting the cool air seep into his body. If he was honest with himself, he knew exactly why he'd kissed her.

He'd thought of little else since he'd witnessed her feeble attempt at burglary. Hell, since that first moment he'd walked into the Martins' kitchen fourteen years ago and spied Granger's gangly little sister reading a book.

Even at fourteen, she had been stunning. She'd innocently followed him around like a puppy, and he'd loved every minute of her schoolgirl adulation. At the time, he'd treated her like his own kid sister, playfully deflecting her attempts at flirtation. With his teenage hormones in full throttle, it had been the hardest thing he'd ever done.

Now, he'd give anything to have that same kind of adulation from her, even though he could never act upon the attraction out of respect for Granger.

With the boat untied, Brandon helped Cara into the craft and then started the engine. She slipped into the passenger seat as they idled out of the marina. In a few quiet minutes, they'd reached the open area of the lake. Brandon kicked up the speed a notch, careful to avoid other boats as they headed out into the dark, moonlit lake.

The awkward silence stretched on; finally, Cara turned to him. "Aren't you even going to ask me why I was doing what I was doing?"

"No, because you've already made it abundantly clear you're not going to give me a straight answer."

Her brows furrowed. "You don't want to know why?"

He glanced her way, watching her red curls blow in the wind. "Doesn't matter."

She stiffened, her jaw firming under his gaze. "You're a hypocrite, you know that."

Brandon slowed the boat so he could face her. "And just how in the hell am I a hypocrite?"

"You claim to be this cool guy, putting on this cooler-than-thou front, when in fact there's nothing cool about you." She closed the distance between them, standing on her tiptoes to bring her closer to his height. "I used to think you walked on water, but I was wrong. You're nothing but a womanizing jerk who couldn't see the truth if it was laid in front of him on a platter."

At her words, he stopped the boat, placing it in idle. "What truth is that?" His gaze dropped to her mouth, the urge to kiss her again tugging at his control.

The boat bobbed and rocked. The sound of gentle waves lapping at the shore in the distance reinforced the fact that they were alone.

"What happened to you, Brandon?" She shoved her hands into her trouser pockets, ignoring his question.

"I grew up, Cara."

She snorted. "Oh yeah, I forgot. Brandon Walker, the big, bad lawyer with the stellar reputation, keeps his nose clean. Doesn't do anything out of line or unlawful."

He wanted to do something out of line right now. The truth would probably shock Cara. Would she be surprised if he acted on his impulses?

What he wouldn't give to be able to strip her naked, slide his aching cock inside her, feel her warmth surround him as he fucked her until she screamed her release. He had visions of bending her over the bow of the boat and taking her from behind, her firm bottom tucked against his groin while he palmed her breasts.

Brandon swallowed hard. He could almost feel his cock gliding in and out of her. He decided to take the coward's way out and play it safe. "You're right! I don't get out of line anymore. That crap ended in my early twenties. I'm not going to apologize for upholding the law. That's my job—if you don't like it, sue me."

Her lips pursed at his choice of words.

"Now, you want to tell me what in the hell you were doing in Bill's home office?"

"Thought you weren't interested."

"Just tell me."

"I was investigating." She shrugged one shoulder. "You know, you and Granger have more in common than just women and football."

"Really? Like what?"

"You both hear only what you want to hear." She gritted her teeth.

He shook his head. "Investigating, hmm? Is that what you call it?"

Cara frowned. Of all people, she expected Brandon to understand. She wasn't looking for his approval of her actions, but she truly thought he'd understand the need to risk everything for what you believe in. Goodness knows he'd taken plenty of risks in his lifetime.

Cara took a deep breath. "At least my actions weren't done for the sole purpose of getting laid."

Brandon drew back as if she'd slapped him. Cara decided she'd probably gone too far. This older, wiser version of Brandon was harder to gauge.

All humor was gone from his eyes. "I'm sorry if the rumors of my behavior upset your virginal sensibilities."

Cara bit the inside of her cheek to keep from screaming in frustration. "News flash, hotshot—I'm no virgin."

"So you told me." He leaned closer until they were a whisper apart. "Well then, honey, for your sake I hope you don't fuck as bad as you pick a lock, because then I'd have to pity the guy you end up with."

Cara stared defiantly at Brandon. His dismissive comments stung her.

She grabbed his shirt with both hands and yanked him forward, her lips pressed hard against his for a moment, before she shoved him away. Cara leaned in close and whispered. "Such a shame you'll never know."

Brandon's nostrils flared as something wild lit his eyes. It was as if she'd thrown gasoline on a fire. Before Cara had a chance to move or breathe, Brandon pulled her into an angry embrace. His lips crashed down upon her just as they'd done in the closet, but this time without the tenderness.

Cara gasped and Brandon took the opportunity to plunder her mouth with his tongue. He swept in, exploring all her hidden areas, before returning to twine with her tongue. The kiss was a challenge, a gauntlet tossed down between them. They were now at battle in a purely sexual way. She wanted him. *Had always wanted him.*

Cara's chest was pinned against a wall of solid muscle. Her nipples puckered beneath her sweater at the slight abrasion of his embrace. Brandon fed deep, while his fingers bit into the tender flesh of her back.

Cara went up in flames. Moisture pooled between her thighs as he changed the tempo of the kiss, taking what she'd been offering him for years. There was no holding back as their bodies melded and squirmed, trying to get closer to one another.

The grip on her back loosened just enough for Brandon to slide one hand from her back, over the flare of her hip, until he reached her bottom. He gripped her ass, cupping her cheek, pressing her sex against his hard erection. His other hand went for her hair.

Cara didn't have the time or inclination to stop him. His fingers splayed over her scalp and then tugged. Her red-headed wig fell away, revealing a blanket of ebony hair. He smiled against her lips, but didn't stop kissing her.

Suddenly there were too many clothes separating them. Cara needed to get closer, feel his body, feel him. She had to have the hard length of him rubbing against her, the scrape of his hair along her legs and over her nipples. She wanted his cock inside of her, riding and rocking with the boat's motion as he thrust hard.

She pulled at his shirt. Her fingers tangled in the material, trembling as she unfastened the buttons. Brandon didn't try to stop her. He seemed too absorbed by her mouth. His hands kneaded her bottom, creating an answering pull at the juncture of her thighs.

His hips bucked as she lifted one leg and wound it around him. A moan escaped from deep in his throat as he moved from her mouth to the fleshy part of her ear. He nipped and licked, teasing her flesh with his magical tongue.

"We shouldn't do this," he murmured against the crook of her neck.

Cara pushed his shirt from his broad shoulders. "You're right," she said, as she nibbled on his collarbone.

One hand released her bottom long enough to massage its way to her throbbing breast. He palmed her, playing dangerously close to her nipple, until he'd driven her nearly mad with need.

"Brandon," she whispered, "I want you."

He growled and quickly caught the edge of her sweater, lifting it over her head and letting it drop.

Shaking and out of breath, they divested each other of their clothing, pausing only long enough for Brandon to grab a condom. Cara pulled away from him to look her fill. His thighs were muscled, with a spattering of golden brown hair, leading to a nest of curls which held his jutting cock.

Cara swallowed hard. He was magnificent. Neither man she'd been with could compare to the serpentine specimen before her. He was huge. His thick cock curved in slightly, due to its impressive length. The plum-sized crown flushed crimson under her gaze, growing impossibly longer and thicker.

Cara's stomach tightened with the sensation of a thousand butterflies taking flight. Her heartbeat stammered, then sped to overdrive.

She reached out, hesitating for a second before curling her fingers around his intimidating girth. Cara ran her free hand over the wide expanse of his pelted chest, taking care to tease his disc-like nipples along the way.

She flicked one and then another, as Brandon sucked in a labored breath. She wanted to lick, nibble, and explore every square inch of him. Before Cara could act upon her thoughts, she found herself guided back to the stern of the boat and flat on her back.

Brandon dropped to his knees and reverently kissed her stomach, paying special attention to the nerves surrounding her belly button. Cara giggled and then sighed as his tongue plunged inside.

"Do you have any idea how many times I imagined seeing you like this?" he asked, between hot, moist kisses. His warm hands covered her breasts, plucking her nipples.

Cara moaned as an answering throb started between her legs. "Probably as many nights as I spent in bed fantasizing about you." She reached for him, reveling in the feel of his skin beneath her fingertips.

He kissed his way to her mouth, tasting her, feeding upon her flesh, as if the mere act of doing so would sustain his life. His tongue flicked over her nipples, causing them to tighten to the point of pain.

By the time he reached her mouth, Cara's need had risen to *destructive*. His lips came down upon hers, crushing, punishing. They attacked each other like rabid wolves, fighting to get closer, to dominate.

Brandon's tongue dipped into her mouth, demanding a response, and Cara gave it to him. Her bones seemed to melt within her body. She became liquid inside and out, melding to his hard form. Her nails bit into his skin. Somewhere in the back of her mind, Cara knew she was marking him, claiming him.

Brandon tore away from the embrace, air heaving into his lungs as he made his way down to her waist, nipping and licking an erotic path to her woman's center. He glanced at her from beneath lowered lashes as he hovered above her raven curls. His eyes glazed and the muscles in his neck strained, as he appeared to fight his baser instincts.

"I can't wait to taste you, Cara."

Cara gasped, his words electrifying her already-charged senses.

The moisture glistening off the curls between her spread thighs seemed to capture Brandon's attention, drawing him toward her achy flesh. He groaned, inhaling as he buried his nose in the soft curls.

Her legs began to tremble as his tongue flicked out to taste her. Brandon glanced up one last time, his hazel eyes glinting with savage need, before his grip tightened. He proceeded to plunder her feminine folds, laving and sucking, teasing the swollen flesh with his lips and teeth, taking care to avoid her clit.

Cara's fingers sank into his hair, gripping his skull for support. The muscles in her neck gave out and her head fell back against the floor of the boat as he ravished her flesh. Her nipples tingled under the cool night air, yet from the waist down she was on fire.

"Brandon, please . . . you're killing me." Cara begged, teetering on the edge of release.

He growled, burying himself deeper into her sex. The second Brandon sucked her throbbing clit into his mouth, Cara exploded. She cried out as wave after wave of sensation lapped at her body. The boat rocked and so did her world, as her womb clenched and released, matching her channel's rhythm.

The sensations were too much—he was too much. She needed more of a connection. Cara glanced down, her gaze locking to Brandon's face as he continued to stroke and draw out her orgasm.

Cara reached down, grabbing Brandon's arms, pulling him up until his body covered hers. He trembled as he settled between her spread thighs.

"Brandon, I n-need you. Now!"

He moaned, reaching for the foil wrapper to sheath himself before positioning the head of his cock at her entrance. Cara shrieked as he drove inside of her, filling her completely.

She tried to breathe, to think, but her whole universe centered on where their bodies lay joined. He was so big, so thick, that she felt stretched to her limits. Cara met Brandon's eyes. The intensity of the connection she saw there frightened and excited her.

His thrusts were long and deep and torturously slow. He fucked her with his whole body, rolling his hips, rocking them both with a primal rhythm. It didn't take long before she recognized the familiar pressure building inside her once again.

Cara had read about multiple orgasms, but never thought she'd ever experience them. Sweat beaded Brandon's brow as his movements took on new urgency. He reached down, lifting her legs, urging her to grip his waist, as he plunged impossibly deeper into her.

Cara couldn't seem to stay focused. His determined face kept fading in and out of her line of vision as the tension inside her grew. Brandon released one leg long enough to reach between them and find her clit. He circled the bud, once, twice, three times, and then she was falling. The lake, the city, everything but the man moving on top of her faded away.

Brandon grunted, increasing his speed. He thrust a couple more times before following her over the edge with a gruff bellow.

They lay, panting in each other arms, still joined. Neither was in a hurry to separate as the magnitude of the moment sank in. Suddenly, as if remembering where they were, Brandon pulled out of her and stood. His cheeks flushed a deep red as he looked at her boneless form on the boat floor.

"What have we done?" There was no disguising the confusion in his voice or the shattered expression on his face.

Three

There were no comforting words as Cara stumbled to her feet and dressed. In fact, there were no words at all—just awkward silence. Hell, he could barely look at her. The clenched jaw and furrow between his brows left no doubt that Brandon regretted making love to her.

Cara's stomach tightened. She sat, hugging her knees to her chest. She'd imagined Brandon and her together many times, but not once had the scenario ended this way. She had wanted this, wanted him, more than anything. She still did, and no matter how much Cara searched her conscience, she felt absolutely no regrets. In fact, she'd do it again in a heartbeat.

How could she convince the man beside her, who jerked his pants and shirt on, that making love hadn't been the biggest mistake of his life?

Dressed, Brandon took the boat out of idle and started toward the cove. His face was set in a permanent frown as he guided them across the lake to Granger's houseboat. If he gripped the wheel any tighter, Cara was convinced it would snap in two.

Granger, being the creature of habit that he was, had his

boat anchored right where they thought it would be. It didn't surprise Cara in the least to see him standing on deck, his hands resting on his hips, a scowl marring his normally handsome face.

Her brother had her coloring, just like the two younger siblings in her family, Keegan and Rory. Cara's twin brothers had earned quite a reputation about town and were fondly known as the "double sins." She could only imagine how they came about the nickname—but preferred not to.

Granger glared as they approached, his gaze darting to Brandon, then back to her. Her heart gave a jolt. *Did he know?*

"What in the hell took you guys so long?" Granger asked, exasperation in his voice. "I was about to call out search-and-rescue."

Brandon looked away, avoiding Granger's gaze. "We had engine trouble." He glanced at Cara, his expression daring her to contradict him.

She nodded to her brother.

Granger blinked. "Anything serious?"

"Nope, it overheated, just needed some oil." He tossed a rope to Granger. "It's been taken care of."

"Are you sure it's out of your system?"

Brandon dropped the fender he'd been holding. His gaze shot once more to Granger and then to Cara. He nodded, reaching down to slip the fender buoy between the boats.

With that done, he faced Granger. Cara knew her brother might very well be a pain in the ass, but he wasn't dim. There was enough tension floating in the air to sink both boats. She stuck out her hand for Granger to help her onboard. He did so reflexively.

Brandon jumped up on the deck of the houseboat, his fingers gripping the rail. Guilt surged through him as he attempted to hold Granger's gaze. Was that suspicion in those familiar blue eyes, or was he just being paranoid?

He knew there was no way his best friend had guessed what they'd been up to, or else he wouldn't be standing. Granger would've knocked the stuffing out of him as he deserved.

He followed the siblings into the main cabin, which doubled as both living room and galley kitchen. A brown, water-resistant carpet covered the floor, while tweed cushions shoved over hidden storage areas made up a couch. A small wooden plank functioned as both table and an emergency bed. There was a three-burner stove for cooking and a full-size refrigerator in the galley. Brandon made his way to the refrigerator and threw open the door to grab a beer. He twisted off the cap and began chugging.

"Thirsty, buddy?" Granger smiled and shook his head.

Brandon snorted. "Would anyone else like one?"

"Sure," Granger and Cara answered in unison.

He grabbed two more beers and then walked to the small table. Cara had scooted to the center cushion, which left him to either stand or sit down next to her. If he stood, it would draw even more attention to a situation that he'd just as soon forget.

Forget? Was that possible? Even now, he could not shake the image of Cara looking at him, a sigh escaping her parted lips as he thrust inside her. Brandon ran a trembling hand down his face. Dear God, what had he done?

He released a pent-up breath and sat. Her leg accidentally brushed against him and Brandon stiffened, his body reacting in an instant to her nearness.

"Are you all right? You don't look so good," Granger asked.

Brandon tugged at his shirt collar. "I'm fine, just a little tense from the journey."

Granger laughed. "I'm sure seeing Cara shocked the shit out of you." He pulled her into his arms in a brotherly hug, until she playfully punched him in the arm to release her.

Brandon cleared his throat. "Yeah, seeing her was quite a surprise."

Granger chuckled. The resemblance between the two siblings was uncanny, but the temperament couldn't have been more different. Granger had no middle moods, while Cara's well ran deep.

"I guess I should have told you she was back, but where's the fun in that?" He grinned, snagging a beer from in front of Brandon.

The action brought Brandon's attention back to the problem at hand. He was embarrassed and ashamed for having betrayed his best friend, but he couldn't bring himself to regret making love to Cara. It had been quite simply the best sexual experience of his life. And that thought scared the living hell out of him.

Brandon twisted the cap from the remaining bottle and handed it to Cara.

"Thank you," she whispered, as she accepted the beer. Her gaze flicked to his for a second before focusing on the table.

Brandon couldn't really blame her for being upset. He'd practically leapt off her the second he'd come. He wasn't about to admit he'd panicked over the intense emotional connection he'd felt—and the instant guilt. Hell, as teenagers, he and Granger had nearly pummeled every prepubescent boy who had ever looked sideways at her.

His throat tightened as he considered his motives back then. It had seemed brotherly enough at the time, but was it? Or had it been the fact he didn't want any other guy around?

Cara's body had been like nothing he'd experienced before. She'd been open and refreshingly candid in her responses, which only fueled his need, driving him on to take, to claim.

Her soft moans and keening cries still echoed in his mind, calling out to the primitive male inside of him. Just thinking about her had him growing hard.

"Right, Brandon?"

Brandon's gaze snapped to Cara. She'd asked him something or said something and was looking for him to agree with her. The problem was, he'd been so preoccupied with thoughts of her, he hadn't heard a word she'd said.

Damn!

"I'm sorry, could you repeat the question?"

Cara's brow arched and she gave him a knowing smile. Brandon felt heat spread across his face and prayed Granger didn't notice the exchange. He took another sip of beer. Why did Cara have to be so gorgeous? Those blue eyes framed by long, dark lashes. Her full lips that were still swollen from his kisses. Ebony hair that could shame the finest silk. It wasn't just her striking appearance. There was something about Cara that made her different—special.

"I was just telling Granger how we explored every option while trying to fix your boat."

Brandon coughed, choking on the beer. Her tone told him the exploring she referred to had nothing to do with his boat. "That's right," he squeezed out from between tight lips as he took another swallow of beer. If he didn't slow down, he was going to cop a buzz from one beer.

Granger stared at them both for several seconds before speaking. His assessing gaze had Brandon shifting in his seat, while Cara seemed oblivious. When it came to ignoring her brother, she had years of practice.

Brandon's cell phone rang, easing the tension.

Granger snickered as Brandon glanced at the number. "Who's stalking you this week?" His eyes sparkled as he turned to Cara. "Brandon hasn't changed much in all these years. He's still quite the gigolo, right, bud?"

"Right." The statement stung. What in the hell was he

thinking? Granger was *right*. He may have slowed down over the past few months, but his track record with women remained lousy. He'd never made it longer than a few months. Hell, he didn't even know if he could. Cara deserved better than that. She deserved better than him.

Granger smiled, punching Brandon playfully in the arm. Brandon turned, forcing a smile to his face.

"Well, let's get down to brass tacks. What in the hell happened tonight?"

Brandon's gaze left Granger and focused on Cara. "You'll have to ask her."

She glanced up, a challenging smile flitting at the corners of her mouth.

Brandon swallowed hard. He sent out a prayer to the powers that be that for once in her life Cara kept her mouth shut. His prayers were answered as she began to speak.

"I sort of crashed William Cavanaugh's Christmas party."

Granger's gaze narrowed. "What do you mean, sort of?"

"I scaled an eight-foot wall, made my way around his pool, and stepped in through the back door." Cara shrugged nonchalantly and then took a sip of beer.

"You *what*?" Granger stood, his hands planted on the table in front of him. "This was supposed to be a simple paperwork case. It shouldn't have required fieldwork. What in the hell were you thinking?"

Cara faced him, her features tightening with angry lines. "I thought I was doing my job. Getting the proof I needed for my client." She stood, matching her brother's stance. "I thought I was doing exactly what you'd do in the same circumstance."

Brandon stared at them, unable to suppress his smile. "That's not the best part of the story," he goaded, enjoying the mini-flashback to childhood.

Granger glanced at him before glaring once again at Cara. "What else?"

She hesitated. "I needed proof and figured there was only one place to find it."

"And where was that?" Granger's tone had dropped to deadly as he waited for his sister to answer.

"In his filing cabinet."

Granger pinched the base of his nose as if to ease some of the tension raging through him. "You mean to tell me you broke into a suspect's home files?"

"No."

"Then what happened?" Ice filled his voice.

"I couldn't get the damn lock open."

Granger growled, fisting his hands at his sides until his knuckles cracked. "I swear to all that's holy, Cara, if I wasn't your big brother, I'd paddle your ass."

Brandon laughed. "That's actually what crossed my mind."

Granger glared at him, obviously not in the mood for jokes. Brandon held up his hands in defense. "Don't look at me. I'm the one who got her out of there before Cavanaugh caught her. It's a good thing I work a lot of cases with the man and know the layout of his house."

Granger's jaw clenched and released, then he gave Brandon a curt nod. "Thanks, bro."

"No problem." Brandon tipped his beer. Trouble was, he knew he had a big problem, and she stood next to him, refusing to back down from her brother.

"Why did you do something so stupid?" Granger bit out, his frustration directed at Cara.

She looked at Granger as if he'd grown a third eye in his forehead. "The case! Have you heard nothing I've said?"

"Yeah, you're talking about the senile old bat, right?" Granger spat.

"She's not senile!" Cara exclaimed.

Granger shook his head. "I don't know what you're out to prove."

"Guys," Brandon interrupted, "not that this doesn't seem

like old times here, but I still don't know what's going on, so could you both sit down and let's try to talk this out like adults?"

"Fine!" they shouted, a second before plopping down like two miffed teenagers.

"Why don't you start from the beginning," Granger coaxed, his voice calming a little.

She crossed her arms over her chest. "I tried to, but you insisted on interrupting me with your pigheaded bullying."

"Cara!" Brandon snapped.

"Fine." She stared at her hands for a few seconds as if gathering her thoughts. "Eliza Rosemary came into the office a few days ago, looking for someone to represent her case. Since he considered it useless, Granger gave it to me."

Granger shifted, his face flushing under the truth. "I'm going to put on some coffee." He rose and walked to the little kitchenette, his bare feet silent on the carpeting. "Tell Brandon what she's paying you with," he suggested, while he filled the kettle with water and leveled out scoops of coffee.

Cara blushed, her gaze dropping to the table before settling on Brandon. She pursed her lips a moment longer, then muttered, "Cookies."

Brandon leaned in, convinced he'd misunderstood her. "She's paying you in *what*?"

"Chocolate chip cookies," she said louder with more conviction.

Granger threw his head back and howled with laughter. Brandon chuckled under his breath, then reached beneath the table to squeeze Cara's hand.

"I think that's sweet," he murmured.

Cara jerked her hand from his grip. "Don't patronize, Brandon. It doesn't suit you. If what Eliza says is true, this Cavanaugh colleague of yours is a fraud and a thief."

His smile faded. "I was serious, and you want to be careful with unsubstantiated accusations about Cavanaugh. He's a pitbull.".

"Cookies!" Granger shouted again, drawing their attention to see him wiping the tears of laughter from his eyes. "And you wonder why I passed on the case."

Cara glared and rose to her feet. "You might have been able to turn an eighty-two-year-old woman away, but I couldn't. Money isn't everything, big brother."

Her anger made her face glow, reminding Brandon of the moment she'd reached orgasm in his arms. His breath caught as he glanced down at the front of her sweater, just able to make out the hard ridge of her nipples jutting beneath the iridescent fabric. The urge to strip her naked and ravish her again struck hard.

He turned to Granger before he had a chance to consider how it'd look. "Knock it off, Granger!" Brandon demanded. "I don't care why she took the case. I want to know why she was at Cavanaugh's party."

Cara gaped at Brandon. She couldn't help it. In all the years he'd been coming over to their family home, she'd never seen him stand up to her brother in her defense. He'd always taken Granger's side.

Something had shifted internally.

She'd felt it the second their bodies joined this evening. Obviously, the impervious Mr. Brandon Walker had, too. The realization thrilled her.

Granger frowned for a moment before appearing to dismiss it. *Typical Granger,* she thought. He placed coffee cups on a tray with cream and sugar before bringing everything over to the table.

Cara poured them each a steaming mug, then continued. "Eliza Rosemary was—is—a client at your law firm.

Cavanaugh's client. She came to me concerned about . . . ir-regularities. I thought it would be a simple enough case, and besides, it was my chance to get out of the office. Prove myself." She punctuated the end of her sentence with a glare aimed at her brother, who proceeded to stick out his tongue before taking a sip of his coffee.

"That's mature." She mimicked his actions.

"You don't have to prove yourself to anyone," Brandon murmured.

Cara glanced his way before continuing. "Anyway, when I started looking into Eliza's finances, I noticed a discrep-ancy—well, several, actually. At first glance, she looks solid money-wise, nothing missing. Her holdings are vast and ex-tremely lucrative. The problem is, she hasn't been able to account for a lot of her assets."

"Is she senile?" Brandon asked quietly.

"She's about as senile as I am." Cara's comment met with two sets of raised male eyebrows. "You both know what I mean." She rolled her eyes.

"Go on." Brandon urged, then blew on his coffee.

Cara stared, mesmerized by Brandon's pursed lips. The simple act of cooling his coffee brought back memories of his hot breath blowing across her nipples. His firm lips graz-ing her skin. Her gaze wandered to his strong hands; those long fingers had slid inside of her, teasing, torturing, and taking her body to new heights of ecstasy, until she'd have surrendered her soul if he'd asked.

Cara shifted in her seat, glancing once more at his face. Brandon must have sensed her staring, because he looked up in time to catch her watching him. A beat later, his lips curved in a secretive smile.

Cara cleared her throat. "On paper, Eliza's worth a small fortune, yet she has nothing to show for it but a Sun City cottage and a chocolate-colored '76 Cadillac. Eliza's theory is that someone at the law firm is getting a little jiggy with the books."

"Jiggy?" the men asked as one.

Cara exhaled. "Her words, not mine. She's watched *Men in Black* a few too many times."

"Eliza Rosemary sounds like quite an interesting lady. I'd like to meet her."

"Brandon, I don't think that would be a good idea."

His gaze caught hers and held. "I'm not *asking,* Cara. I'm *telling.* Set up an appointment with Ms. Rosemary as soon as possible. If there's a problem within the firm, I want to know about it."

She nodded stiffly.

"But I can tell you right now, there isn't. The law firm of Kazman, Williams, and Blake wouldn't do anything which could possibly smudge their prestigious reputation—that includes hiring a thief." Brandon exhaled, setting his cup down. "I work with Bill Cavanaugh on a number of cases. I consider him not only a colleague, but somewhat of a friend. He may be a bit pretentious, but he doesn't bilk little old ladies out of their estates."

"We'll see." She took a sip of coffee. "I hope you're right."

"I am."

Cara didn't reply.

"Well, gang, I don't know about you guys, but I'm exhausted." Granger stood, taking the coffee tray with him. "It's been a long day and it's turning into an even longer night."

Cara glanced up, meeting her brother's sleepy gaze. "I'd have thought you'd be used to these hours by now."

"Very funny, sis." He leaned down and kissed her cheek, before adding, "This isn't over. You know that, right?"

Cara shot him a look that would have felled a lesser man.

Granger simply laughed as he walked to the kitchen to clean up.

"Brandon, are you spending the night?" Granger asked, not looking up from his task.

Brandon looked at Cara for a second before replying. *Don't do it,* his mind all but screamed. "I guess so."

"Cool." He smiled. "Grab your usual spot. Your swim trunks are in the drawer."

"Thanks, bro."

"Don't mention it."

Brandon spent a fitful night dreaming of Cara. In his dream, he'd taken her on the couch, in the shower, on the counter, and on the floor. He'd awoken in a cold sweat, more than a little angry with himself, to the sounds of splashing water. His body was in a permanent state of arousal.

It had taken him a few seconds to realize where he was. When that occurred, the previous night's events came crashing down upon him like a lead weight. He'd slept with his best friend's little sister. He was slime. Hell, he was worse than slime. He didn't even rank with sludge.

Last night Cara had managed to single-handedly press every one of his hot buttons. He'd known better than to mix sex with emotions; being burned in the past had taught him that.

Yet within seconds, sweet little innocent Cara had done what no other woman in the past five years had managed—she'd gotten to him. Okay, maybe she wasn't so sweet. Definitely not so little anymore, she'd filled out in all the right places. As for innocent, after last night he'd strike that assessment from his mind. She definitely had enough experience to whet his appetite for more.

Not that his desires needed any extra help; by the time

Cara turned eighteen, he'd thought of little else when he was around her.

The splashes grew louder.

Brandon kicked off the wool covers, pulled on a pair of swim trunks that he always kept on Granger's boat, and then padded down the hall. He could hear loud snoring coming from Granger's room at the bow. He laughed to himself. Some things never changed. His best friend always could sleep through anything.

As Brandon entered the living room area, he could hear singing accompanying the splashing water. He smiled as he recognized the off-key voice. Cara was singing. Robert Palmer's "Simply Irresistible," if he wasn't mistaken.

Brandon chuckled again as he crossed the small area into the kitchenette. He needed coffee and time to gather his thoughts before he faced Cara again.

Because her case involved the firm and his associate, there was no way he'd be able to avoid her, at least while the investigation was ongoing. Not that he wanted to avoid her, but he knew he should.

Being around Cara would only lead to further temptation, which in turn would increase their chances of being caught. Brandon knew that was a risk he couldn't take. Granger would never forgive him. Hell, he'd probably never forgive himself.

The situation needed to be addressed and dealt with swiftly. Just like his law cases. Quick. Clean. To the point.

With coffee in hand and his mind percolating, he stepped out into the bright Arizona sunshine. Cara swam a short distance away, her face tilted toward the sun with her eyes closed. He watched her for several minutes, enjoying the gleeful expression on her face as she sang without self-consciousness.

He'd always envied that about her. She could let go, at the drop of a hat, and just be herself. He'd never been able to do that, too concerned with what his peers might think if he did. It had been one of the reasons he'd loved hanging out at the Martins' house.

The sun sparkled off Lake Pleasant's surface, reflecting the surrounding hillsides like a mirror. The air was crisp and dry, a perfect Arizona winter day. Saguaro dotted the desolate landscape, while a turkey buzzard circled lazily above the houseboat, reaffirming the fact that life did indeed exist in this harsh desert environment.

Cara glanced up from the water as if she'd sensed his presence. She smiled and waved, urging him to join her. Brandon looked over his shoulder. The cabin still lay in darkness. There were no sounds, except the constant snuffles of Granger's snores.

Cara approached, swimming briskly. "Are you going to join me?" she asked, a bit breathless. Her ebony hair lay slicked back from her face, accenting her features, while droplets of water clung to her lashes.

Brandon's gaze followed the outline of her body. He dropped his coffee. God help him, she was naked.

Exhilaration shot through him, tightening his muscles, sharpening his vision. His immediate response lingered on the tip of his tongue like a decadent dessert. He squatted down until he could run his hand in the water, while he tried to get his emotions in check and his heart to slow down.

It took a second for Brandon's mind to register the water's temperature. It was freezing. "I don't think so. It's a little on the frigid side for me."

Cara grinned again. "Oh, come on, don't be such a baby. I'll keep you warm."

"That's exactly what worries me." He laughed, glancing over his shoulder to be sure Granger hadn't risen.

"Lighten up, Brandon." Cara splashed him, and then swam the short distance to the boat.

Brandon's breath caught as Cara climbed the ladder onto the deck of the houseboat. Her pale skin glowed rich pink from the cool water. As she passed him, her ripe bottom swayed from side to side, like the wagging finger in his mind, reminding him to walk away.

So why hadn't he moved?

Cara knew she played with fire, teasing Brandon, but she couldn't help herself. She needed to be near him, feel the press of his warm, hard body against hers. She'd spent most of the night replaying the previous evening in her mind. He wanted her to pretend they'd never had sex. Unfortunately, that idea didn't work for her.

She'd experienced a taste of what was possible. There was no way she'd forget last night. It had been the greatest sex of her life. How could he ask her to walk away now that she'd held him in her arms? The plain and simple truth was she couldn't—and wouldn't.

Brandon may very well want to ignore what happened last night, but Cara wasn't about to let him forget. It may have started out as angry lust, but sometime during the sex something changed, shifted between them. She'd felt it all the way to her core, and from his expression at the time, so had he.

She turned to watch him. He gaped at her, muscles tense, eyes glazed. Sex with this man reminded Cara of frosted donuts—both were deliciously decadent, but in the end probably bad for your heart.

Not that this knowledge would deter her from the course she'd decided on. She would solve this case for her client and somehow land one of the valley's most eligible bachelors. The trick was to convince Brandon that they belonged together.

Cara made her way to the on-deck shower. She flipped a

switch and waited for the water to heat. Brandon was used to making deals, at least while at work. Perhaps she'd strike a bargain that would benefit them both.

She glanced out of the corner of her eye in time to see Brandon grip the railing of the houseboat. The delicious play of muscle beneath tanned skin made her hot blood simmer.

With Granger dead to the world, she took the opportunity to entice Brandon even more. Cara stepped under the warm water, arching her back as the droplets sluiced over her body.

She heard a gasp and then peeked out from beneath her lowered lashes to see Brandon frozen in place. His hazel gaze had locked onto her nipples and his mouth had parted as if he'd attempted to taste her from where he stood. His normally placid expression took on a mixture of lust and pain.

"W-What in the hell do you think you're doing?" he hissed under his breath.

Cara brushed her hair back from her face with her fingertips, before clearing away the excess water. "What does it look like I'm doing?"

"Granger could come out here any moment. Someone on another boat could see you."

Her eyes flashed wide. "That's the excitement of it, don't you think? The danger of being caught."

"No," he growled out. The front of his swim trunks tented from his growing erection. "I thought I told you we can't risk doing this again."

Cara took a deep breath and then released it, sending her nipples quivering from the action. Brandon swallowed and took a step closer.

"I know what you said, but I've made different plans." She reached for the bath gel and began soaping herself.

He took a few more steps forward, his gaze riveted on her actions. "Care to fill me in?"

She smiled, playfully flicking some of the suds onto the deck. "When the time comes . . ." she paused. "Until then, I was hoping you could fill *me* in." Cara arched a brow, challenging him as she rinsed the soap away. She had no idea how strong his control was or if he'd take the bait. Fortunately, she didn't have a long wait to find out.

Brandon closed the distance separating them. His large hands came down upon her shoulders, before sliding along her arms. He held her for a few seconds as his mouth found hers. His kiss deepened as his thumbs began to stroke and tease her marbled nipples, before moving onto her throbbing clit.

He groaned as his tongue touched hers. He tasted of coffee and man, strong, bold, and full of passion. Brandon circled and flicked her hooded flesh, ratcheting the tension inside of her. Cara sank into his embrace, her body running hot and cold, raw and achy. She wanted him inside her, filling the emptiness that he'd left behind.

His fingers firmed, unrelenting in their course to bring her pleasure. Cara pulled back from the kiss, her breath coming in panting gasps, her body rocking with seismic intensity as her orgasm hit.

Her fingers ran over his chest, sinking into his flesh, tangling in the soft, brown curls. She reached for the waistband of his swimming trunks and tugged. Brandon stopped her before she could get them off.

"I don't have protection with me and I don't want to wake Granger by going back in the cabin to get the condoms."

"We won't need condoms for what I have in mind."

Cara didn't give him a chance to respond. She slowly lowered to her knees, scraping her nails along his sides as she did so. He flinched, but didn't recoil. She reached the waist-band of his trunks once more and then pulled them out and over his straining erection.

In the dark, he'd been impressive, but in the daylight, he was what wet dreams were made of. Cara licked her lips and felt every muscle in his body tighten in anticipation. She glanced up at his face, which had now flushed a deep rose. With his gaze on her, Cara stuck her tongue out and ran it along the length of his cock.

Brandon's hips bucked and his fingers curled at his sides. Raw energy surged through him, as he seemed to fight the urge to touch her. Cara curled her hands around the base of his shaft a second before taking him fully into her mouth. He tasted wet and salty, wholly male.

The air came rushing out of his lungs as she began to move, gently sucking at the same time. His hands came to her head, but he made no attempt to guide her. She set the speed and pace, taking him deep and then teasingly shallow. Brandon left everything up to her.

It didn't take long before the muscles in his thighs began to tremble. Cara dropped one hand away, so she could cup his sac. She massaged and stroked while continuing to pleasure him. Brandon's breathing shattered and he moaned.

"Cara, if you don't stop, I'm going to come."

She smiled around his length, not bothering to pull away.

"I mean it, Cara, I can't last much longer."

Cara looked at Brandon's face. His eyes were at half-mast. His gaze scorched, telling her without words how much he wanted her. There was so much caring, so much history, so much *love?* Her heart skittered. Cara sped up her move-ments, tightening her grip at the same time.

"Enough!" Brandon groaned. His fingers tightened on her head as he pulled Cara to her feet, before she had a chance to finish.

"You're incredible, you know that?" He brushed the side

of her face with the back of his knuckles, then kissed her tenderly.

"I'd like to think so." She smiled. Cara stared at him, wondering if he had any idea how much that liquid hazel gaze revealed to her.

Four

Brandon woke Granger to say good-bye. He'd told himself his best friend's face was flushed from sleep and not from observing any of his and Cara's on-deck activities. Granger would certainly have called him on it or at the very least punched him for touching his little sister, wouldn't he?

He hadn't missed the winks the siblings exchanged before he and Cara climbed into the powerboat to head back to shore. Cara had changed clothes. She wore the sweater from last night and a short black skirt, which showed off her long, supple legs.

It took forty minutes to reach the dock and five more to get to the car. He kept his gaze glued to the water ahead, as he tried without success to ignore Cara's fabulous legs.

By the time Brandon sat behind the wheel of his Jaguar, he realized the exchange between the siblings had probably been a case of his own guilty conscience. Or at least he should be feeling guilty, but he wasn't. His eyes strayed to Cara's legs, as he tried desperately to forget what they'd felt like wrapped around his waist, squeezing him as he plunged inside of her. He could almost feel her thighs gripping his head as he lapped at her flesh.

Unfortunately, lust wasn't the only emotion powering through his body at the moment. Brandon didn't want to look too closely at what he was feeling. He knew it would scare the life out of him. So instead, he focused on the drive. They would reach Eliza Rosemary's home in Sun City within fifteen minutes, depending on the blue-haired express.

He and Granger had tagged every road leading into Sun City the "blue-haired express" due to the average age of the drivers, most of whom were in their seventies.

Eliza Rosemary lived in a modest cottage surrounded by freshly tilled beds of desert flowers. Bright orange and red blooms lit up her front yard, while along the side of the house purple reigned supreme. Two giant saguaros stood like sentinels on the rock-surfaced lawn. Happy green shutters surrounded the spotless windows, while a bright coat of white paint decorated the walls.

The place seemed peaceful and welcoming compared to the urban sprawl of the valley surrounding the little oasis. No other house on the block looked anything like Eliza Rosemary's home.

Cara approached the door first, her hand raised and ready to knock. Before she could make contact with the surface, the door flung open and a little white-haired, gold-spectacled woman appeared in the frame. She had a rosy-cheeked face, which led downward to a slight yet spry body.

"It's about time you got here. I've been expecting you for days."

Brandon chuckled.

Cara smiled and grabbed Eliza's hand. "Now, Eliza, I told you I wouldn't come by until I had more information to share."

"And do you?" The woman's bushy brows arched and her face lit up with excitement.

Cara glanced toward Brandon. "Not exactly . . ."

"Well, why not?"

Brandon stared in amusement as Cara fidgeted under the woman's watchful gaze.

"Does it have anything to do with the looker standing behind you?" The old woman's gaze fixed on Brandon. She studied him for so long, Brandon started to sweat. It wasn't near as much fun having Eliza's gaze focused on him.

"Brandon's here to lend his expertise."

"And what expertise might that be? Perhaps you just keep him around because he looks good." She shrugged. "Some men are just better off naked and mute. The sooner you learn that, Cara, the better." Rosemary patted Cara's hand.

"Eliza Rosemary!" Cara pulled away. "Shame on you."

The old woman just laughed and winked at Brandon, completely unrepentant.

"Oh hush, we all know it's the truth." Eliza stepped aside and waved them into her home.

Brandon couldn't keep the smile from his face. Eliza Rosemary was a pistol, and she reminded him an awful lot of his grandmother, God rest her soul.

Following the women inside, Brandon thought the home resembled what the inside of a gingerbread house would look like. Deep red cushions covered the chairs and couch. Throws of yellow and orange blanketed the arms of the furniture. The walls held decade upon decade's worth of photographs, highlighting a life well lived.

The odor of cookies wafted in the air, reminding Brandon he hadn't eaten. His stomach growled as Eliza walked into the kitchen, then quickly returned carrying a tray of fresh-baked chocolate chip cookies.

"Cara dear, I forgot the coffee and milk. Could you retrieve it for me?"

"Sure thing, Eliza." Cara trotted into the kitchen as Eliza guided Brandon into the living room.

"It'll take a minute or two for her to find the milk, because I hid it."

He frowned. "Why in the world would you do that?" Brandon worried that perhaps Cara had misjudged Eliza Rosemary's competency.

"To give us time to get acquainted, dear. And for me to find out what your intentions are concerning Cara." She sat in a nearby chair, glaring at him over the gold rim of her glasses. "Have a seat." She extended a gnarled finger, pointing to the couch across from her.

"My intentions?" Brandon sat without thinking; his emotions teetered on the edge, creating turbulence in his mind. "There's nothing going on between Cara and me—we're just old friends."

"Can it, sonny! I may be old, but I'm not senile." She pursed her lips. Somewhere in the house, a clock chimed eleven.

Brandon shifted on the cushions under her scrutiny. Finally, he released a pent-up breath. "I don't quite know what's going on," he admitted. "But I'll never hurt her."

Eliza smiled sweetly. "Good. Now, would you like a cookie?" She tipped the tray, offering the cookies.

Brandon reached for one. Eliza's claw-like hand hooked him, the innocent-looking grip belying a strength and speed not normally associated with little old ladies. "You'd better be telling me the truth."

Cara padded back into the room carrying a tray loaded with the milk, coffee, and some cups. The change in Eliza was astonishing, as if someone flicked a switch inside of her. "Take a cookie, dear." She released Brandon with a smile.

He hesitated for a moment before taking one from the platter. Cara's assessment had been correct. Eliza was far from incompetent.

"Eliza, did you know someone put your milk in the cabinet with the pots and pans?" Cara asked, her gaze narrowing in suspicion.

Eliza giggled. "Oh, goodness me, I'd forget my head if it wasn't attached." Her gaze shifted from Cara to Brandon, where it settled, silently letting him know that she was holding him to his word.

They spent the rest of the afternoon listening to Eliza recount her concerns and suspicions. By the time Brandon walked Cara to his car, his original dismissal had grown to concern. He'd look into Eliza's account for Cara, but he still couldn't believe that the firm mishandled Ms. Rosemary's estate. Why would anyone swindle a nice old lady?

If her accusations ended up being true, would that mean he worked for a disreputable company? That wasn't possible, was it? And what of his associate and sometime partner Cavanaugh? Brandon was proud of his own reputation, but everything he'd worked so hard to achieve would be ruined if his fears turned out to be the truth. He had to find out.

Of course, if he were caught snooping in files that weren't his, the firm would probably have him disbarred. Damn it, he'd worked too hard to get to where he was to allow that to happen.

The only solution that he could see was to prove Cara and Eliza wrong. It wouldn't be pleasant for any of them. He knew that by doing so, he'd probably destroy Cara's chances of ever getting another meaningful case at the Martin Detective Agency. The thought of hurting her left a bitter taste in Brandon's mouth.

He drove for several minutes in silence. From the direction he headed in, Cara knew he was taking her back to her car. Now was the time to strike a bargain with him. Hopefully, he'd be distracted enough to agree.

"Brandon, I know you've said we shouldn't have sex again

and you're probably right." Cara absently played with the leather seam on his gearshift, as she stared at his profile.

Her gaze wandered over his broad shoulders, along his flat stomach, to rest upon the impressive bulge in his pants. She bit her lip as her body recalled the feel of his thick length sliding inside of her, riding her body until they'd reached a fevered pitch, then tumbling them over the edge of oblivion. Cara crossed her legs to stave off the sudden ache, as need slammed into her. She wanted him again—now!

Brandon glanced at her face, then her fingers, following their movement for a few seconds before focusing once more on the road. His expression seemed to harden before her eyes.

She couldn't tell what he was thinking, but Cara knew she had to turn his wayward thoughts around. "Relax, Brandon. It was just sex."

His head whipped around. "Is that what you think?"

Cara took a shaky breath, then shrugged.

Brandon's gut clenched. He'd had sex for its own sake, but this was more than that. He'd enjoyed their time together. So much so, he didn't want to share her with anyone. How could she be so casual? Just the thought of Cara having sex with another man had him thinking murderous thoughts.

What would it be like having her night after night? It didn't matter, because he wasn't about to find out. Possessiveness was an emotion he tried to avoid and it was already building inside him.

What harm would come from a few more days? The insidious little voice in his mind whispered. Granger had called him a gigolo on the houseboat. The label reminded Brandon of why this was such a bad idea. He'd end up hurting Cara, just like he'd hurt all the other women in his life.

When pushed for an emotional connection, he'd walk away as before, as he always did.

But Cara wasn't asking for an emotional connection, was she? This was about sex, wasn't it? He'd had no problem separating the two things in the past. Brandon didn't want to think about the fact that it bothered him intensely that Cara could do the same.

"Are you listening?"

Her voice snapped him back to the problem at hand. If he backed off, she'd take that sweet ass of hers to some other guy. And if he stuck around, then he risked losing her and his best friend in the end. Brandon couldn't allow her to walk away, at least not yet, possibly not ever. He kept that information to himself. He wasn't ready to deal with it just yet.

Cara smiled triumphantly.

"I haven't said a word."

Her grin widened. "You didn't have to."

Why did he feel as if he'd just walked into a trap of his own design? Brandon shook his head.

Cara slapped her hands onto her lap. "Okay, where do we start?"

"We start by me dropping you off at your car," Brandon replied, "and then I'm going to head into the office and see what I can dig up."

"I can go, too."

He turned onto the highway. "I don't think that's such a good idea, Cara."

"Why? This is my case." She crossed her arms over her chest, hiding her delectable breasts from his line of sight.

"It may be your case, but you asked for my help." He glanced in his side mirror before making a lane change. "If you want my help, you're going to have to do things my way. Besides, the last thing we need is for Bill Cavanaugh to see us together again."

"It's a Sunday. He's not going to be in."

"Maybe, maybe not. We can't take that chance."

She huffed. "You're as bad as Granger."

Brandon glanced at Cara and smiled. "I know—that's why you like me."

Cara arched a brow. "No one said I liked you."

"Maybe not in so many words." He shrugged. "But I know damn well—you wouldn't have slept with me if you didn't like me. It's not your style."

She leveled her gaze on him. "It's been ten years since you last saw me. Who's to say my style hasn't changed?"

For a second, tension filled Brandon's chest; then he caught a glimpse of Cara's eyes sparking with fire, and he laughed. "Some things never change, you brat." He winked at her before exiting the freeway and making the turn onto the street running parallel to Cavanaugh's gated community.

The yellow banana, as she called her Camaro, sat in front of one of the privacy walls. Probably the same one she'd scaled the night before. A piece of paper shoved under the windshield wiper fluttered in the desert breeze.

"Looks like you've got a ticket for your trouble." Brandon shot Cara a glance.

She sat forward in her seat and looked over the dashboard in the direction of her car. The second she spotted the offending paper, she frowned. "Fudge!" She sank into her seat, her chin resting on her hand.

"Hey, look on the bright side."

She glared at him. "There's a bright side to parking tickets?"

"Yep." He pulled in behind her car and parked, but didn't kill the engine. "At least they didn't tow it."

"Very funny." She smirked at him as she undid her seat belt. "What am I supposed to do while you're at the office?"

"Go through Eliza's files again and highlight all the assets you can't identify."

"I've already done that."

"Then do it again. We need to be absolutely sure." He turned to face her. "I'm taking a big risk going through Bill's files. We're on several cases together—if there's a problem, it's not just his reputation that'll take a beating."

Cara hadn't understood until this moment how closely Brandon worked with Cavanaugh. They may not be best friends, but they obviously had a good relationship built on mutual respect.

With a sinking feeling, she realized she'd unwittingly put Brandon in a terrible position. If he found the proof she needed, he'd be losing a close colleague and quite possibly his position within the firm. She had to end this now. There was no way she was going to be responsible for Brandon losing his job. She cared too much about him to allow that to happen. She'd work the case on her own.

"Brandon, perhaps this isn't such a good idea. I don't think you should be getting involved."

His hazel eyes widened and his expression grew stern. "Why? You haven't gotten cold feet already, have you?"

Cara opened her mouth to speak, but closed it as his words sank into her mind. He wasn't talking about the case or his job. He was talking about them. Her heart thumped in her chest. The beats grew louder and louder until she'd swear he could hear them. Cara reminded herself that this was not the time to be selfish, no matter how much she loved him. The realization slammed into her. She felt no panic, only resignation.

"I think I need to release you from your commitment." There—she'd said it. Cara sighed.

Brandon's eyes narrowed and his face flushed beneath his tan. The muscles in his body tensed as he gripped the steering wheel as if it were a life raft. "You release me? That's big of you." Anger tainted his words, along with . . . *hurt?*

"Cara, if you had no intention of going through with this, I don't know why you went through this big production." He released a ragged breath. "I don't like being teased and played with. I'm not a kid."

"I'm not playing with you." She stammered. "I just thought, considering the position I've placed you in, that maybe it would be best for you if we called the whole thing off."

"Best for me, huh?"

"Yes," she murmured.

"Let me decide what's best for me, okay?" He ran a hand through his hair and over his face. "Are you that afraid of what I might find?"

Anger surged through Cara. The big dope didn't understand that she was trying to protect him. "I believe my client is correct."

"And I believe you're both wrong, so let me get the documents to prove it."

"Fine!" Cara opened the car door and jumped out, slamming it behind her. She strolled around the vehicle to his window, then tapped on the glass. The window lowered with a slight hum.

"Yeeess?" he asked, his face the picture of insulted arrogance.

Cara casually glanced at her watch. "It's two now. I'll meet you at your place at six-thirty and I'll bring Chinese. I expect to have a full report when I arrive."

"Is that so?" Brandon arched a brow, his gaze slipping to her lips. "What if I have plans?"

Seeing the heat in his eyes, Cara turned away from the window and strode to her car. She opened the car door, turning at the last second to look at him. "Change them."

With that, she slipped behind the wheel, started the engine, and drove off with the ticket flapping in the wind.

Brandon drove into the parking lot at the law firm of Kazman, Williams, and Blake. Pulling into his customary space, he casually glanced around the lot to see if he spotted any of Bill's flashy sports cars. His gut clenched over what he was about to do. He'd never betrayed anyone in his life. *Except Granger.*

Brandon uttered an expletive and slipped from behind the wheel. He strode toward the building. With any luck, few people would be in today. He swiped the electronic lock and then stepped into the marble-floored lobby. Mahogany paneling covered the walls and a fountain made of gold-leafed sprites sat in the center of the room, pouring fifty gallons of recycled water every ten seconds.

The sound, normally soothing, did little to ease the tension taking up residence between his shoulder blades. A security guard sat behind a desk on the right. Brandon showed him his key and then walked the short distance to the elevator doors and pressed the button.

The doors opened with a smooth *whoosh.* Brandon stepped inside, and then pressed number nine. The elevator chimed as it reached each floor, punctuating his sense of dread.

The elevator came to a gentle stop and the doors slid open, revealing the plush ninth floor. Mahogany lined the walls, the same as in the lobby. Opulent emerald-green carpets trimmed in gold blanketed the floor.

Brandon made a right. Bill Cavanaugh's office sat at the end of the hall, next to his own. Whether it was nerves or just plain chickening out, Brandon went to his own office first. The lights were off in Bill's, indicating no one was there.

After a couple of deep breaths, he proceeded to Cavanaugh's office. He gave the area a quick look-around before opening the door and stepping inside. Cavanaugh had an extra filing cabinet they both used for their shared cases and another for his own use. Brandon bypassed the shared files, going straight for Bill's personal ones. If he was up to no good, there was no way he'd leave the files for Brandon to access.

He reached for the drawer and pulled. The cabinet didn't budge. "Oh, of course." Brandon shook his head and turned, striding to Bill's desk. He'd seen Cavanaugh open these files often enough to know the key was in the left-hand drawer. Conflicted, Brandon cursed again as he slid the drawer open. A set of keys lay beneath an invoice. He snatched them up and quickly returned to the locked file cabinet.

The first key Brandon tried didn't work. He moved to the door, checking up and down the hall before returning to try another key.

The fourth key seemed to be the charm. It slid into the lock, opening it with a faint click. Brandon pulled the drawer open and began to scan the names.

"Come on, come on," he muttered to himself.

He found Eliza Rosemary's file shoved in the back, toward the end. Brandon grabbed it, then glanced into the hall once more before making his way to the copy machine.

Five excruciatingly long minutes later, he had his copies. Brandon tucked them into his jacket pocket, then strolled back to Bill's office. He slipped the file back into the drawer before closing and locking the cabinet. His hand was reaching for the desk drawer when he heard a cough coming from the hallway.

He had just enough time to toss the keys inside and shut the desk drawer, before Bill Cavanaugh appeared in the doorway. Brandon glanced around Bill's desk and pretended to search for something.

Bill's oily, dark features scrunched as he stepped back to look at the name on the door as if to assure himself that he was in the right place. "What in the devil are you doing in my office, Walker?"

"Oh, Bill, hi." Brandon met his gaze, willing his face to remain expressionless. "I can't seem to find the files on the Wilmington case. I thought maybe you had them."

Bill stared at him for a few seconds before finally relaxing. "I put them in our joint file cabinet."

"I must have missed them. I thought maybe you'd left them on your desk."

Cavanaugh frowned. "How long have we been working together?"

Long enough to have me wondering why I'm questioning your ethics and not my own.

"You know I never leave files out." Cavanaugh continued.

"I know. I guess it's been a long weekend." Guilt slammed into Brandon. He was betraying one friend for another. It didn't matter that Bill wasn't technically a friend, but more like a close colleague. The difference meant little under the circumstances.

He hoped that once he'd cleared Cavanaugh's name, Bill would forgive him. The best-case scenario would be that he never found out.

Brandon made his way to the office door. As he was about to pass, Bill stopped him. "Aren't you forgetting something?"

Brandon tensed. "What?"

Bill arched a brow. "The files you came for."

"They're not that important. I'll get them tomorrow."

Cavanaugh's eyes narrowed for a moment, then he smiled. "Rough night, eh?" he laughed. "You never said how it went with that luscious redhead." Bill nudged Brandon with his elbow. "Did you ever make it to the Hyatt?"

Brandon flinched. He had the overwhelming urge to slam Bill into the door for talking about Cara as if she were an easy piece of ass. Bill knew he wasn't the type to talk about the women he dated. At the most, he'd shared vague tidbits with Cavanaugh. The thought of saying anything about Cara made him doubly uneasy.

What they'd shared had been far too intimate to cheapen by office gossip. But Brandon knew he'd have to say something or Bill would become suspicious, if he wasn't already. So he said the first thing that entered his mind—the truth.

"We never made it that far."

Bill laughed, clapping him on the shoulder as he walked past. "You are such a lucky dog, Walker. That woman had an ass on her that wouldn't quit."

Brandon turned, every muscle in his body tensing as anger surged through him. "She's more than a piece of ass to me. Got it?" He poked Cavanaugh in the chest for emphasis. What in the hell was the matter with him? He wasn't the territorial type when it came to women. Yet Brandon had been so mad that he'd spoken without thinking.

Cavanaugh seemed dumbstruck for a moment. "Sure, pal, anything you say."

"Good." Brandon forced a smile and then walked a few feet further to his office. Before stepping inside, he paused. "Hey, Bill."

"Yeah." Cavanaugh poked his head out of his office door.

"Have you ever heard of a lady named Eliza Rosemary?"

Cavanaugh's expression went from open to closed in a half-second. "Yes, why do you ask?"

Brandon shrugged casually, feeling anything but. "She left me a couple of voice messages by accident. I was just wondering if she was your client."

Bill's lips thinned. "Yes, she's my client."

"She sounds like a handful, from the messages." He knew that was the understatement of the century. Eliza was a walking, talking mini-microburst.

"She is," he answered hesitantly.

"Do you share responsibility for her with anyone else?" Brandon prayed that Cavanaugh would say yes.

"No, I acquired her on my own." He frowned. "Do you want to tell me why you have a sudden interest in a senile old lady?"

Brandon forced a smile. "Just making conversation."

Cavanaugh's jaw tightened. "Well, make it somewhere else. I've got work to do."

Brandon saluted Bill a second before Cavanaugh slammed his office door closed. No doubt, he was checking on the file Brandon had copied earlier. Of course, there was still a very good possibility that Bill was innocent, but if so, why had he reacted in such a queer manner?

Brandon drove home listening to Miles Davis pour out of his Alpine speakers. The music normally soothed him, but not today. It would take a month for the knots in his neck and back to ease after this nightmare settled. Brandon pictured Cara's face. Okay, the entire situation wasn't bad. He'd managed to fulfill a boyhood fantasy last night and this morning.

His body tightened, remembering the way she'd taken him into her mouth. He pulled into his driveway and hit a button on his visor. The garage door opened and Brandon pulled in to park. He grabbed his jacket, double-checking the inside pocket to be sure the copies he'd taken of Cavanaugh's papers were still there.

Brandon glanced at his watch before punching the alarm code in to disarm the system. It was four-thirty. In two hours, Cara would be here, full of questions. He hoped like hell he'd have the answers.

Brandon walked across the kitchen to the refrigerator, quickly snatching a beer before striding down the hall to his home office. He flicked on the light, then went and sat behind the maple desk.

He took a long swig of beer, then put it down to dig into his pocket for the photocopies. By the time he'd finished going over the pages, an hour had passed, the beer sat empty, and his stomach had turned to stone.

Money was definitely missing, but from all accounts, Eliza was still an extremely wealthy woman.

Thirty more minutes went by, and Brandon remained no closer to figuring out the financial puzzle. What he did know was there was enough evidence to cast aspersion upon his reputation. Guilt by association. Being a lawyer, he knew that better than most. If he handed over the files to Cara, his career may very well be over.

"Shit . . . shit . . . and double shit! Bill, what have you done?"

Brandon dropped the papers and walked to the shower. He stripped quickly, not bothering to wait for the water to heat before stepping under the spray. Anger reverberated through him in invisible waves. He didn't like being manipulated, first by Bill and then by Cara. He'd been a fool to think he could help her and remain unscathed.

He let the water beat down upon him, never flinching as the drops pelted his skin. He was mad at himself. He'd been compelled to go to the office to get the files Cara needed for her case. Why hadn't he simply refused her?

Because you love Cara, always have—always will.

Where in the hell had that come from? Brandon turned the water to COLD, attempting to cool his amorous thoughts.

He'd tried to place the blame for everything squarely on Cara's delicate shoulders, but he knew better. He would not have done any of this if he hadn't needed to know the truth for himself. Cara was the beautiful, raven-haired catalyst, and nothing more.

Now the question was, would he give her the information he'd found?

Five

Cara knocked on Brandon's door at exactly six-thirty. It had been excruciatingly difficult to wait and not show up earlier. The smell of soy sauce and teriyaki wafted in the air, causing her stomach to growl.

Her grip tightened on the bag containing their dinner. Brandon opened the door before the third knock, dressed in jeans and a black T-shirt that lovingly stretched across his wide chest like a second skin.

His feet remained bare, giving her a glimpse of his sexy toes. Cara had never considered toes sexy until she'd seen his. They were long, hairless, and perfectly shaped. In a word—sexy.

Brandon's whiskey-colored hair was damp and slightly slicked against his head, giving her an unobstructed view of his long, dark lashes and his glittering hazel eyes. His sharp gaze watched her, hesitant.

"Are you all right?" he asked.

"I'm fine." Cara felt heat spread across her face. She'd been staring at him like a lovestruck teenager . . . again.

Brandon brushed a hand through his hair, sending several locks standing on end. "Come in." He stepped aside for her to enter.

"Did you find out any information on the case?" Cara couldn't keep the hopeful note from slipping into her voice.

"No." He padded down the hall.

She frowned. Brandon had never been a very good liar. In all the years she'd known him, he'd never gotten a single fib by her. Instead of pressing, she stepped around him and strode toward the kitchen. At least, she hoped she was heading toward the kitchen. She hadn't been here in ten years. The place had been brand-new then.

She remembered the sense of pride and accomplishment Brandon had felt when he invited her family over to see it. He'd just gotten out of law school and been hired by Kazman, Williams, and Blake. The two-bedroom, ranch-style house had been a celebratory splurge—or, as her father was fond of saying, an investment.

Cara set the bag of food down on the marble counter and began opening and closing cabinets until she located the plates. She opened the bag. The smell of teriyaki chicken rose from the first steaming container. She proceeded to pull out Mu Shu pork and braised beef from the other boxes.

"Are you hungry?" Brandon asked, staring at the bounty.

Cara rolled her eyes. "You know Chinese doesn't stick to the ribs, so I ordered a lot. To be honest, I wasn't sure what you liked anymore."

His eyes flashed and his gaze strayed to her face a moment before traveling down the length of her body and back up. Brandon licked his lips. "You know exactly what I like."

Her pulse skittered, but she refrained from smiling. Cara stuck her finger in the teriyaki sauce, then raised it, holding it in front of Brandon's handsome face. Teriyaki juices dripped down the length of her finger, while she waited for him to respond.

His gaze locked on her face and then onto her hand, his nostrils flaring as he seemed to fight his natural instincts.

"Just one taste," she coaxed, extending her hand an inch closer, knowing one taste would never be enough for either of them.

A growl erupted from Brandon's chest as he closed the distance between them. His hand grasped hers as he slipped her finger into his mouth to lick the savory teriyaki juice, paying special attention to the tender, webbed flesh between her fingers.

Cara closed her eyes as fiery sensations shot through her body, hardening her nipples and dampening her silk thong. Brandon continued to feed on her flesh until her clit twitched in response, aching under his libidinous assault.

Brandon released her hand after dropping a kiss onto her fingertip. His hands went immediately to her waist. He lifted Cara, placing her bottom on the center island, between the open boxes of Chinese, before releasing her.

"I thought you were hungry?" she asked, her voice dropping to a seductive purr.

He smiled at her, a feral light shining in his eyes. "Oh, I am." He nodded, affirming her suspicions. "Just not for food."

Brandon brushed the food aside. He grabbed a nearby barstool, then stepped between her thighs. "Now, where were we?"

Cara didn't get a chance to answer. His lips came down upon hers, his tongue demanding entrance, probing her mouth, like his cock would soon be doing to her body.

She leaned into his kiss, her breasts flattening against his hard chest, as nipple met nipple. Brandon's hands slid along her sides, then grasped the material of her shirt, separating their mouths only long enough to remove the offending material. Cara followed suit with his T-shirt, her fingertips pressing his flat, disc-like nipples until he moaned.

Then he was at the buttons on her pants and within seconds Cara was wearing nothing but her underwear. He made quick work of her bra, tossing it on top of the rest of her clothing. She went to remove her thong, but he stilled her hands.

"Leave it on for now." His finger ran the length of the damp strip of cloth and Cara shuddered.

"You're overdressed." She glanced at his jeans, admiring the bulge beneath his zipper.

"I'm going to leave my jeans on for a while or we'll be over before we've had a chance to begin." He grinned.

Cara giggled. "Ready to go off?"

"Like a rocket."

She licked her lips. "We wouldn't want that."

"No, we definitely wouldn't." Brandon dropped to his knees, bringing his face eye level with Cara's feminine heat.

He glanced up at her from beneath lowered lashes. "What do we have here?" He blew a warm breath over the front of her thong.

Cara gasped, squirming in anticipation.

"Sit still. If you move, I'll stop."

"Now who's being the brat?" she asked.

Brandon grinned.

The muscles in Cara's body tightened as she fought the urge to move. She wanted his lips upon her. She wanted his tongue parting her folds, lapping at her center, exploring her tender clit. Instead, he began to nibble on her inner thigh. Cara's mind and body rioted. Heat soared through her, streaking like lightning to her extremities.

"Brandon, please."

His tongue darted out, cooling the places he'd just nibbled on. "Did you know your skin tastes as sweet as watermelon on a hot summer's day?"

Cara bit her bottom lip. Her hands went to her throbbing nipples and she began to circle and lightly pinch them, trying to get some relief from the tension building inside of her.

Brandon slipped a finger inside her waistband, then pulled it to the side, exposing her dark thatch of curls. He leaned forward and inhaled.

"Musky, womanly—mine," he proclaimed, and then licked the exposed skin, skirting the edge of her folds.

Cara's head dropped back, her body no longer her own. From far away, she heard a rip and felt the material of her thong pull away from her body. Exposed, naked to his exploration, she spread her legs farther apart.

Brandon growled as he buried his face between her thighs. His tongue darted out, tasting her flesh, searing her mind. He licked and sucked, swirling his tongue around her clit with maddening accuracy. He followed her folds down to her entrance, where he circled her opening again and again, without delving inside.

Cara released her nipples, her hands digging into the island countertop. Her head tossed from side to side as she drew nearer to release.

"I love the smell of you, Cara. The taste. It's different—you're different. I love the feel of your body as it tenses with desire. I could fuck you day and night, and never grow tired of exploring you."

Brandon flattened his tongue against her clit and hummed. The vibrations caused Cara to scream. He held his tongue in place while he pushed a finger into her moist entrance, curving it just enough to hit her G-spot.

Cara shattered, exploding into a million pieces without moving an inch. Her orgasm roared through her, making her feel as if the world had just dropped out from beneath her feet.

Brandon stood, his finger still buried inside her. His lips grazed her nipples, teasing her, building her need once again.

"Brandon?" his name came out breathless on her lips.

He lifted her from the countertop. Cara's legs automatically slipped around his waist, her arms around his neck, as he carried her effortlessly into the bedroom. Each step brought his finger deeper into her body. Cara groaned as Brandon placed her onto the bed, and then gently rolled her onto her stomach, before pulling her to her hands and knees.

"I've been wanting to take you like this from the moment I laid eyes on you in Cavanaugh's office."

Cara glanced over her shoulder to watch Brandon remove his jeans. His cock rose long and thick from his tanned body, demanding her attention. Cara swallowed hard, her body growing needy once more. Brandon reached for a condom in the side table and quickly sheathed himself.

His hands closed around Cara's hips, drawing her bottom toward his massive erection. The crown of his shaft slipped inside of her entrance, stretching her, teasing her aching body with his fullness. Cara's knees threatened to give out. She tried to push back and deepen his penetration, but he held her in place.

"Not yet," he gritted out between clenched teeth. Brandon rolled his hips, slipping an inch deeper into her vise-like channel. His body trembled as he fought to maintain control and not pound inside of her like a wild beast.

He'd imagined this moment so many times and in so many ways. He stroked Cara's bottom, her soft skin like silk beneath his fingertips. She groaned as he made a shallow thrust inside of her.

"Brandon, you're driving me crazy."

"That's the idea." His breath hissed out.

Of course, he was killing himself in the process. One hand released her hip and slid to her breasts. Brandon palmed the full globes, relishing the feel of her nipples as they stabbed his palm.

Cara bucked back, sheathing him completely. Brandon groaned, unable to hold back. He speared into her, taking her deep, his thrusts greedy. He released her nipple, sliding his hand down her slightly rounded stomach until he reached her swollen nub. He stroked her clit in time with his thrusts, driving them both to the edge of insanity and back again.

Cara's orgasm slammed into her body and she collapsed, taking Brandon down with her. His body tightened, his sac drawing up near his abdomen as he came hard. The sound of their rapturous cries filled the room as the smell of musk and sweat rose in the air.

Brandon rolled off Cara, scooping her into his arms at the same time. They lay spooned together, his chest to her back, dozing in the afterglow of their lovemaking.

That's what it had been, *making love*. Somewhere over the past couple of days, they had left casual sex behind. If he was honest with himself, Brandon knew their first time together had been anything but casual. He liked the feel of Cara in his arms. His heart clenched as he imagined her there for all time.

His mind flashed to the papers in his office. Could he keep her if he chose not to disclose what he'd found? No matter what excuses leapt to his tongue, he knew it wouldn't be possible to maintain a relationship built on deception. He exhaled. Her warmth crept into his body, into his heart, melting away the last of his resistance.

They made love on and off throughout the night, each time reaching a higher peak, a deeper level of intimacy. Cara fell asleep in his arms, her rosy lips swollen from his kisses, her cheeks flushed from her orgasms.

As the first tendrils of daylight peeked above the mountains, Brandon knew he'd fallen hard. He loved her. There was no longer any doubt in his mind. He'd have to face his best friend Granger and let him know. But how? How could he tell Granger and expect him to believe that this time with Cara was different? Hell, he could hardly believe it himself.

The thought of disappointing her or, worse yet, breaking her heart, terrified him. He had no point of reference when it came to long-term relationships. Goodness knows his parents didn't set any kind of example. Could he make this relationship last? Brandon didn't know, but he'd damn sure try.

He stared in awe at her sleeping form for a few seconds before leaning his face into Cara's hair and breathing deep. Her scent was like inhaling sunshine. He kissed the side of her head, tenderly. "I love you, always have," he whispered before slipping from the bed and heading to his office.

Brandon gathered the Cavanaugh files from his desk and strode to the kitchen, where he placed them in Cara's purse.

Cara heard Brandon's whispered confession as he crept out of bed. Her heart soared with the news. She'd dreamt of this moment for years. Brandon Walker loved her, almost as much as she loved him. Had always loved him.

She heard him coming down the hall and quickly closed her eyes. Brandon slipped back into bed and pulled her close. His early-morning erection nudged her bottom, awakening her body. They made love slowly, tenderly, his shaft sliding in and out of her while their gazes remained locked, melded together as one.

Brandon was sound asleep as Cara dressed and left for work. She grabbed her purse on the way out, stopping long enough to leave him a note in her feminine scrawl. *I love you, too.* The note was simple and to the point, saying everything she wanted to convey in four little words.

Showered and eager to go, Cara entered the Martin Detective Agency. Granger was out for the day, so he wouldn't be around to bug her. She opened her purse to grab her lipstick and found the papers Brandon had shoved in there instead.

Cara spent much of the morning poring over the files. She

worked right through lunch with still no luck. She couldn't find anything out of place in Eliza's accounts. Could she have been wrong? Had she wanted this case so badly that she created something that wasn't there? She shifted in her chair, feeling the tender muscles that Brandon had so thoroughly used last night. She almost groaned at the thought of taking him into her body.

"Focus, Cara!" she said to herself.

If nothing out of the ordinary existed in Eliza's accounts, then what about the titles? Cara scanned the titles and then began entering them into her computer database. It took a few minutes of downloading, but the answer that appeared in the tiny window shocked her.

"Caught you," she whispered triumphantly.

Cara reached for her phone and punched in Brandon's work number. The phone rang a couple of times before he finally picked up.

"Good afternoon, beautiful. I got your note." His voice rumbled on the other end of the line.

Cara smiled for a moment, basking in the sound of his rich, masculine voice. "Good—what did you think?"

"I think I need to see you in person to convey my thoughts clearly."

She didn't miss the teasing note in his voice. Neither did her body. Her nipples tightened and she felt herself growing wet.

"Down, girl," she muttered to herself.

"What was that?" Laughter filled his voice.

Cara cleared her throat. Now was not the time to get sidetracked. "I've figured out how Cavanaugh's been stealing from Eliza."

Silence came from the other end of the line.

"Brandon, are you there?"

"Yeah, I'm here," he replied. "How did he do it?"

"You're never going to believe this. It was never hidden. It was in plain sight all along."

"Cara, just tell me." The playfulness slipped from his voice, leaving behind the attorney.

"He's kept everything in Eliza's name," she said. "The cars, the houses, a boat. You name it, she owns it all."

There was a long pause on the other end of the line. "That son of a bitch," Brandon said finally.

Cara twisted the cord of her phone around her fingertips. "I've phoned Eliza and told her I'd pick her up in about an hour. I had her call Cavanaugh and tell him to meet us at his house. I mean *her* house," she corrected, waving her hand in front of her face. "Oh, you know what I mean."

"Give me a little time and I'll meet you both there. I don't want you confronting Cavanaugh alone."

"I've already paged Granger."

"All the same, I want to be there. The bastard has ruined my reputation along with his own. It'll be a miracle if the firm survives the scandal."

"I'll see you there." Cara hung up the phone. She didn't bother to tell Brandon there probably wouldn't be any scandal. She hoped that she'd kept everything silent enough to avoid one.

Eliza was waiting on the front lawn with her purse in hand, along with a tin of cookies. Cara chuckled. They were probably her final payment. Eliza opened the passenger door to Cara's car and slipped inside.

"Let's go get him!" Eliza cried out as if she were heading into battle.

Cara reversed the car out of the drive and they were on their way.

Brandon trudged toward Harold Kazman's office. The senior partner's secretary sat at a large desk outside the corner office, guarding against unwanted guests. As Kazman's cousin, Ruth considered everyone, including associates at the firm, beneath her.

"Ruth, is Mr. Kazman in? I need to speak with him."

The woman arched a blond brow. "Mr. Kazman left strict instructions not to be disturbed."

Brandon stared at the blond-haired woman with the perfect silicone breasts. Coifed in the finest New York fashion, she sat behind her desk like a queen. Her well-manicured nails tapped impatiently on the mahogany.

"Ruth, I need to see Mr. Kazman immediately. It's imperative. Now call him or I'm going in."

She took an exaggerated breath and released it, as if the mere act of asking was an inconvenience, then spoke into her headset. "Mr. Kazman. Brandon Walker wishes to see you. No, he doesn't have an appointment, but he says it's important."

Ruth stared at her nails, listening to the voice in her headset. "Are you sure, sir? I can send him away." She paused. "All right, I'll send him in."

Ruth glared at Brandon. From the slight flush on her high cheekbones, he could see this galled her.

"You may go in," she said, dismissing him with a waggle of her fingertips.

Brandon winked and she huffed, turning away to look at her desktop, as if the plant on her desk had suddenly become more interesting than their conversation. Brandon smiled and entered Harold Kazman's office.

Kazman stood when he saw Brandon. Meeting him halfway, Kazman shook his hand, then guided Brandon to a nearby chair.

"What can I do for you, my boy?"

"I really don't think I should sit, sir."

Kazman waved his hand in the air. "Nonsense, take a seat."

"If you insist."

The man's bushy eyebrows furrowed. "I do."

Brandon sat as Kazman reached his seat behind the desk. Dread took up permanent residence in his stomach. He was about to lose the career he'd busted his ass creating, and there wasn't a damn thing he could do about it. Once Kazman found out he'd worked on several cases with Bill Cavanaugh, all that would be left for Brandon to do is pack his personal items and leave.

"Sir, I'll get right to the point."

"Please do."

Brandon took a deep breath. "It's come to my attention that Bill Cavanaugh has been diverting funds from at least one of his clients and using it for his own personal gain."

Kazman's expression grew stern. "That's a very serious charge you're leveling upon a colleague, not to mention libel, if you're wrong."

"I understand, sir." Brandon shifted in the plush leather chair. "But I'm not wrong."

"Do you have proof of these charges?"

"Yes, sir, I do."

Kazman sat back in his chair, his fingers steepled at his chin. "Didn't you work with Bill Cavanaugh on several cases?"

Here it came. The axe was about to fall on his head. He'd just shattered one reputation in order to shed another. Brandon braced himself, not missing the irony. "Yes, sir."

The man arched a brow. "And yet, you still came to report this incident?"

"Yes, sir."

Kazman leaned forward and pressed a button on his desk. "Ruth, get me Ronald Williams and Jack Blake on the phone. Now!"

"Y-yes sir, Mr. Kazman." A flustered Ruth stuttered out on the other end of the line.

Within moments, the two men were on the conference line, listening to the details that Brandon laid out. They interrupted on occasion to ask a question here and there. Otherwise, they kept quiet, absorbing the news.

"Brandon, could you leave the room for a moment?"

"Of course, sir." Brandon stood and walked to the door. His heart lay heavy in his chest while he tried to decide what he should do first, pack his desk or head straight for Cavanaugh's so he could punch the man squarely in the face.

He stood out in the waiting area. Ruth seemed so nervous she actually chewed on her expensive set of acrylic nails. A couple of minutes passed, and then Ruth's headset beeped.

"I'll send him in right away, Mr. Kazman."

Brandon entered Kazman's office. He knew his fate was sealed by the expression on Kazman's face; being informed by the senior partner was only a formality.

"Brandon," Kazman's voice boomed.

Brandon frowned. "Am I being terminated, sir?"

Kazman laughed, his brown eyes sparkling in mirth. "Not exactly."

Brandon stilled. "If you're not firing me, then what?"

"I've talked it over with the other senior partners, and on behalf of Kazman, Williams, and Blake we'd like to extend our thanks."

"Thanks?" Brandon asked.

"Yes, you've averted a scandal."

"You're welcome, sir, but I'm not sure I understand."

"The last thing we need the public thinking is that we are untrustworthy." Kazman continued. "Our integrity is all that separates us from the other law firms in town. We will prosecute Cavanaugh to the full extent the law permits. But this coming from within is a good thing."

"Good thing?" Brandon tried to follow Kazman's reasoning.

Kazman chortled. "Absolutely! God alone knows what

would have happened if some newspaper had dug this up."
He shook his head. "This is us taking care of our own business, our own clients. Way to go, my boy."

Kazman stood and came around his desk. "We'd like to offer you partnership in the firm."

"Partnership?" Brandon couldn't believe what he was hearing.

"Son, is there something wrong with your hearing? You keep repeating everything I say to you."

"No, sir." Brandon choked and then laughed. "Just surprised, sir."

Kazman clapped him on the back. "Congratulations. We'll make a formal announcement tomorrow. In the meantime, I'll call Judge Moreland. He can get a warrant issued with a minimum of fuss."

"Okay, great. Thank you, sir." Brandon felt numb as he left Kazman's office. He couldn't believe it. He hadn't lost his job after all. Instead, he'd been made partner. His biggest dream since leaving law school. *Just wait till I tell Cara the news,* he thought, and smiled, amazed at how quickly his mind had jumped to her.

Cara and Eliza were already at Cavanaugh's house when Brandon arrived. From the look on Bill's face, they'd verbally beaten him to a pulp. When Cavanaugh saw Brandon, he leapt to his feet.

"Walker, tell these women they're insane, especially the old lady."

"Watch it, buster, or I'll get jiggy with you," Eliza threatened, her gnarled fist raised in the air.

Brandon fought to keep a straight face. He turned to the man he'd worked with for over seven years. "How could you, Bill? I trusted you."

Cavanaugh stepped back. "You don't think I . . . how could you believe . . . I want my attorney."

"Good idea." Brandon snorted.

Granger walked in the door a moment later. "Did I miss the party?"

Brandon smiled. "Nope, you're just in time."

"Good." Granger stepped forward. "There's a couple of black-and-whites outside to take this scumbag away."

Brandon saw Cavanaugh put his head in his hands.

Granger turned to go out the door.

"Granger, hold up a minute. I need to talk to you." Brandon glanced at Cara and Eliza to be sure they didn't hear their conversation. They appeared deep in discussion, probably about what would happen next.

Granger stared at Brandon, an amused expression upon his face. "What's up?"

Brandon walked a few feet away, motioning for Granger to follow.

Granger glanced at Cavanaugh. "If you move," he glared at the man, "I'm going to let them take turns kicking the shit out of you. Got it?"

Cavanaugh's eyes widened as he glanced at Eliza and Cara. He nodded and backed up until he was leaning against the wall.

Granger joined Brandon. "Now, what's up?"

Suddenly nervous, Brandon shifted on his feet. "You know, we've been best friends for years, right?"

Granger's lips twitched. "Yeah."

"And I wouldn't do anything intentionally to ruin what we have."

"Yeah." Granger bit down on his lip.

"I, uh, I mean to say, Cara and I . . . are . . . uh . . ."

Granger threw his head back and laughed. "I know."

Brandon's eyes practically bugged out of his head. "How did you know?"

Granger stopped laughing long enough to look at him. "That day on my houseboat."

Heat rushed to Brandon's face. "But you were sleeping," he accused.

"Not with all the racket you guys were making on deck." Granger grinned. "I knew something was up the night before. You both acted guilty as hell. Besides, it's about time. The two of you have been making eyes at each other for years."

Brandon shoved his hands into his pockets. "Shit, bro. I didn't mean to . . . I mean—I didn't think—"

Granger leaned in, stopping his words. "One thing," he paused, "you break her heart and I'll kick your ass."

Brandon smiled, extending his hand. "Deal."

"I mean it." Granger grabbed Brandon's hand and squeezed. "She's not one of those bimbos you're used to hooking up with. She's my little sister."

"I know."

Their eyes met and held, each man weighing and measuring the other. Granger must have seen something in Brandon's expression, because he smiled again and released his hand.

Brandon and Granger returned to the spot where Eliza and Cara stood chatting away.

"What are they going to do with him?" Cara asked, glaring at Cavanaugh.

"Take him to the police station and get him booked for fraud and grand larceny to begin with and whatever else we can come up with. I'll meet you back at the office afterward—okay, sis?"

Cara nodded.

Eliza reached for Cara's hand and patted it. She looked around, her eyes widening as her gaze took in the cavernous room. "So all this is mine?"

"Sure is." Cara smiled.

"Those fancy cars in the driveway, too?"

"Yep." Cara giggled.

After a few moments, Eliza turned to face the small group, zeroing in on Granger. "Handsome, if this place is mine, then would you please get this asshole," she pointed to Cavanaugh, "out of my house."

The group burst into laughter.

"Yes, ma'am." Granger grabbed Cavanaugh by the arm and led him out of the house.

"As for you, dearie . . ." Eliza reached for the cookies she'd brought and handed them to Cara. "These are for you."

Cara's smile widened. "Thanks, Eliza, it's been my pleasure." Cara put the cookies down on the counter. "I guess I'd better take you home, unless you want to spend a little time exploring your new digs."

Eliza chuckled and glanced around once more. "This place is lovely, but it's too big for me," she sighed. "I think you should have it."

"Yeah, right." Cara laughed. "Eliza, quit kidding around."

The old woman stilled. "I'm serious."

Brandon stepped forward. "Eliza, I don't think you realize what you're saying." He spoke to her as if she were a child.

Eliza's face grew pink as she turned on him. "Honey, don't let the white hair fool you. This old bird is not stupid." She poked him in the chest. "I'll expect you to draw up the papers if you want to be my new attorney."

"Yes, ma'am." Brandon stepped back, grinning.

Cara grabbed Eliza's hand. "Eliza, I can't accept this house as a gift."

Eliza's brow furrowed. "This isn't a gift, dear. This is payment for your services," she said. "You didn't really expect me to pay you in cookies, now, did you, dear?"

Cara could only gape in response.

Eliza strode over to the sets of keys hanging from a rack by the door. "Are these keys for those cars?"

"Yes," Brandon answered.

"Will this start that . . . Lamborg . . . Lamborg, that black sporty thing in the driveway?"

Brandon looked at the key and then back at Eliza. "Yes, ma'am, it will."

Eliza smiled and winked. "Good. You kids have fun. I've got some freeway to burn up." With that, she slipped out the door, leaving Brandon and Cara staring after her.

"I'm not sure Eliza's ready to drive a Lamborghini. Do you think we should go after her?" Cara asked, her voice tipped with concern.

Brandon shook his head. "No." He smiled. "I've got a better idea." He grabbed Cara's hand and led her up the stairs and down the hall to Cavanaugh's home office.

"What are you doing, Brandon?" Cara asked as he opened the closet door and shoved her in, following behind.

His arms closed around her as he brought her body flush against his. Brandon's lips brushed her ear as he whispered, "I'm picking up where we left off."

The drapes over his motel room's window pulled open, Eli McKenzie stood and stared through the mottled glass, squinting at the starburst shards of sunlight reflected off the windshields of the cars barreling down Highway 90 in the distance.

Second floor up meant he could see Del Rio, Texas, on the horizon, and to his left a silvery sliver of the twisting Rio Grande, a snake reminding him of the venom he'd be facing once he harnessed the guts to cross.

The room's cooling unit blew tepid air up his bare torso, making a weak attempt at drying the persistent sheet of sweat. Sweat having less to do with the heat of the day than with the choking memory of the poison he'd unknowingly ingested on his last trip here.

An accidental ingestion. A purposeful poisoning.

Someone in Mexico wanted him dead.

The only surprise there was that no one but Rabbit knew Eli's true identity. Wanting to dispose of an SG-5 operative was one thing, but he hadn't been made. Which meant this was personal.

This was about his covert identity, his posing as a member of the Spectra IT security team guarding the compound across the border.

An identity he'd lived and breathed for six months until the nausea and dysarthria, the diarrhea, ataxia and tremors turned him into a monster. One everyone around him wanted to kill.

He'd tried himself. Once.

Rabbit had stopped him and sent him back to New York and to Hank Smithson, the Smithson Group principal, to heal. Eli owed both men his life, though it was his debt to Hank that weighed heaviest.

Hank, who plucked men in need of redemption off their personal highways to hell and set them down on roads less traveled. Roads that took the SG-5 operatives places not a one of them wished to see again after reaching the end of their missions.

Places like the Spectra IT compound in Mexico.

Scratching the center of his chest, Eli shook his head and pondered his immediate future. He and Rabbit were the only ones inside the compound not working for Spectra. Outside was a different story.

And there had been one person nosing around and causing enough scenes to make a movie.

Stella Banks.

Stella Banks with her platinum blond hair and battered straw cowboy hat and legs longer than split rail fence posts. She was an enigma. A private investigator who dressed like a barrel racer and looked like a runway model.

She kept an office in Ciudad Acuna, another in Del Rio. He knew she was working the disappearance of her office manager's daughter, Carmen Garcia. The girl was fourteen, and like so many of the others gone missing recently, a beauty.

She was also currently being held inside the compound, waiting to be shipped away from her family and into a life of prostitution courtesy of Spectra IT. Or so had been the case last Eli had checked in with Rabbit.

The room wasn't getting any cooler, the day any longer, the truth of what lay ahead any easier to swallow. Like it or not, it was time to go. Once across the border, he'd make his way south a hundred kilometers in the heap Rabbit had left parked in a field west of the city.

As much as Eli longed for a haircut and a shave, he wouldn't bother with either. The scruffy disguise went a long way to helping him blend in, to hiding the disgust he never quite wiped from his face.

Considering the condition of the car and the roads, he was looking at a good two hours of travel time. One hundred and twenty minutes to go over the plans he'd worked out with Rabbit to take down these bastards.

Plans trickier than Eli liked to deal with but which couldn't be helped. Not with the lives of twenty teenaged girls on the line.

His plans for Stella Banks he hadn't quite nailed down.

He needed her out of the way.

Before he got rid of her, however, he needed to find out what she and her outside sources could add to what Rabbit had learned on the inside.

Only then would Eli make certain she never interfered in his mission again.

He was alive.

And he was back.

That son-of-a-bitch was back.

Stella Banks curled her fingers through the chain links of the fenced enclosure and watched him leave the compound's security office and cross the yard to the barracks.

She couldn't believe it. Not after all the trouble she'd gone through—and gotten into—to get rid of his sorry kidnapping ass for good.

Next time she'd forgo the poison and use a bullet instead.

Here's a look at Nancy Warren's latest
romantic comedy for Brava,
TURN LEFT AT SANITY
available now from Kensington . . .

"Don't you think we'll end up more frustrated if we keep talking and it doesn't go anywhere?"

"Well, last night would have been too soon, but now . . ."

Now, what? Joe came up with an answer for her. "Now I've passed the Miss Trevellen school of larceny and good manners?"

She laughed aloud. Out of her peripheral vision she could see that Gregory Randolph had the hood up on Joe's car. How long did this disabling business take? She was in a cold sweat, gulping her cocoa like it was courage-giving whiskey.

Greg was bent over the open hood of the car, his white T-shirt gleaming against the darkness. *Please let him get the job done quickly.*

A computerized *ping* broke the strained silence in the office and Joe said, "Ah, my e-mail."

He started to turn his chair around to his computer, which faced the window, which looked out on a man screwing with his car.

She had to stop him. No time to think. She stuck her foot out and stopped the chair mid-twirl.

"Emmylou, I need to get that," Joe said, an edge to his voice.

"But I need you," she said, hoping that her voice sounded husky with passion and not strained by panic.

He opened his mouth, no doubt to tell her to get a grip, or at least wait until he'd read his e-mail. She couldn't let that happen, so she launched herself at him, sloshing cocoa mug and all.

"Whaa—" he managed before her lips clamped over his.

Blindly she managed to get her mug onto the desk top so her hands were free, then she plunged them into his hair, making a human vise to keep his head from turning. She opened her legs around his and snugged up tight onto his lap.

It was a move born of desperation and if he pushed her off him, which she was pretty certain he'd do, she'd end up sprawled on her butt all over the rug and when he turned around, he'd view more than his e-mail.

She expected to go sailing through the air and hit the rug ass-first. She expected outrage when he caught sight of Greg out there messing with his car. What she hadn't expected was that after a startled second of total stillness, Joe would kiss her back.

Oh, not just kiss her, but make love to her mouth.

His passion exploded around her and in her, sparking her own. She nipped at his lips, grabbed the back of his head to pull him closer, felt his mouth so hungry on hers, on her skin, his hands in her hair, on her neck, racing over her back.

". . . want you," he said and the echo of those words played over and over in her head. *Want you, want you, want you . . .*

Heat began to build in the three-point triangle of nipples and crotch. If Dr. Beaver was right, she had a dandy little electrical circuit running between those three hot spots.

He moaned with hunger, or maybe that was her, hard to tell over the pounding of her heart.

He pulled at the buttons on her shirt, fumbling open the top one, and then the second, while she waited in a fever of impatience. She forgot why she was doing this, forgot everything but the fact that she needed this man and she needed him now. He got the rest of the buttons undone, not smoothly but fast, then pushed the sleeves down her arms to her wrists and stopped, so she ended up with her arms bound behind her, a circumstance he seemed to enjoy.

With some wriggling she could easily free her arms, but he looked so pleased with himself she let well enough alone.

"I like you in this posture," he explained with a devilish glint in his eyes. The fatigue had vanished and he pulsed with energy. "Your breasts thrust forward, and your busy hands still. No bread baking, flower arranging, cookie cooling. All you can do is sit there and let me touch you."

Take a sneak peek at MaryJanice Davidson's
"Ten Little Idiots," in
"WICKED" WOMEN WHODUNIT
coming in March 2005 from Kensington . . .

"This is all Jeannie Desjardin's fault," Caro declared to the hallway.

Lynn Myers blinked at her. "Who—who's Jeannie Desjardin?"

"My friend. She's this awesomely horrible woman who generally revels in being bad. You know—she's one of those New York publishing types. But every once in a while she gets an attack of the guilts and tried to do something nice. Her husband and I try to talk her out of it, but . . . anyway, this was supposed to be *her* Maine getaway. But she gave me the tickets instead and stayed in New York to roast along with eight million other people." *And the yummy, luscious Steven McCord,* Caro thought rebelliously. *That lucky bitch.* "And now *look,*" she said resisting the urge to kick the bloody candlestick. "Look at this mess. Wait until I tell her being nice backfired again."

"Well," Lynn said, blinking faster—Caro suspected it was a nervous tick—"we should—I mean . . . we should call the— the police. Right?"

Caro studied Lynn, a slender woman so tall she hunched to hide it, a woman whose darting gray eyes swam behind magnified lenses. She was the only one of the group dressed in full makeup, pantyhose, and heels. She had told Caro during the first "Get Acquainted" brunch that she was a realtor from California. If so, she was the most uptight Californian Caro had ever seen. Not to mention the most uptight realtor.

"Call the police?" she asked at last. "Sure. But I think a few things might have escaped your notice."

"Like the fact that the storm's cut us off from the mainland," Todd Opitz suggested, puffing away on his eighth cigarette in fifteen minutes.

"Secondhand smoke kills," Lynn's Goth teenage daughter, Jana, sniffed. A tiny brunette with wildly curly dark hair, large dark eyes edged in kohl (making her look not unlike an edgy raccoon), and a pierced nostril. "See, Mom? I told you this would be lame."

"Jana . . ."

"And secondhand smoke *kills*," the teen added.

"I hope so," was Todd's cold reply. He was an Ichabod Crane of a man, towering over all of them and looking down his long nose, which was often obscured by cigarette smoke. He tossed a lank section of dark blond hair out of his eyes, puffed, and added, "I really do. Go watch *Romper Room,* willya?"

"Chil*dren*," Caro said. "Focus, please. Dana's in there holed up waiting for *les flic* to land. Meantime, who'd she kill?"

"What?" Lynn asked.

"Well, who's dead? Obviously it's not one of us. Who's missing?" Caro started counting on her fingers. "I think there's . . . what? A dozen of us, including staff? Well, four of us—five, if you count Dana—are accounted for. But there's a few of us missing."

The four of them looking around the narrow hallway, as if expecting the missing guests to pop out any second.

"Right. So, let's go see if we can find the dead person."

"Wh—why?" Lynn asked.

"Duh, Mom," Jana sniffed.

"Because they might not be dead," Caro explained patiently. "There's an old saying: 'A bloody candlestick does not a dead guy make,' or however it goes."

Jana was startled out of her sullen-teen routine. "Where the hell did *you* grow up?"

"Language, Jana. But—but the police?"

"Get it through your head," Todd said, not unkindly. "Nobody's riding to the rescue. You saw the Weather Channel . . . before the power went out, anyway. This is an island, a private island—"

"Enjoy the idyllic splendor of nature from your own solitary island off the Maine coast," Lynn quoted obediently from the brochure.

"Don't do that, it creeps me out when you do that."

"I have a photographic memory," she explained proudly.

"Congratufuckinglations. Anyway," Todd finished, lighting up yet another fresh cigarette, "the earliest the cops can get here is after the storm clears, probably sometime tomorrow morning."

"But they have helicopters—"

As if making Todd's point, a crack of lightning lit up the windows, followed by the hollow boom of thunder so loud it seem to shake the mansion walls. The group pressed closer to each other for a brief moment and then, as if embarrassed at their unwilling intimacy, pulled back.

"They won't fly in this weather. We're stuck. Killer in the bedroom, no cops, power's out. The perfect Maine getaway," Todd added mockingly.

"It's like one of those bad horror movies," Caro commented.

"Caro's right."

"About the horror movies?"

He shook his head. "Let's go see who's dead. I mean, what's the alternative? It beats huddling in our rooms waiting for the lights to come back on, doncha think?"

"What he said," Caro said, and they started off.